"Got a score to settle!"

"Your brother would still be alive if you hadn't sent him to blow a hole in my back, Young." Landford's voice was amazingly calm.

Hatred pulled at Upton Young's dark features. His hand swooped downward.

Landford's .45 was out quicker than the eye could see. At the same time he lowered his crouch, the gun hand bracing oddly against his thigh. He fired with blinding speed.

Young grunted heavily as the slug tore into his chest. His gun hand had not cleared leather. The second to fall was the man to Young's right. The third man was mortally struck, but not before he got off one shot.

A lance of fear shot through Jimmy Blackburn's body as he witnessed the showdown—and he saw his friend Landford go down.

The Badge Book 2
THE FACELESS MAN

THE BADGE: BOOK 2

★

THE FACELESS MAN

★

Bill Reno

™ Created by the producers of
Stagecoach, Wagons West,
White Indian, and Winning
the West.

Book Creations Inc., Canaan, NY · Lyle Kenyon Engel, Founder

BANTAM BOOKS
TORONTO · NEW YORK · LONDON · SYDNEY · AUCKLAND

THE FACELESS MAN

*A Bantam Book / published by arrangement
with Book Creations, Inc.*

Bantam edition / December 1987

*Produced by Book Creations, Inc.
Lyle Kenyon Engel, Founder*

ISBN 0-553-26785-X

Published simultaneously in the United States and Canada

PRINTED IN THE UNITED STATES OF AMERICA

O   0 9 8 7 6 5 4 3 2 1

THE FACELESS MAN

★ BADGE ★

From the moment it appeared in 1873, the Colt Peacemaker was the weapon of choice throughout the West. Firing a metallic cartridge rather than powder and ball, the .45-caliber revolver generally came with a 7½-inch barrel, though an easier-to-draw 4¾-inch model was favored by gunfighters.

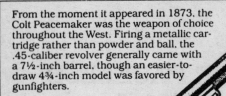

Guns That Tamed The West

Henry Deringer, a Philadelphia gunmaker, designed and gave his name to the original 1825 gun that saw service in the pockets and up the sleeves of countless western gamblers and gunfighters. Pictured is the Remington Over-and-Under .41, a two-shot, double-barreled model.

★ Book 2: The Faceless Man ★

RON TOELKE '87

Chapter One

Sarah Blackburn wiped her hands on the apron tied around her slender waist and proceeded to plant the store-bought candles in the double-layer chocolate cake. Seventeen of them. Projecting her lower lip, she blew at the wisp of blond hair that insisted on falling onto her forehead.

Seventeen, she thought. *How can Jimmy possibly be seventeen years old? Why, it seems like just yesterday. . . .*

Sarah's hazy-blue eyes were captured by something she saw through the kitchen window. On the plains due east five tiny dots were silhouetted on the horizon against the crystal Colorado sky. Something cold coursed through her. Dropping the candles still in her hand, she ran to the door.

Stepping into the yard, she scanned the corral and barn, searching for movement. Seeing nothing, she looked westward, shading her eyes against the lowering sun. The jagged Rockies stood tall and still, as if waiting for the sun to descend upon them. The sun-dappled waters of the Poudre River moved listlessly beneath the lengthening shadows of the giant cottonwoods lining the western bank.

With mounting panic Sarah glanced again toward the five dots as they approached and grew larger. She ran around to the north side of the house and looked over the grassy meadow. The horses and cattle were grazing lazily in the slanting sun.

Circling the house eastward, she hurried toward the corral. Her nervous fingers fumbled with the sliding latch on the corral gate. She had always had trouble with the stubborn thing. It would not budge. Cupping her hands around her mouth, she shouted in the direction of the barn. "Will!" No answer. "*Will!*" Still no answer.

Bending beneath the top pole of the corral fence, she crawled through, then dashed across the corral and yanked open the barn door. As it grated on rusty hinges, Sarah screamed, "*Will! Will!*" The barn was dark and quiet.

1

A wave of panic washed over the frightened woman. Just as she screamed her husband's name again, a door on the opposite side of the barn flew open. A rectangular shaft of light illuminated the inside of the dark structure and was instantly filled with the shadowed frame of Will Blackburn. "What is it, Sarah?" he asked, moving toward her.

"They're coming!" she cried, reaching for him.

Folding her trembling, fragile frame in his muscular arms, he said, "Are you sure?"

"Who else would it be?" she replied, digging her fingernails into her husband's back. "There are five of them!"

Fourteen-year-old Daisy and twelve-year-old Myra appeared in the door their father had just entered. "What is it, Mama?" asked Daisy.

"Wait here," came the heavy voice of Will Blackburn.

Freeing himself from Sarah's grasp, the big man moved through the barn door and stepped out into the corral. He didn't need to ask from which direction they were approaching. He knew.

Squinting for focus, Blackburn set his eyes eastward. The five dots that Sarah had seen now assumed the shapes of horses and riders. A sick feeling hit Blackburn's stomach.

Turning toward the barn, he said, "Sarah, get inside the house. I want you girls to climb up in your room and stay there. Don't make a sound. Those men riding this way are bad. Now go on."

Daisy's face twisted. "But Daddy—"

"Now!" snapped Blackburn.

As the girls slipped through the pole fence, Sarah looked into her husband's ashen face. "All these years I've dreaded this moment," she said with quivering voice. "What can we do, Will?"

Blackburn's face was fixed with grim lines. He eyed the approaching riders again. "Get into the house, honey," he said, tight-lipped.

"Do you want your guns?" she asked.

"I can't fight it out with five men. I'll just have to talk 'em out of it."

"I'll stay out here with you."

"No." Blackburn's voice was firm. "Those men have been locked up for twelve years. You're a beautiful woman. They'll—" Blackburn wiped his brow with his sleeve and adjusted his sweat-stained hat. "Please, Sarah. Get in the house and stay there. Make the girls stay in the loft. No sounds. Go on now."

The big man opened the corral gate for his wife and walked her toward the house. As they reached the yard he stopped and squared his broad shoulders. Sarah gave him a painful look and went into the house.

Alone, Will Blackburn faced the oncoming riders. He could not make out their features yet, but there was no question in his mind who they were. They were keeping their promise. The bitter memory was still raw and painful on his mind.

Time slid back. . . .

It was a mild April day in 1860. Will Blackburn had just closed the deal on a two-hundred-acre farm ten miles due west of Topeka, Kansas. He had signed the papers on the front porch of the gleaming white farmhouse. Leaving his lawyer with the land agent to tie up the loose ends, he rode toward town. Blackburn was elated and proud of himself. After all, how many men twenty-nine years old had a two-hundred-acre spread?

Sarah would be happy to know the farm was now theirs. They both agreed that the place for Jimmy and the girls to be raised was in the country. Their son would be five in June, and now he could have some animals to care for and begin to learn responsibility.

Bounding over the rolling green hills, Blackburn loved the feel of a good animal beneath him and the wind in his face. Coming up on his right was the gate of Mac Whitaker's place. Whitaker would be his nearest neighbor, with their houses about four miles apart. He had met the man once in Topeka, so as the gate drew closer he decided to take a few moments and say hello to his new neighbor.

Turning through the gate, he guided the nimble bay gelding down the double-rutted wagon trail toward the house, which was situated in a dense stand of poplars, cottonwoods, and willows. As Blackburn drew near the shaded buildings, something out behind the barn caught his eye. Five rough-looking men were clustered beneath a big cottonwood tree.

He could not make out what the men were doing until he rounded the corner of the barn and the whole scene came into view. Mac Whitaker lay in a crumpled heap on the ground. One of the men drove a heavy boot into Whitaker's rib cage as Blackburn called out.

Startled, the five outlaws wheeled and went for their guns. Blackburn studied their faces quickly and kicked the gelding's sides. The frightened animal lunged into the tight group, knocking them down. By the time the men had scrambled to their feet, the bay had skirted the dense stand of trees and was carrying its rider toward the gate.

Blackburn glanced behind him as several shots were fired, but the bullets were only ripping into the trees. He held the bay at a full gallop all the way into town.

Skidding to a dusty halt in front of the sheriff's office, Blackburn charged through the door. "Sheriff!" he gasped breathlessly. "I just left Mac Whitaker's place. There were five men beating him up!"

Sheriff Sy Yeager was seated at his desk, reading his mail. Looking up at the tall man, he said, "Did you recognize them?"

"No," responded Blackburn, "but I'd know them if I saw them again."

"They see you?"

"Yeah. Took a few shots at me, but I rode through them. By the time they got to their feet I was past the trees and out of sight."

Yeager scraped his chair back, grasped a double-barreled shotgun off the rack behind the desk, and said, "Let's go." The lawman shoved some shells in his pocket, bolted through the door, and mounted his horse.

"Think we ought to take some more men?" asked Blackburn, swinging into his own saddle.

"They'll probably be gone when we get there. If not, this twelve-gauge will handle 'em." Yeager spied a man coming down the board sidewalk. Raising his voice, he said, "Henry! Tell Doc Catron to jump in his buggy and hightail it out to Mac Whitaker's place. Old Mac may be hurt!"

Henry nodded and wheeled around.

The two riders left Topeka in a cloud of dust. Blackburn's bay was well-lathered and breathing heavily as they turned through Whitaker's gate and headed for the buildings shaded among the trees.

"Behind the barn!" shouted Blackburn, pointing.

They reined in at the spot where he had seen the five men,

but the place was deserted now. Mac Whitaker was nowhere in sight. Sliding from the saddle, Blackburn studied the rumpled ground where the beating had taken place. There was a smooth path about eighteen inches wide in the soft dirt, which led to the barn.

The two men ran to the barn door, which was standing slightly ajar. Mac Whitaker was lying facedown on the earthen floor. He was breathing but unconscious, his silver hair matted with blood and dirt.

The two men carefully rolled Whitaker onto his back and moaned as they saw his face. The five men had beaten the old man to a pulp.

"One of them was caving in his ribs when I rode up," said Blackburn. "Does he have a wife, Sheriff?"

"She died several years ago. He lives alone."

Standing up, Yeager pulled a saddle blanket from a shelf. He rolled it neatly and placed it under Whitaker's head. "Why don't you find some water, Will? We'll do what we can till Doc Catron gets here."

Within thirty minutes the unconscious form of Mac Whitaker lay in the buggy next to Dr. Sam Catron.

"You go ahead, Doc," said Sy Yeager. "Will and I are going to check their tracks. Soon's we get a line on what direction they headed, we'll be in town to form a posse. Those skunks are going to pay for this."

Less than two hours later Will Blackburn walked through the back door of his small frame house in Topeka. The winded and weary horse was in the shed, glad for the rest.

Jimmy and Daisy were playing with some boxes on the floor. Sarah was holding the baby, sitting in a rocking chair. She looked up and smiled as her husband entered the room. "Did we get it?" she asked apprehensively.

"What's that?" asked Blackburn, tossing his hat on the table.

Sarah's brow furrowed as she focused on his face. "Will, what's wrong? Didn't the sale go through?"

"The what? Oh. Yes, honey. Yes, we got the farm."

Young Jimmy, almost five years old, shouted and danced with glee. Although two-year-old Daisy did not understand Jimmy's ecstasy, she clapped her hands and giggled.

"Oh, Will, that's wonderful!" exclaimed Sarah, rising to her feet. "But what's wrong?"

Blackburn mopped his moistened brow with a bandanna. "I was on my way home from the farm. I decided to take a minute and stop by old Mac Whitaker's place. You know—tell him we were going to be neighbors."

"Yes."

"I came upon five men beating on the old man. I charged into them with the horse and headed for town. They started shooting—"

"Oh, Will," gasped Sarah.

"I'm okay, honey. I took Sheriff Yeager back out there with me. The vicious brutes were gone, but we found old Mac unconscious. Doc Catron has him at his office now. Says he may die."

"Oh, no," said Sarah softly, shaking her head.

"Yeager's got a posse ready to ride, along with a fresh horse for me. I'm the only one who can identify them, so I've got to go along."

"I understand," Sarah said with a weak smile.

Bending over, he stroked the baby's cheek and kissed Sarah. "I'll be back as soon as I can."

"Be careful, Will," she said.

Blackburn hugged Jimmy and Daisy, picked up his hat, and was gone.

The five Hegler brothers were camped in a dry wash nearly twenty miles south of Mac Whitaker's place.

Luke, the oldest and leader of the gang, bellied up to the crest of the wash and scanned the northern horizon. While Les, Larry, and Lyle busied themselves with preparing supper, Lonnie lay down beside his elder brother. "See anythin'?" he asked, studying the prairie for himself.

Big Luke spit a brown stream into the grass. "Nope. Not yet."

The sun had already disappeared from the western sky, leaving a darkening purple hue over the land.

"Mebbe them Topeka folks won't feel that the old man was worth formin' a posse over," said Lonnie.

"Can't be sure," said Luke evenly. "We beat him up purty bad."

"His own fault," said Lonnie coldly. "If he'd jist tole us where he kept his money, he wouldn't got hisself stomped on."

"We should've caught that tall dude," said Luke. "We'da had more time to search the place."

The gathering darkness left the northern horizon with no signs of life. Luke and Lonnie Hegler returned to the others and sat down to eat.

"One of us'll have to be awake at all times," said Luke, chewing and talking at the same time. "If they come, they'll probably hit us in the dark. If there ain't no posse by sunrise, there probably won't be none."

Lyle, the youngest of the Hegler brothers, volunteered to take the first watch. About midnight a quarter moon appeared in the star-bedecked sky as Lonnie took the second watch and the rest of the bearded, unbathed gang slept peacefully. He was relieved by Larry, whom Les relieved about an hour before dawn. Luke, being the leader, had not taken his turn at watch.

When the rim of the sun peeked over the edge of the earth, Big Luke opened his eyes and blinked. The silhouette of Sheriff Sy Yeager's body stood over him, against the morning sky. Luke sat up with a start. Blinking in disbelief, he stared into the twin barrels of Yeager's shotgun.

"What the—" Luke blurted.

"On your feet!" the sheriff said heavily.

The sound of Yeager's voice penetrated the sleep of the other three. They sat up, gazing in shock at the ten armed men surrounding them.

Yeager drove a boot into Luke's side. "I said on your feet!"

Luke stood and swung around, looking for Les. "How—"

"He's still asleep," said Yeager levelly, nodding toward Les, who was sprawled on the grassy slope. "He was dozing anyhow, so we put a knot on his head. He'll be out for a while."

Big Luke swore. "Dammit, what's this all about, Sheriff? You had no call to whump my brother on the head. We're travelin' men, just movin' through to Oklahoma Territory."

"You know what it's about," said Yeager. "You beat up an old man. Left him on the edge of death. If he dies, every one of you will hang."

Luke Hegler turned his dirty palms upward, hunching his shoulders in a gesture of innocence. "I don't know what you're talkin' about, Sheriff. Old man? We didn't beat up no—"

A long, lanky frame detached itself from the encircling posse. Luke's words dropped off when his eyes focused on the face. It was Will Blackburn.

"It's them, Sheriff," said Blackburn. "I'll swear to it in court."

Judge Anthony Howard set the trial for April twenty-first. Three days before that date Will Blackburn was loading furniture onto a wagon while Sarah was busy in the house, packing fragile belongings into crates.

A nine-year-old boy named Harold Sightler slowly approached the busy man. "Mornin', Mr. Blackburn," he said in a friendly tone.

"Morning, Harold." Blackburn smiled, loading a chair in the wagon bed.

"Bet you were real glad to hear that Mr. Whitaker is doin' better, huh?"

"Sure was, Harold. He came mighty close to leaving this world."

"Too bad about his eyes though."

Blackburn's expression darkened. "Yeah."

"Won't he be able to see *anything*?"

"Doc Catron says only shadows against bright light," Blackburn answered sadly.

"Guess you're the only one can testify against the Heglers, then, huh?"

"Looks like it."

"They're goin' to Leavenworth, huh?"

"Sure hope so."

"How long you think the judge will give 'em?"

"Don't know, Harold. Ought to lock them up and throw away the key." Blackburn started for the house.

"Uh . . . Mr. Blackburn," said Harold nervously.

The tall man paused and turned. "Yes?"

Harold was pulling a wrinkled white envelope from inside his shirt. "I was playin' over behind the jail a while ago. That big man Luke . . ."

Blackburn eyed the envelope. "What about him?"

"He talked to me through the little window with the bars on it. Said he would give me a dollar if I'd run home and get an envelope and pencil and paper. I got it for him. Then he said if I'd bring a letter to you, he'd give me another dollar."

"He give you the money?"

"Yes. Said I shouldn't tell no one though."

Blackburn took the envelope from the boy. "Best you leave it that way then."

"Yes, sir," said Harold. "'Bye."

As the boy skipped away, Blackburn said, "Thanks."

Blackburn noted that the envelope was sealed. Whatever its contents, Harold Sightler had not seen it. Running his index finger under the flap, he removed the note. In large, crooked letters it read:

> If you want to live, you better have a suddin loss
> of memory. Tell them at the trile you made a misteak.
> If you don't, we'll come after you when we get out
> of prison. Even if it's ten years.

" . . . you have there, Will?"

Suddenly Sarah's words gained his attention. She was standing beside him, holding a crate of dishes. It was too late to hide it from her. "Oh, uh . . . a letter."

"From whom?"

"The, uh . . . Heglers," he said, turning the page away from her eyes.

Sarah set her jaw and placed the crate on the tailgate of the wagon. "Let me see," she said, extending her hand.

Reluctantly, the tall man gave her the paper. Sarah's face crimsoned as she read it. Pulling her lips tight, she hissed, "Dirty scum! Wait till the judge sees this—he'll double their sentence!"

"Wouldn't do any good, Sarah. And they know it."

The beautiful face reddened some more. "What do you mean it wouldn't do any good? It's written evidence."

"It isn't signed, Sarah," he said. "Harold Sightler brought it to me. The court wouldn't act on the word of a little boy. We'll just have to forget it."

"Forget it?" she said, wide-eyed.

"Honey, there's no way to prove the Heglers wrote it. They'll get at least seven or eight years. That's a long time. By the time they get out they'll cool off."

"Either that or it'll seethe inside them like a slow poison and they'll come for you with murder in their eyes."

"Tell you what I'll do," he said placatingly. "I'll take it to Sheriff Yeager, see what he says."

"All right." Sarah handed him back the letter. "I think the law ought to know about it."

Blackburn kissed his wife's forehead and walked toward the center of town. Less than an hour later he returned and entered the house. Sarah was on her knees in the middle of the parlor floor, rolling up bedding. When she looked up, he said, "The sheriff's going to take it to Judge Howard and let him see it."

"Good. I hope he reads it to the jury."

While a neighbor watched the children, Will and Sarah took a load of furniture out to their new farm. It was nearly dark when they returned to town. Sheriff Sy Yeager was waiting by the front porch as they pulled up.

The Blackburns saw him smile in the fading light. "Judge says it would be shaky as evidence in court, Will," said Yeager. "But he's gonna keep it in mind."

"Guess that's all we can ask," replied Blackburn.

"If this was back east, I couldn't even have taken the letter to him," said the sheriff. "Things aren't as civilized here." He handed the letter to Blackburn and bid them good evening.

On the morning of April 21, the Blackburns had completed their move to the farm. They drove to town, deposited the children with the same people as before, and made their way to the courthouse.

The trial took less than an hour. The Heglers glared at Will Blackburn with boiling hatred as he sat in the witness box and fearlessly pointed them out as the ones who had beaten Mac Whitaker, leaving him virtually blind. The jury convened for five minutes and returned with the guilty verdict.

Judge Howard stood the convicted men before the bench and gave them a fiery lecture on the ignominy of their dastardly deed. Information had been obtained revealing that all five had been in trouble with the law in their home state of Missouri and were notorious as gunmen. They had done short terms in jails and prisons there.

It was expected by all, including the Heglers, that the judge would sentence them to seven or eight years, with parole possible in four years. Taking into consideration, however, their past and the threatening letter sent to Will Blackburn, Judge Howard ordered them to serve twelve years in the Leavenworth Territorial Prison near Kansas City.

The filthy, unshaven bunch stood in stunned disbelief when

they heard the sentence. They eyed one another, calculating it would be at least six years before any possibility of parole, when the judge hit them with another shocker. Looking at each of them in turn, he added gruffly, *"With absolutely no consideration of parole."*

The gavel popped the desk. The shackled prisoners wheeled and were ushered up the aisle toward the door. The Blackburns sat in the second row of seats next to the aisle. Sarah gripped her husband's arm when Luke Hegler paused, staring straight at him. The black beard emphasized his bared teeth. To Sarah he looked like a huge killer beast.

"So it's twelve years, Blackburn," he hissed. "You better enjoy 'em. When we get out, you're a dead man."

Standing to the rear of the five brothers, Sheriff Yeager spoke up. "Let's go, Luke!"

As he moved off, Hegler kept his virulent black eyes locked on Blackburn's face. Death was in his stare.

Blackburn sat with his arm around Sarah as the courtroom emptied. Her whole body trembled. With pleading eyes she said, "Let's move away from here. Now!"

"We'll talk about it later, honey," he said softly.

Sarah burst into tears. "Oh, Will! What if they break out? They'll come straight here. Please, let's sell the farm. Let's go where they'll never find us!"

"Let's go home," said the tall man. "We'll talk about it later."

The matter of moving was discussed on and off for over a year, always in privacy, never in front of the children. The death threat to their father was kept from Jimmy, Daisy, and Myra Blackburn.

Finally, in May 1861, Blackburn succumbed to Sarah's pleadings, though he insisted the Heglers would find him wherever they went. She knew it was true but said she would feel better if they left Kansas.

By the end of June war had broken out back east, but the Blackburn family had bought two hundred acres of rich farmland six hundred miles from Topeka, in northern Colorado, and were peacefully settled in. The farm was situated some nine miles northwest of Fort Collins on the Poudre River, nestled into the rugged foothills of the majestic Rockies.

Within a year Blackburn had enlarged the small house that went with the place and built several sheds and a big barn. In

Colorado the war seemed far away. Rainfall was plentiful and the soil was good. Talk of the Heglers dwindled to an occasional mention between Blackburn and Sarah after the children were bedded down at night.

One day in October 1862, seven-year-old Jimmy was playing alone in the yard beside the house. He had fashioned himself a toy gun out of a dead branch that had the natural shape of a revolver. Sarah happened to step out on the porch. Unaware of her presence the boy whipped out the gun from under his belt and shouted, "Bam! That's for you, Luke! Bam! Bam! Bam! Bam! That takes care of the rest of you! You're dead now—all five of you!"

A hot shaft pierced Sarah Blackburn's heart. "Jimmy!" she shouted.

Startled, the boy dropped the stick and turned to face his mother. "Y-yes, ma'am?"

"Who were you shooting?" Sarah suppressed her voice, trying to remain calm.

"Nobody," Jimmy said weakly, dipping his chin.

"Then who's *Luke*?"

"Luke?"

"Yes. Who's Luke?"

"He's nobody," said the lad, his words trailing off.

"Jimmy, come here." His mother's voice was firm.

Jimmy edged his way slowly toward the porch.

Bending down and looking him straight in the eye, Sarah said, "I want the truth. Who were the five people you were shooting?"

Jimmy cleared his throat. His mother knew the answer, but she wanted to hear him say it. "Th-the Heglers."

"Now, son, I'm not going to punish you. I want you to tell me how you know about the Heglers."

"I . . . I been awake sometimes when you 'n' Papa have talked about 'em." Jimmy's face clouded. "I'm gonna get me a *real* gun, Mama. I'm gonna kill them dirty skunks before they kill Papa!"

Sarah Blackburn broke into tears and pulled the boy close to her breast. "No, Jimmy," she sobbed. "I don't want you ever to kill anybody. Papa will be all right. Those bad men are a long way from here. They have nine years to go, nearly. By that time they'll forget all about us. Do you hear?"

"Yes, ma'am."

"Now, boy, I don't want you ever to speak of those bad men again. Not even to Papa. Understand?"

"Yes, ma'am."

"Let's just keep it between you and me . . . okay?"

"Yes, ma'am."

From that moment Jimmy Blackburn never voiced another word about the five gunmen. They never left his mind, but their name did not touch his lips.

In less than a week Will Blackburn caught his wife sobbing in the middle of the night. She broke down and told him of Jimmy's toy gun and his knowledge of the Heglers. Blackburn never mentioned the incident to his son.

The years passed quickly. The girls were blossoming into lovely young ladies. On his sixteenth birthday Jimmy announced to the family that when he finished his schooling in Fort Collins, he wanted to go back east and study law. The West was becoming more settled now, and Fort Collins needed a good attorney. His parents were elated, and they actively encouraged him to pursue his desire.

Then came April of 1872. On the morning of the twenty-first Will Blackburn awakened to see his wife sitting on the edge of the bed. She was gripping the covers and sobbing. Her shoulders shook.

Sitting up, Blackburn asked, "Honey, what's wrong?"

As she turned to face him, he saw her deep-blue eyes swimming in tears. With quivering lip she said, "It was twelve years ago, Will."

"What was?"

"The *trial*." Sniffing, she continued, "They'll be out in a few days."

Will Blackburn took his frightened wife in his arms and held her tight.

That had been a month ago. Now it was May 28, Jimmy's seventeenth birthday. Will Blackburn watched Luke Hegler and his brothers coming up the wagon-rutted road, riding five abreast.

Chapter Two

Will Blackburn fixed his gaze on the riders. The Hegler brothers sat heavy in their saddles, hunched slightly forward. Ferret-eyed, bearded beasts in dirty clothes, they had a fierce, menacing look.

Blackburn's rigid shadow stretched long before him. Without turning, he knew Sarah would be watching from behind the curtains. Daisy and Myra would be up in the loft by now. He was glad the only window up there was on the west side. If the Heglers gunned him down, the girls would not see it.

Jimmy! Blackburn suddenly thought of his son, who was working at the south edge of the farm. Noting the length of his shadow, the broad-shouldered farmer knew that Jimmy would be returning soon. He would work till sundown, then head for the house. If there was trouble, the boy might get himself killed trying to fight off the Heglers. Though quiet in nature, he had a fierce temper when riled.

Breathing a prayer, he said, "Dear God, don't let Jimmy come back till this thing is over."

Facing into the western sun, the Heglers eyed the tall form of Will Blackburn. He stood less than fifty yards away, unmoving, ready to face them.

"He ain't got no gun," Lyle exclaimed.

Big Luke spat a dark brown stream. "Wouldn't do him no good," he said coldly. "We'd just kill 'im quicker. I like it better this way. We'll have some fun first. Sun'll be down in less than an hour. We'll make 'im sweat for a while. Kill his family right in front of his eyes. Then at sundown we'll blow him to eternity."

Les Hegler looked at his older brother and gave a dry, humorless chuckle. "I been waitin' twelve long years for this moment. I sure don't want it to end too quick."

Halting their mounts within twenty feet of the man, the Heglers sat glaring at him. Presently Luke said, "We're keepin' our promise, sodbuster. We come to kill yuh."

Blackburn's mouth was dry, and he could feel the pulse throbbing in his temples. "You boys didn't learn anything in twelve years of prison?" he said grimly.

"Little scared, sodbuster?" asked Lonnie.

Ignoring the question, Blackburn said, "Things have changed in twelve years. The law has new and better ways of tracking criminals."

Larry Hegler turned his head back and forth, scanning the land. "You're a long ways from anybody, sodbuster. We can slaughter you like a hog and hang you up to cure. Be a long time before somebody finds your salty carcass."

"Yeah." Les chuckled. "We'll be long gone afore anybody knows yer dead. Ain't no law gonna ketch us."

"Yes they will," said Blackburn firmly. "You'll hang."

Lonnie laughed. "I think the big man is skeert spitless, boys. While he's tossin' threats his guts is churnin' like buttermilk in his belly."

A flash of heat touched Blackburn's temper. "You talk big," he said, staring down Lonnie Hegler. "You're pretty tough, aren't you?"

Lonnie's face stiffened.

Blackburn's mind was working. There was no question that these men had ridden over six hundred miles with one intent: to ride away, leaving him dead. Maybe . . . maybe if he goaded one of them into a fight, they would be satisfied just to leave him with less blood and some broken bones. It was worth a try. He thought again of Jimmy. *Please stay out in that field, Jimmy. Please.*

Baring his teeth, he said to Lonnie, "Yeah. You're pretty tough. You're a big man with a gang around. But get any one of you alone and your backbone turns to jelly."

Lonnie spun a look at Luke, who eyed him blankly.

"What did you big brave men go to prison for? Beating up a helpless old man. And it took five of you to do it."

Lonnie Hegler looked at Luke again.

Blackburn's voice became louder. "What about *you*, big mouth?" His eyes fixed on Lonnie. "Ever fight a real man?"

Quietly, Luke shifted in the saddle and said, "Sounds like a challenge, Lonnie. You gonna take it up, or does big brother have to fight your battles fer yuh?"

Lonnie Hegler was just under six feet tall but like all the Heglers was heavyset, tilting the scales near two hundred twenty pounds. He leaped from his horse and charged Blackburn like a maddened bull. He forgot that he had been in the saddle for hours, his legs stiff. Awkwardly, he stumbled into Will Blackburn's rawboned fist.

The remaining Hegler brothers quickly dismounted as Lonnie flopped to his back, shaking his head. The four hesitated as Lonnie rolled to his knees and stood up. He swayed slightly, then charged the farmer again.

Blackburn balanced himself, sidestepped deftly, and chopped the thick-bodied man with a savage blow to the jaw. Lonnie slumped to the ground and lay still.

"Get up, Lonnie! Kill 'im! Kill 'im!" the brothers shouted. But Lonnie could not get up.

The four remaining brothers looked at one another and suddenly started forward, surrounding the farmer. Blackburn could not fight them all, and he was powerless as three of the Heglers grasped his arms and swung him around. "Hit 'im, Luke!" screamed Lyle.

Blackburn tried vainly to shake loose as Luke closed in on him and began to pound him in the belly, doubling him over. Suddenly the side door of the house flew open. "Stop it!" screeched a female voice.

Sarah Blackburn was holding a shiny Winchester .44. A red ribbon was tied to the barrel. From the wooden stock a tag dangling by a string read: HAPPY BIRTHDAY JIMMY.

Sarah's face was livid with rage. "Let go of him! Get off our property! *Now!*"

With blinding speed Les Hegler palmed the revolver in his holster, thumbed back the hammer, and touched the muzzle to Will Blackburn's head. "Drop it, lady," he growled, "or I'll blow his head off!"

Sarah's eyes grew wide. She hesitated only a moment before she lowered the rifle.

Instantly Luke moved to the woman, snatched the rifle from her hands, and smashed it against the porch step. Flipping the broken gun to the porch floor, he shoved Sarah inside the house. Looking over his shoulder, he said, "Bring the farmer in here."

The sun was dipping behind the jagged peaks as Will Blackburn was slammed into a straight-backed chair. In the loft overhead, two terrified girls looked down unseen.

Sarah moved to the cupboard and leaned against it, her face a mask of terror. Added fear touched Will Blackburn. He was helpless to protect his family.

Lonnie Hegler had regained his senses and stumbled into the large kitchen. He flashed the farmer a hot look of hatred. Luke stood over Blackburn. Curling his upper lip, he said, "You got some kids, ain'tcha?"

Blackburn lifted his sagging head. His eyes grew cold as steel. "You harm my children . . . I'll kill you all."

"Now, you ain't in too good a position to do that," rasped Luke, leveling his gun muzzle on Blackburn's face. "Where are yer kids?"

"Your beef is with me, Hegler," snapped Blackburn. "They didn't testify against you. I did."

"You don't have to remind me, mister," said Luke, placing the muzzle against Blackburn's forehead. The hammer was still cocked.

Sarah gasped. Her whole body trembled.

"Maybe if we work your little woman over, you'll produce the brats."

Blackburn's eyes widened as Luke nodded his head toward Larry. The ugliest Hegler lunged for Sarah, sank his fingers into the neck of her dress, and gave a yank. Pain shot through her lower back as she slammed into the cupboard counter. The dress tore in a straight line, exposing her shoulder. Quickly she grasped the torn piece, moving it into place while sliding along the cupboard.

Larry moved toward her again when suddenly Myra screamed from overhead.

Sweat beaded on Blackburn's forehead. The barrel of Luke's gun was pressed tight against the skin. Both girls could be heard whimpering in the loft.

Luke eyed the ladder that led to the girl's sleeping quarters. With hungry eyes Larry was inching toward Sarah.

"Larry," said Luke. "Pump some lead into the loft."

"*No!*" shouted Blackburn.

Sarah screamed as Larry adeptly fanned his revolver, pointing the muzzle straight into the loft.

Myra died instantly. As the blue smoke sifted upward,

Daisy crawled to the edge and put one hand on the top of the ladder. Stretching head and shoulders over the loft's edge, she breathed one last word, "Mama" . . . and slumped down. Her head and one arm dangled lifelessly.

Sarah, frenzied to desperation, grabbed a knife from the counter and drove it into Larry's shoulder. When Larry screamed, Luke swung his gaze in that direction. Blackburn batted the gun from his head and it fired, sending the bullet into the wall. He knocked Luke down with a body blow and grasped for the man's gun.

At the same instant Lyle drew and fired at Sarah. The bullet tore into her heart. She slammed into the cupboard from the impact, then dropped limply to the floor.

Les and Lonnie both shot Blackburn at the same time. He collapsed on top of Luke, who quickly crawled out from under the man's weight.

"Let's get outta here!" bellowed Luke, snatching up his gun.

The five men dashed out into the dusk, Larry trailing blood. While they scrambled for their horses, Will Blackburn raised his bloody frame from the floor and staggered to a rolltop desk. Sliding open a drawer, he grasped a Navy Colt .44 and stumbled to the door. Leaning against the jamb, he lifted the gun with effort. The killers were just spurring their horses as he sighted on the man closest to him and squeezed the trigger. The gun bucked against his palm. Lonnie Hegler stiffened in the saddle, hung there for a brief moment, then fell to the ground. Four men reined around. Will was trying to steady the gun in his hands when Luke aimed and fired. The blood-soaked farmer dropped to the floor, lying half in the house and half on the porch.

The outlaws studied the crumpled form of Lonnie Hegler lying motionless on the ground.

"He's dead," said Luke. "Let's go."

"What are you talkin' about, Luke?" said Les. "We can't jist leave him there. We gotta bury him!"

"Ain't time," snapped the older brother. "All that shootin' is bound to bring neighbors. 'Sides, we gotta get Larry to a doctor. Ain't nothin' we can do fer poor Lonnie now. Draggin' his corpse with us ain't gonna do nothin' but slow us down. Now let's git!"

As the Heglers became black dots in the east again, Will

Blackburn groaned and rolled belly down. Painfully, he struggled to pull his knees beneath him.

Nearby, Lonnie Hegler's body twitched, shifted, and twitched again. Slowly he rolled over, trying to lift himself.

Earlier in the afternoon Jimmy Blackburn had climbed from the wagon and surveyed the southern pasture. His father had been right. The cattle *had* broken down the fence around the haystack. One of the posts was snapped off, and the barbed wire lay slack and tangled on the ground.

The fenced area had actually held six stacks after the third cutting last September. They were down to one, but it would easily last until the first cutting in about three weeks—that is, if the fence was repaired so the cattle couldn't eat everything up.

A dozen or more were inside the area now, chomping at the sun-bleached hay. Jumping from the wagon, Jimmy ran into the enclosure and chased the pesky creatures back into the pasture. Before starting on the fence, he took a pitchfork from the bed of the wagon and gathered up the hay that the cattle had scattered. This done, the tall, lanky youth returned the pitchfork into the wagon bed and removed one of the fence posts he had brought along.

As he worked the stump of the broken fence post loose, Jimmy paused and eyed his gangly body, self-conscious of his lean frame. Sometimes he was annoyed by a superabundance of elbows, knees, and feet, but he had just turned seventeen, and his dad said this awkward stage would pass in another year or so, or at least that's the way it had been for his dad. Jimmy hoped that someday he would be as strong and well-proportioned as the senior Blackburn.

Folks were already remarking how much he resembled his pa. "Spittin' image," one old-timer called it. As he worked, Jimmy smiled to think of how just this morning his mother had made him and his father stand back to back after breakfast. She had laid a hand on each head and exclaimed, "He's only an inch shorter, Will. Time he's eighteen, he'll be taller than you!"

Jimmy's dad had laughed, cuffed him lightly on the chin, and said, "Then I'll have to call *him* sir!"

Stretching the barbed wire fiddlestring-tight and pounding down staples, the lean-bodied youth wondered if his father

had bought him that new Remington rifle for his birthday.
He'd sure put out a strong hint about it the last time they
were in the gun shop at Fort Collins.

The last staple was driven, and it was still a while before
sunset. Jimmy entertained the thought that maybe if he got
back early, his mother would let him sample his birthday
cake before supper. He was sure it was chocolate, his favorite.

Jimmy loaded the tools in the wagon bed and was about to
climb aboard when he heard a calf bawl. Running his eyes
westward toward the sound, he squinted against the lowering
sun and spied a calf caught in a shrub thicket by the river.

Guiding the wagon to the spot, Jimmy jumped from the
seat and talked comfortingly to the calf as he approached. The
little beast had worked its way in tightly.

The sun was dipping behind the jagged peaks when the
calf, freed from its prison, bawled and ran stiff-legged toward
a gathering of cattle. Jimmy climbed back into the wagon and
yawned, stretching his long length.

Suddenly, from over the ridge toward the house, came a
series of gunshots, making a staccato echo across the broad
valley. The youth froze and, pointing his face northward,
strained his ears.

Another shot came, followed instantly by several more.
Panic bolted through Jimmy Blackburn. One word escaped
his lips as he snapped the reins: "Heglers!"

As the wagon bounced across the open fields another shot
cracked the air, followed by one more. Topping the crest of
the ridge, Jimmy eyed the familiar cluster of buildings in the
gathering dusk. A group of riders was galloping hard toward
town.

He angled across the hay meadow, swung around the west
end of the corral, and headed for the house. Rolling the
wagon to a thundering halt, he tensed to alight. Jimmy's gaze
shot first to a big man who lay across the wagon ruts, struggling to work his gun out of its holster. There was a red spot
on the back of his shirt.

Quickly the youth's eyes fell on his father, blood-soaked,
swaying on his knees on the side porch. Will Blackburn was
trying to bring his gun to bear, facing the big man on the
ground.

Lonnie Hegler now had his gun in hand, striving with
difficulty to thumb back the hammer.

With lightning speed Jimmy reached behind him, grasped the pitchfork, and leaped from the wagon. With the pitchfork poised, and having no thought for his own safety, he lunged for Hegler, charging straight into the gun muzzle. Lonnie ejected a mortal cry as the tines pierced his throat. He fell over, blood gurgling. The fork handle swayed in its vertical position as the youth ran to his father.

Blackburn had fallen and was sprawled in a mass of blood on the porch. Numb with terror, Jimmy knelt beside him. "Pa!" he screamed. "Pa! Don't die!"

Will Blackburn's face was pale with death. He coughed once and said, "Heglers," coughed again . . . and died.

Jimmy could not believe his eyes. This couldn't really be happening. Certainly it was just a bad dream. He told himself he would wake up soon and the nightmare would be over. His brain came back to reality as he found himself shaking his father's body and crying, "Pa! Pa!"

Easing down on his haunches, the terrified youth released the body and looked at his hands. They were crimson-smeared and sticky. Wiping the blood on his pants, he stepped over the inanimate form of his father and fixed his eyes on the open door of the house. It was dark in contrast to the still-fading light outside. The deathly silence told him what he would find.

Avoiding the pool of blood on the threshold, Jimmy moved inside. The stillness of the room was oppressive, foreboding. It took only seconds to find his mother in the gathering gloom. As he knelt beside her inert form, a coldness formed in the middle of his chest, then spread slowly through his entire body.

Standing up, Jimmy scanned the room. Suddenly he knew where to look. Stepping away from his mother's body, he swung his gaze toward the loft. Daisy's head and arm dangled lifelessly over the edge. He climbed the ladder. There was enough light coming through the window to see Myra. She lay on her back, eyes wide open, staring sightlessly toward the angled ceiling.

Jimmy moved back down the ladder in a stupor. He heard nothing but his own heartbeat. It was as if he were in a vacuum, a timeless void of dismal gray. There was a bitter, brassy taste in his mouth.

Meticulously he lighted a lantern, carried his mother's

body to the open area of the kitchen, and stretched it out on the floor. Climbing the ladder again, he eased Daisy's body over the edge of the loft, cradled it in his arms, then descended and laid the lifeless form beside his mother. Then he carried Myra down and laid her next to Daisy.

The lantern sitting on the kitchen table spread a rectangular shaft of light onto the porch. As Jimmy moved through the door his eye caught a reflection of something shiny. He stooped over and picked up the broken rifle. The red ribbon still clung to the barrel, and the tag still dangled from the stock. Jimmy angled the tag toward the light and silently read the words.

Lowering his hands, he let the gun slip from his fingers and fall to the floor. With effort, he dragged his father's slack frame inside and laid it next to his mother.

The night breeze came through the open door as Jimmy lowered himself into a straight-backed chair and fixed his vacant gaze on the bodies on the kitchen floor. The only sound in the room was the monotonous ticking of the clock on the wall.

The lantern had ceased to burn sometime during the night. At dawn the growing breeze moved the open door slightly, causing the hinges to squeak. The clock ticked on. Jimmy Blackburn remained in the chair where he had been all night. The numbing coldness that had been in his body was gone. With the dawn came a hot, seething hatred. His bloodshot eyes were aflame with molten fury. If it was the last thing he ever did, he would kill the Hegler brothers. Suddenly he remembered. He *had* killed one already.

Rising stiffly to his feet, Jimmy stepped outside. The sun was exposing its flaming rim on the eastern horizon. He walked off the porch, noting that his father's blood had soaked into the dry wooden floor and turned a dull brown.

The pitchfork was still standing vertically, Lonnie Hegler dead on his back. His cold, stiff fingers grasped the tines that pierced his throat.

The outlaw's saddled horse stood near the corral, where the Blackburn horses had gathered inside the pole fence. Jimmy fetched the horse and led it to the spot where Lonnie Hegler's corpse lay. Closing his fingers on the fork handle, he yanked it out of the dead man's neck.

As he tossed the pitchfork aside his gaze fell on the Frontier Colt .45 lying on the ground. The hammer was in its place; Lonnie's weak thumbs had not eased it back. Jimmy picked it up and wiped off the dew with his sleeve. The weapon felt strange to his hands. He was a crack shot with a rifle but had never used a handgun. Somehow it felt good to hold it.

Jimmy's eyes dropped to the gun belt encircling Lonnie's hips. The holster was tied to the dead man's thigh with a thin leather thong. Laying the gun on Lonnie's pulseless chest, he released the belt and holster. It was evident that the gun and holster were well used.

Pulling the belt around his hips, Jimmy Blackburn was reminded of his lanky, slender body. Even with the belt latched in the last notch it wouldn't stay on his hips. With the holster and belt dangling in his left hand, he retrieved the Colt with his right. His mind went to the four remaining Hegler brothers.

The hatred inside him flared afresh. Standing there in the early morning sun, James William Blackburn made his murdered family a vow. Looking toward the house, he shook the gun and said through clenched teeth, "I'll get them, Pa! You tell Ma and my sisters—I'll get them!" The muscles in his jaw corded as his face reddened. "You hear me, Pa? I'll get 'em. I'll kill every one of 'em!" Then he shoved the revolver into the holster and laid it on the ground.

Lonnie's horse nickered in protest as Jimmy lifted up the dead man and slid him across the saddle. The bay mare did not like the smell of death and made her disapproval known by snorting, dancing about, bobbing her head. Jimmy tied her securely to the corral fence, lashed the body in place, then picked up the gun and moved toward the house.

The coldness came back to his breast as he stepped through the door and eyed the bodies once again. Jimmy wished he could cry. Maybe if he could cry, the pain in his heart would subside.

His gaze fell upon Daisy and Myra, lying side by side in death. Just before he left the house yesterday morning, both girls had kissed his cheek, saying "Happy birthday, big brother!" A lump formed in his throat as his eyes swung to the cupboard counter.

Jimmy walked to the cupboard and looked down at the

cake. Six store-bought candles stood upright in it, forming a partial circle. He counted the remaining candles scattered on the cupboard. Eleven.

His face twisted in anguish. The lump in his throat turned hot. Jimmy stumbled to the table and collapsed into a chair. Dropping his head into his arms on the tabletop, he sobbed and cried for twenty minutes.

The emotional pressure inside the youth was eased as he dried his tears.

Methodically, Jimmy walked to the nearest bedroom and returned with two blankets. He covered the bodies and eyed Lonnie Hegler's gun and holster lying on the chair where he had put them. Hanging the belt over his shoulder, he stepped outside and pulled the door shut. Crossing the wagon-rutted yard, he entered the corral and saddled his own horse. He placed Lonnie's gun belt in the left saddlebag.

Leading the chestnut gelding to where Lonnie Hegler's mare stood, Jimmy untied the reins from the pole fence. He attached a six-foot lead rope to the reins and mounted the chestnut.

As Jimmy rode toward town his face was as hard as the rocks of the ancient mountains that loomed up behind him. Yesterday he had turned seventeen. Today, though he still bore the body of a youth, he was a man . . . a man old for his time.

Chapter Three

The Colorado sun was lifting itself past its mid-morning perch in the sky when Jimmy Blackburn crossed the bridge over the river just north of Fort Collins. As he rode up Main Street Jimmy noticed a crowd gathered in front of the Great Northern Hotel. Above the hum of the crowd he could hear women wailing.

Reining in at the edge of the gathering, he peered over the heads from his higher vantage point. Two men were sprawled on the street. At the side of them a couple of women knelt in the dust, sobbing.

Jimmy lifted his eyes to Sheriff Floyd Cashman, who sat on the hotel porch, leaning against a pillar, his shoulder a bloody mass. Dr. John Moon was attending him.

Jimmy's attention was then drawn to another man, who was lying on the board sidewalk. It was Cashman's deputy. Like the men in the street, he was dead.

Abruptly someone in the crowd pointed out Lonnie Hegler's corpse draped over the mare's saddle. Folks were turning to look. Someone eyed Jimmy and said, "It's the Blackburn boy."

Frank O'Brien, a short, stocky Irishman with silver hair, was the chairman of the town council. Detaching himself from the crowd, he approached Jimmy. He eyed the dead man, then set his gaze on the youth. "Jimmy, what happened? Who's this?"

Jimmy's face was sullen. "Gang of killers murdered my family," he said grimly. "Hegler brothers." Throwing a thumb over his shoulder, he added, "This is one of them."

O'Brien's jaw slacked. "You mean they killed your pa and ma?"

The somber youth nodded. "Daisy and Myra too."

O'Brien eyed the blood on Jimmy's pants. "They cut you up, son?"

"No, sir. That's Pa's blood."

Still stunned, Frank turned to the crowd. Lifting his voice, he said, "Folks, them same dirty sidewinders murdered Will and Sarah Blackburn. Their girls too."

Sheriff Floyd Cashman's head came up.

O'Brien continued. "Young Jimmy here brought one of 'em in. Deader'n a hammer!"

The crowd pressed around Lonnie Hegler's inert form, leaving the two women sobbing beside their dead husbands. The sheriff slowly came to his feet.

"I'm not through with you, Floyd," said Doc Moon with irritation. "Gotta tie a sling around your neck."

"In a minute, Doc. I have to look into this."

While the wounded lawman held one arm with the other and walked slowly between the bodies in the street, Jimmy said to Frank O'Brien, "You mean it was the Heglers that killed these men? Shot the sheriff?"

"Sure was, son. Not more'n a half hour ago."

"Jimmy," said Cashman as he approached, "did I hear right? The Heglers killed your whole family?"

Jimmy's throat went tight. He looked at the sheriff and nodded.

Looking at Lonnie, Cashman said, "This is one of the brothers?"

"Yes, sir," the youth said.

Cashman observed the bullet hole in Lonnie's back. "You kill him, son?"

"Yes, sir. Pa put the bullet in his back. But I killed him."

"I don't understand," said the sheriff, grimacing and adjusting his arm.

"I wasn't at the house when the killing started," Jimmy explained. "I was working over the ridge until about sunset, when I heard shooting. Time I got there, the gang was riding away. Guess they thought Pa was dead. Seems when they started to ride out, Pa shot this one in the back. When I got there, he was lying on the ground trying to shoot Pa again. So I . . ." Jimmy cleared his throat. "Put a pitchfork through his neck."

Frank O'Brien sank his fingers in Lonnie Hegler's hair and snapped the head up. The crowd gasped as O'Brien exposed the purple punctures in Hegler's throat. One of them had split the Adam's apple.

"What about the bodies of your family?" Cashman asked.

"Going to bury them on the place, sir," replied Jimmy. "I want Reverend Ashworth to do the preaching."

Reverend Donald Ashworth, pastor of the First Baptist Church, stepped forward. "I'd be honored, son," he said. "We'll do it just like you say."

The sun hung in the middle of the sky the next day as Reverend Ashworth finished his prayer. The four mounds were nestled under a group of cottonwoods near the river.

Jimmy stood dolefully, shoulders drooped, as neighbors and friends filed by, offering their sympathy. Frank O'Brien and Sheriff Cashman waited until the last mourner had gone. Moving to the youth and flanking him on either side, each man laid a hand on his shoulder.

"If there's anything we can do, Jimmy," said O'Brien softly, "all you have to do is tell us."

Jimmy lifted his head and tried to smile. "Thanks."

"The posse will catch them, son," said Cashman. "Just wish I could've gone with them. But with this bum arm I—"

"Sheriff," Jimmy butted in, "when I mentioned the Heglers yesterday, you seemed to know them."

"U.S. marshal's office in Wichita sent me a bulletin on them . . . and some posters. They went on a killing spree just as soon as they got out of Leavenworth. Marshal knew they were headed west. Sent the information ahead to every sheriff and town marshal in western Kansas and Colorado."

"The posters? With pictures of them?" asked Jimmy.

"Yep."

"Could I take a look at them?"

"You won't need to, son. The posse will have the Heglers in Fort Collins in person shortly."

"You seem mighty confident."

"They'll do it, Jimmy. I'll send somebody out to fetch you when the posse gets back. Even if they're dead, you can take a good look at them."

Fire touched Jimmy's eyes. "If they're alive, I want them, Sheriff. One at a time, I want them!"

"Now, son, it's up to the law to administer their punishment," put in O'Brien. "Don't you worry. If the posse brings any Heglers back alive, they'll hang. You can count on that."

"And you can watch it happen," added the sheriff.

A sullen look formed on Jimmy's face. "What if the posse doesn't catch them?"

Cashman's brow furrowed. "They will, son. They will."

O'Brien and Cashman went to their horses. As they settled in their saddles, the lawman said, "You'll hear from me, Jimmy, just as soon as the posse returns."

Wordlessly, Jimmy nodded. Cashman did not like the look in the boy's eyes. Shaking his head, he threw O'Brien an uneasy glance and spurred his horse. O'Brien followed, hurrying to catch up.

The brokenhearted youth remained at the graves for over an hour, the burning hatred inside him suppressing any tears. Then he slowly turned, walked across the field, and entered the barn. His saddle was centered on the gate of one of the stalls. Unbuckling a saddlebag, he produced Lonnie Hegler's gun belt.

His face an expressionless mask, Jimmy left the barn and entered a nearby shed, which was his father's workshop. After fumbling for a moment in an old toolbox, he pulled out a metal punch. Placing the belt flat on the workbench, he lifted a hammer off the wall and punched an additional hole in line with the others, so that the belt could be further tightened.

Grimly, he wrapped the belt around his lean waist and buckled it. He shook his head. It was still too loose. Removing it, he lined the point of the punch an inch left of the new hole and hit it with the hammer. This time the belt fit tightly on his hips.

Somehow Jimmy knew that the posse was going to fail. Or was it a deep-seated hope that they would? Merely looking at their dead bodies, or even watching them dangle by a rope, would not satisfy the vindictive craving that possessed his soul. The heartless beasts had murdered his family in cold blood. Certainly, he thought, it was only right that he should exact punishment on them. The son of Will and Sarah Blackburn and brother of Daisy and Myra Blackburn ought to have the gratification of personally obliterating his family's murderers from the face of the earth.

Jimmy waited twenty-four hours, but still no word came from the sheriff. The posse had had two full days. If they had not caught the Heglers by now, he decided, they never would. He saddled up and rode to town. Lonnie Hegler's gun lay in the saddlebag. The chestnut gelding thundered over the bridge, and two minutes later Jimmy slipped from the saddle under a sign that read:

LARIMER COUNTY SHERIFF'S OFFICE
AND JAIL
FLOYD B. CASHMAN, SHERIFF

The tall youth ducked his head as he entered the office. Floyd Cashman was at his desk, clumsily cleaning a rifle with his good hand. He looked up at the stolid face.

"Posse back yet?" asked Jimmy curtly.

"Not yet," answered Cashman, meeting the boy's gaze.

"Little slow, aren't they?"

"Heglers had a healthy start, son."

"I want to see their pictures."

"Now, Jimmy," said the sheriff with irritation, "you're not going after those killers. You take the law into your own hands and there'll be a posse after *you!*"

"All I said is that I want to see their pictures. Can I see the pictures of the men who murdered my family?"

Reluctantly, Cashman slid open a drawer and slapped four posters on the desk.

Jimmy Blackburn's eyes narrowed and his countenance flamed as he stared at the repulsive image of Luke Hegler. Slowly he sifted through the four posters, scrutinizing the features of each man, filing them in his mind. Recognizing them would not be difficult. There was a strong family resemblance. Lonnie had been no different, and Jimmy had seen him with his own eyes.

Floyd Cashman stood up as the youth handed him the posters. "Jimmy," he said, "I don't want you—"

The sheriff was interrupted by the sound of horses reining in outside. He stepped around his young visitor and flung open the door. Jimmy followed the sheriff outside.

The weary and dusty posse had returned empty-handed. Cashman waited silently as the appointed leader dismounted slowly and looked at the sheriff with red-rimmed eyes. "They got away, Floyd," he said solemnly. "We lost 'em somewhere this side of Fort Morgan. Just plain disappeared."

"Where you think they're headed?" the sheriff asked, disappointment in his voice.

"Didn't the bulletin say they were from Missouri?"

"Yeah. Joplin."

"I think they must be heading home then," said the posse leader. "Bartender in Eaton said he overheard 'em talkin' about going home. Wanted to tell somebody about their brother dying."

A hot voice spoke from behind Floyd Cashman. "I'll find them!"

Cashman whirled, facing Jimmy. Decision steeled the youth's dark eyes. The muscles in his lean jaw were set.

"You'll do no such thing," the sheriff said bitingly.

"You're going to let them get away?" snapped Jimmy.

"I'll wire the authorities in Joplin," Cashman said hastily. "They can arrest them and bring them back here to stand trial."

Jimmy's face was like frozen granite. "Like I said, I'll find them."

Cashman swore. "You fool. They'd cut you down before you could bat an eye. These aren't green kids, Jimmy. They're hardened criminals. Killers. Every one of them is fast with a gun. Especially Lester. You read the posters. You wouldn't stand a chance."

"I'll find a way," said Jimmy, tight-lipped.

"Jimmy, if you shoot 'em in the back, the law will hang you for murder."

"I won't shoot them in the back, Sheriff. I promise. I want to see their ugly faces just before I shoot them. I want them to know who I am. I plan to tell them why I'm killing them, just before I do it."

Cashman shook his head disdainfully, then said to the posse, "You boys go home and get some rest. Thanks for trying." He turned to Jimmy and, squeezing the boy's arm with his good hand, said, "Come into the office a minute."

Stiffly, Jimmy moved ahead of the sheriff into the office. Cashman closed the door and faced him hard. "All right," he said sharply, "let's say that somehow you are able to get so good with a gun that you kill all four of the Hegler brothers. Let's say you face 'em fair and square—all at once, or one at a time—and walk away without a scratch. What then?"

"Then I'll be satisfied. I'll come home, sell the farm, and go to law school, like I was aiming to do."

Cashman closed his eyes and shook his head. "No you

won't, son. No you won't. If you take out the Hegler brothers, your life will never be the same. *You* will never be the same."

Jimmy began shaking his head.

The lawman dug the fingers of his free hand into the boy's shoulder. "Listen to me! Once you strap on that gun and use it, there's an irreversible law that goes into effect. *You can't take it off*. If you live through that first gunfight, if you live to drop the gun back in the holster, you'll have to use it again—either as a gunfighter or as a lawman."

Jimmy looked unmoved.

"Once you face down a man with a gun, there's always another who'll want to challenge you. If you kill him, there'll be another one. And another. And another. Sooner or later one'll come along that's faster than you. He'll gun you down. You'll lie dead or dying in a pool of your own blood while he walks away."

Cashman tightened his grip on Jimmy's lean shoulder. "Are you listening, son?"

"I'm listening," he replied levelly.

"You're listening . . . but do you *hear* me?"

The youth's face showed no emotion. He looked at the sheriff blankly.

"Is that what your mother would want, son? Do you think it would please your pa? You ending up one day in a pool of your own blood . . . the victim of a life that you foolishly forced on yourself? So you kill the Heglers. Will that bring your family back?"

Jimmy managed a weak smile. "I understand your concern for me, Sheriff," he said softly. "And what you say may be true. But, you see, it's *you* who doesn't understand."

"What do you mean, son?"

"Has your whole life been blasted to bits by a bunch of murdering dogs? Have you had your pa and ma and sisters brutally killed, and walked in to find their bloody bodies?"

"Well, no, Jimmy, but—"

"Then you don't understand. And that's all right. How can you? You'd have to wear my boots to understand."

"I can lock you up, boy," Cashman said, letting go of Jimmy's shoulder.

"On what charge?" retaliated the youth.

Cashman's face reddened.

"I may only be seventeen, Mr. Cashman, but I know you can't jail me unless I've broken the law."

"I can call it protective custody," snapped the sheriff.

"Who are you protecting?" rasped Jimmy. "The Heglers? They're not after me. I'm after them."

Cashman wiped a hand over his mouth. His brow furrowed. "Okay, son. I can't stop you. But don't forget what I said. You can't take the gun off once you strap it on. You've got two choices then. Wear it to uphold the law, or wear it to keep killing other fools like yourself until you get shot down. There's no turning back."

Jimmy turned and walked to the door. He opened it, paused, and made a half turn. "Sheriff . . ."

"Yes, Jimmy?"

"You have a wife and a couple of kids, don't you?"

"Uh huh."

"I hope nobody ever does to them what the Heglers did to my family. I hope you make it all the way through life and never have to know what's going on inside of me."

Cashman wiped his mouth again.

"Though you don't understand," continued Jimmy, "please accept that I have to do what I have to do."

"All right, son," said the sheriff, nodding. "All right."

Jimmy stepped through the door and started to pull it closed behind him.

"Jimmy . . ."

The youth paused in the doorway. "Yes, sir?"

Cashman smiled feebly. "Good luck, son."

The door closed, and Jimmy Blackburn was gone.

For exactly one week, six hours a day, Jimmy Blackburn stood between the house and the barn on the very spot where Lonnie Hegler had died. There, he practiced drawing Lonnie's Colt .45. Again and again and again he drew and snapped the hammer on an empty chamber. He had heard of men trying to learn the fast draw with the gun loaded and blowing their feet or legs off. Jimmy would not load the gun until he was satisfied with the adeptness of his hand.

Every fiber in his being screamed for him to head for Missouri. But the youth knew that he must discipline the fiery passion that burned within. When he came up against the Heglers, he had to be ready.

A second week passed. It seemed to Jimmy that he was now lightning fast. He had not dropped the gun since the third day—hadn't so much as fumbled it for a week.

The youth had never seen a fast-draw shoot-out. He wished that he had. At least there would be something with which to compare himself. One thing was certain—he must practice. Practice hard. Practice until he felt that his hand would fall off.

At the end of the third week Jimmy lined bottles and tin cans on the corral fence and loaded the gun. He drew and fired fourteen times before he hit one object. By the time he had used up all the bullets in Lonnie's belt, he had hit only one bottle and two tin cans.

The discouraged youth saddled his horse and rode to town to buy more ammunition. He was satisfied with his progress on speed, but what good was speed without accuracy? If he outdrew an opponent and didn't hit him, he'd be dead before he could thumb back the hammer, aim, and fire again.

It was Saturday, and Fort Collins was alive with people. The country folks were in town to shop, gossip, and drink. Reining in at the gun shop, Jimmy dismounted and threaded his way through the crowd toward the door. Two or three people looked at him with pity and spoke. He nodded in return and entered the shop, where several men stood around talking. One of them said, "In Estes Park?"

"Yep," answered another. "Monday at noon."

"Why Estes Park?" asked one.

"'Cause that's where Landford killed Farley's brother when they shot it out last October. Farley's been practicin' the fast draw. Feel's he's ready, so he up and challenged Landford to his face in front of a crowd in Denver. Trailed him there just to issue the challenge."

"How come Spence Landford didn't make Farley go for his gun right then and there?" came another voice.

"Somebody ast 'im that. Said he'd give Farley the privilege of dyin' on the same spot where his brother did."

Jimmy listened intently. The name Spence Landford rang a bell, and that morning eight months before leaped into his memory.

It had been a crisp October day. Jimmy and his father had hauled a load of hay from the fields to the barn. Will Black-

burn was pitching it from the wagon into the loft, and Jimmy
was inside, carrying the hay back and stomping it down.

The elder Blackburn swung a forkful off the wagon as his
eye caught sight of a rider approaching the house. He squinted,
trying to bring the man's face into focus. Then he shoved his
pitchfork into a pile of hay and, looking up at Jimmy, said,
"You stay here, son. I'll be right back."

Jimmy had leaned out the loft doors, curious as to the
identity of the visitor. His mother had come out of the house
and was engaging the man in conversation. His pa joined
them, and Jimmy heard him call the rider "Chuck."

Must be Chuck Farley, Jimmy thought. Chuck was the
youngest son of Jed Farley, a neighboring farmer to the
north. He was in his twenties and, like his older brother
Chad, was a bit on the wild side. Jimmy had never met either
of the Farley boys, but he had heard stories about them. His
mother called them rude, mouthy, and cocksure. Sarah Blackburn wanted none of their influence on her son. As the visitor
talked to his parents, Jimmy picked out a word now and then
but could not get the gist of the conversation.

After several moments his mother reentered the house.
Chuck Farley wheeled his horse and rode off. Will Blackburn
returned to the hay wagon and picked up the pitchfork.

"Who was that, Pa?" asked Jimmy, playing dumb.

"Jed Farley's boy, Chuck," Blackburn said nonchalantly.

"What'd he want?"

"His pa asked him to stop and see if I'd help with a barn
raising on Monday."

"Oh."

Will Blackburn's voice carried a casual tone, but Jimmy
was not fooled.

"Is that all he wanted?" he asked curiously.

"Uh . . . yeah. Yeah. That was it. Now get back to stompin'
on that hay."

Jimmy knew to leave well enough alone and said no more.

That evening at the supper table, amid the usual family
conversation, Daisy popped up with, "How come Chad Farley's going to try to kill that man, Pa?"

Will's eyes flicked to those of his wife. Sarah glanced at her
daughter, frowned, and looked back at her husband as if to
say, *I don't know how she found out.*

Daisy's father said, "How'd you hear about it?"

"Myra and me were at the window. We heard Mr. Farley tell the two of you all about it. He sure seemed proud that his brother had become a gunfighter."

Sarah saw the puzzlement on Jimmy's face. Looking at her husband, she said, "Might as well tell them, Will. It's best that you explain it to Jimmy."

Blackburn took a long sip of coffee and set his eyes on his son. "Seems that gunslingers have become heroes in the West lately. Young fellows your age have a tendency to put them on a pedestal. But they're nothing but predators who ride around seeing who they can outdraw and kill next."

"Your pa and I want you to see these gunmen for what they are, Jimmy," put in Sarah. "I don't want you to look up to them or see them as heroes. They are evil men." Her features grew hard, as they seldom did. "I don't want you ever to pick up a handgun, Jimmy. Rifles are for hunting game. They provide food. But pistols are for killing men."

Jimmy nodded. "I understand, Mama. I've got no hankering toward that sort of thing."

"How come Chad Farley's going to try an' kill that man, Pa?" asked Daisy, repeating her question.

"Because Spence Landford is a top gun, honey," said her father.

"What's that mean?"

"Spence Landford is fast and deadly with a gun. Wherever he goes, people fear him. Those who know no better worship him as a tin god."

"It means he has killed other men," said Sarah. "That's really something to admire, isn't it?" The caustic tone in her voice was unmistakable. "How could a mother stand it, knowing her son was a cold-blooded killer?"

Will Blackburn took another swig of coffee. "Chuck was telling us, Jimmy, that his brother Chad has now killed three men. Thinks he's ready to go against the likes of Spence Landford. Said Chad just got word that Landford is over Estes Park way. The two of them are lighting out in the morning for Estes Park. They won't be back in time for their pa's barn raising, so Chuck asked if I'd go help."

"Chad won't be back at all," said Sarah. "That Landford will kill him for sure."

" . . . can I do for you, Jimmy?" The words of Mr. Sand-

ers, owner of the gun shop, filtered into Jimmy Blackburn's
thoughts.

"Oh, uh . . . I need six boxes of .45s, sir," said the boy,
startled back to the present.

Sanders arched his eyebrows. "You gonna start a war?"

Jimmy laughed nervously. "No, sir. Just learning to handle
a Colt .45. Have to be able to protect myself now that Pa's
gone."

Sanders face sobered. "Oh. Sure, son. I understand."

Jimmy paid for the cartridges and wove through the crowded
room toward the door. Pausing, he eyed the man who was
giving out most of the information. "Mister, did you say the
gunfight between Landford and Farley would be Monday at
noon?"

"Yep, me boy," replied the man. "Same day of the week
and time on the clock as when Spence killed Chad Farley.
Chuck says it'll be different this time."

"Only thing different this time," said a man in the crowd,
"it'll be Chuck spurtin' blood instead o' Chad. That Landford
is like angry lightnin'!"

After leaving, Jimmy stopped at Dan Hoffer's place on the
way home and asked Hoffer if he would check on the cattle
once a day until he returned. He gave the neighboring farmer
no details, saying only that he had to be gone a few days on
important business.

It was important business all right. Will Blackburn had left
behind his life savings, and Jimmy was determined to use
some of it to hire the famous Spence Landford as a tutor.
First Landford would teach him how to draw and shoot, and
then upon graduation, Jimmy would ride straight for Missouri.

Chapter Four

J immy rode into Estes Park just before sundown on Sunday. He quickly learned that the mountain town's three hotels were full. Word of the upcoming shoot-out between Spence Landford and Chuck Farley had spread far and wide.

Jimmy knew that even in June the nights were cold at this altitude. He decided to nose around town and see if he could get a look at Spence Landford. Later he would head out of town and try to hole up in some rancher's barn.

The main street of Estes Park was thronged with people. The single subject of conversation was the big gunfight at noon the next day. By simply moving about and listening, Jimmy learned that people had come from as far as Cheyenne and Denver to watch Spence Landford perform.

Jimmy was appalled. Why were people so bloodthirsty? What could be entertaining in watching a man die? Who would ride for miles just to see— Suddenly the seventeen-year-old boy realized that he was part of this crowd. Hadn't he himself spent the better part of a day riding to this place?

He pondered on it for a moment, then assured himself that with him it was different. After all, he wasn't coming here for entertainment. This was cold, hard business. These people had no Heglers with which to even a score. Their families had not been gunned down in cold blood.

Estes Park had four saloons. Jimmy waited until dark and then entered the one called the Lucky Miner. It was filling fast, but Spence Landford wasn't there. If he were, everybody would know it. Though Jimmy had never seen the famous gunfighter, he was sure there would be much made over him wherever he went.

The town lamplighter was making his rounds as Jimmy returned to the street. Already the air was taking on a chill. As he approached the Salty Dog Saloon, he heard a loud,

bellowing voice from within. He stepped up to the swinging
doors and peered over. Seated at a table with a saloon woman
on his lap was Chuck Farley.

Swinging a beer mug and scattering foam, Farley said
loudly, "Yes, sir, tomorrow at two minutes after twelve noon
the whole town of Estes Park is gonna know who's the fastest
gun in these parts! And by the next day they'll be talkin'
about it in Denver and Cheyenne."

Farley took a gulp of beer, slammed the mug on the table,
and used his sleeve to wipe away the foam from his mouth.
He slipped the woman's hand into his and said, "There it is,
honey! You're holdin' the hand that's gonna blow Spencer
Landford to kingdom come!"

As the crowd laughed, Jimmy turned away. For sure
Landford was not at the Salty Dog.

He checked out the Pink Lady next, but the gunfighter was
not there. The last one was the Big Brown Jug. To his
disappointment Jimmy did not see Landford in that saloon
either. Stepping to the bar between two rowdy-looking cowboys, he motioned to the bartender.

"What'll it—?" The bartender stopped short. "Hey, boy,
you're too young. Now don't you try to tell me—"

"I'm not wanting a drink, sir," cut in Jimmy. "I was wondering if you could tell me something."

"I'll try. What is it?"

"Is Mr. Landford in town yet?"

The bartender nodded. "Rode in 'bout midafternoon. But
you ain't gonna find him hangin' out in a saloon."

"No?"

"He stays at the Water Wheel Hotel when he comes to
Estes. Ain't nobody gonna lay eyes on him now, until about
one minute to twelve tomorrow. He's a quiet bird. Sorta
keeps to himself."

"Oh," said Jimmy, disappointed. "Thanks."

The bartender nodded with a tight smile, and the youth
turned and passed through the louvered double doors to the
street. Gaiety permeated Estes Park. Blood would be shed
tomorrow, and everyone was excited.

Jimmy had left his horse at the lower end of town. He
decided to ride out to a ranch he had passed about five miles
northeast of town and see if they would let him sleep in the
barn.

Suddenly his gaze settled on a sign overhead. It swung slightly in the cool evening breeze. By the light of the streetlamps he read the big black letters:

WATER WHEEL HOTEL
ROOMS TO LET
DAY-WEEK-MONTH

Jimmy paused and glanced into the lobby. Maybe . . . He shook his head and started down the board sidewalk. Abruptly he halted. Setting his jaw with determination, he turned and retraced his steps.

"We ain't got no rooms," blurted the little white-haired clerk as Jimmy entered the hotel.

"I know," replied Jimmy. "Just want to know what room Mr. Landford is in."

"None of yer business," snapped the clerk. "And if you like your face the way it is, you'd better not be botherin' him. He's not seein' anybody."

At that moment a boy emerged from the hotel dining room carrying a tray of food. "W-what room's he in?" he nervously asked the clerk.

The old man tossed Jimmy a suspicious look, then turned to the delivery boy. "Three. But be sure you announce that you're bringing his supper, boy, just as soon as you knock. He doesn't cotton to visitors."

Ignoring the clerk's shouted protest, Jimmy followed on the heels of the delivery boy. As they reached the top of the stairs Jimmy slowed his pace and watched the boy move toward Spence Landford's door. The old clerk was mumbling to himself at the bottom of the steps.

The delivery boy stopped and looked back at Jimmy. "What are you doing?" he whispered.

"Just want to see what he looks like," answered Jimmy.

The nervous youth looked at the tray, the door, then back at Jimmy. "You want to give this to him?"

"Sure," said Jimmy.

"Thanks," said the delivery boy, shoving the tray into Jimmy's hands. With that he bounded down the stairs.

As Jimmy stood before the door that bore a large number three, two cowboys stepped out of a room farther down the corridor, talking loudly. By the dim lights on the wall Jimmy could see that they were drunk.

He had raised his hand to knock on the door when one of the drunks said, "Hey, Gil, lookee there. Ish hot food!"

"Sure 'nuff," replied the other one, reaching toward the wall for support. "I'm really hun'ry, Sam. Let's see whut's on the tray."

Jimmy braced himself for trouble. "If you men want to eat, go down to the dining room. This is supper for Mister—"

Sam staggered up to Jimmy, and the boy could smell the man's putrid breath.

"We'll take that, sonny."

As Sam reached for the tray, Jimmy lifted it higher. At the same moment Gil sprang forward, swung his hand up, and hit the tray hard. It slammed against the door, smearing the large number three with coffee and gravy. Dishes clattered and smashed to the floor.

"Guess we'll have to work thish shtupid kid over, Gil," said Sam, struggling to keep his balance.

The door swung open just as Sam aimed a fist at Jimmy. The agile youth ducked the wobbly punch, and Sam stumbled into the tall, slender man who stood in the doorway.

Spence Landford sank his fingers into Sam's shirt and said through clenched teeth, "What's going on here?"

Jimmy turned and looked into the rugged, angular face of the famous gunfighter. Landford had coal-black hair with a touch of gray, and a heavy mustache. "I was just bringing your supper, Mr. Landford. These two drunken idiots—"

"That's my supper all over the floor?" snapped Landford.

"You can still eat it," said Gil. "The floors in thish hot—hotel are really clean."

Landford's mouth tightened ominously. Dropping Sam, he took two steps and swung a lightning fist into Gil's face. The drunk went down like cut timber.

Suddenly Jimmy saw that Sam had drawn a gun and was swinging it on Landford's back. The gunfighter whirled in time to see Jimmy kick the gun from the drunken man's hand.

Angry, Landford lifted Sam upward, swung him around bodily, and belted him in the jaw. Sam collapsed on top of his unconscious partner.

Heavy footsteps thundered on the stairs, as Estes Park's

marshal came on the scene, followed by a deputy. The marshal glared at the mess and the sprawled bodies, then fixed his gaze on Spence Landford. "I oughta jail you, Landford," he said heatedly. "Every time you gunslicks come to town there's trouble."

Landford returned the cold stare. "I was in my room minding my own business, Marshal. This young fellow was bringing my supper from the dining room. These two slobbermouths laying on the floor started the trouble. Why don't you jail *them*?"

The marshal ignored the gunfighter's question and turned his attention on Jimmy. "I don't know you, boy." Looking him up and down, he said, "You don't work at this hotel. How come you were bringing Landford his supper?"

Jimmy didn't know what to say. "Well, I, uh—"

"He's a friend of mine, Marshal," cut in Landford.

The boy's eyes widened as he looked at the gunman.

"What's your name, boy?" demanded the lawman.

"Uh . . . Jimmy. Jimmy Blackburn."

"Where you from?"

"Over by Fort Collins," replied Jimmy.

Sam and Gil were beginning to stir. The marshal turned to his deputy. "Tom, get these two birds out of here." Fixing his eyes on Spence Landford, he said, "I wish you'd have your blood-spilling in some other town."

"I didn't choose the place, sir," said Landford evenly. "Mr. Farley wants it to be here."

The lawman wheeled to aid his deputy in moving the drunks toward the stairs. Looking over his shoulder, he said, "If you're still alive when the smoke clears tomorrow, I want you out of town by twelve-thirty. You hear me?"

"I hear you, Marshal."

Landford waited until the four men passed from sight, while Jimmy took in every inch of the gunman's frame. The two were exactly the same height. Landford was slender and rawboned. Jimmy estimated the man might outweigh him by fifteen pounds. The youth studied the exact position of Landford's gun belt, the way the holster was thonged to his thigh, the angle of the gun.

"I'm hungry, Jimmy," said Spence Landford. "Have you had your supper?"

"No, sir," replied the gangly youth.

"How'd you like to have supper with me?"

Eyes still wide, Jimmy said, "Well, I, uh—"

"I only eat with my friends, you know," said the gunman, smiling.

"But, Mr. Landford, I—"

"Any man who kicks a gun from a killer's hand and keeps me from getting shot in the back is my friend."

Jimmy knew that Spence Landford could have drawn and fired at Sam before the drunken man could have pushed the hammer back. However, he'd take the credit. Things were working out better than he had expected.

Landford extended his hand, and Jimmy smiled as he clasped it. "Okay, Mr. Landford—let's eat. I *am* hungry!"

Spence Landford and Jimmy wolfed down their supper in the hotel dining room as curious spectators watched and whispered. Everyone knew the famous gunfighter. Jimmy felt like a celebrity himself. He had never so much as *seen* a famous person, much less had supper with one.

While they ate, Jimmy remembered his mother's warning about gunfighters. *All bad*, she had said. Spence Landford was a little reserved, obviously self-contained . . . but he didn't seem bad. Not at all.

As the coffee was served and the crowd diminished, the rugged-faced gunslinger said, "Jimmy, how come you were bringing me my tray?"

Jimmy felt a bit bolder by now, and without hesitation he answered, "Because I wanted to meet you."

"Gunfighters are the scum of the earth, boy. I can tell you've had proper raising, good breeding. Why would you want to shine up to the likes of me?"

"It'd take me a while to explain it," offered Jimmy, scooping up some more apple pie.

"I got nothing to do till noon tomorrow, 'cept catch a little shut-eye." Landford motioned his empty coffee cup at the waiter, who promptly took care of it. The gunfighter eased his chair back a few inches, produced a cigarillo from a shirt pocket, and put a match to it. He pulled out another one and said, "Smoke?"

"No, thank you, sir," said Jimmy, shaking his head. He marveled that Landford was so calm with a shoot-out impending.

Jimmy used the better part of an hour telling his story to the famous gunfighter. He began with what he knew of the

Hegler trial twelve years ago in Topeka and brought it up to the moment.

"So, you see, Mr. Landford," he said with an expression much older than his years, "you've got to teach me how to draw and shoot."

Landford was slowly shaking his head before the boy's words were all out. "Not on your life, son," he said firmly. "You let the law handle it."

Jimmy's face flushed. "It ain't up to the law," he snapped. "It's up to *me!*"

"Jimmy, I'm sorry about your family. Really sorry. But I don't run a school for greenhorn kids. I'm not gonna help you get yourself killed."

Leaning across the table, Jimmy said, "I'll pay you. My pa left plenty of money."

"Not for a million dollars, kid," said Landford, getting to his feet. "I don't want you on my conscience."

Jimmy stood up, his face dark and sullen.

"You have a place to stay?" asked Landford, tossing a ten-dollar gold eagle on the table.

"Yeah," lied Jimmy stiffly.

"Why don't you get a good night's sleep, then head for home at sunup?"

"I'm staying for the gunfight," said the youth.

"Be better if you went on home."

Jimmy started toward the door as Landford headed for the hotel lobby. "See you at noon tomorrow," said Jimmy.

"Okay, son. Suit yourself."

The doorknob felt cold in Jimmy's hand. As the door came open Spence Landford paused at the lobby entrance and said, "Jimmy . . ."

"Yes, sir?"

"Thanks for kicking that gun."

Jimmy studied the man's smile and smiled back. "You're welcome," he said, and stepped out into the night.

The mountain air bit through his thin shirt as Jimmy swung into the saddle and rode out of town. The moon was a thin sliver in the starlit sky overhead. He pulled his collar up and put the chestnut into a trot. He searched his brain for some way to change Spence Landford's mind but could think of nothing.

The youth's teeth were chattering as he rode through the

gate of the B-Slash-C Ranch. It would feel mighty good to get out of the night chill. His heart sank as he neared the house and buildings and saw that not one window showed a speck of light. He wished now he had told Landford the truth. Maybe the gunfighter would have let him bed down on the floor of his room.

The big barn, just past the house, loomed invitingly against the night sky. The cold youth decided to go ahead and sleep in the barn without permission. Certainly no one would deprive a peaceful traveler a place out of the cold.

Suddenly, as he passed the house, a big sheepdog bounded off the porch, barking its head off. The chestnut shied nervously. "Shh, boy!" Jimmy whispered to the dog, but it didn't do any good. The dog continued to charge back and forth, raising a racket.

"Shh!" said the boy. "Nice doggie. Nice doggie."

Abruptly a heavy voice roared over the barking of the dog. "You on the horse! Put yer hands, up. *Now!*"

As Jimmy lifted his hands, a square-built form emerged from the shadows. "Sonny Boy!" the man said to the dog. "Hush now."

Satisfied that things were under control, the big dog walked briskly back to the house.

"What you doin' on Claiborne property, mister?" the voice growled.

"I was just needing a place to bed down for the night, sir," said Jimmy, trying to stop his teeth from chattering. "There was no light in your windows, so I figured you were all asleep."

Another man's dark form appeared. "What is it, Russ?" he asked the big man.

"Got us a prowler, Ned," answered Russ Pittman.

"I'm not a prowler, sir," said Jimmy, trying to make out the features of the man's face. "I told you—"

"Get off the horse. Nice and easy," commanded the big man.

A light appeared in an upstairs window of the house as Jimmy lowered his cold, trembling frame to the ground.

"Get his gun, Ned," said Russ Pittman.

Ned Sears fumbled in his pocket and thumbed a match into flame. "He ain't got no gun, Russ," said Sears. "Why, it's just a teenage kid."

Pittman stepped closer. "Looks like you're right, Ned. How come you're out alone like this, boy?"

"I . . . I came over from Fort Collins, sir," replied Jimmy. "Have business in Estes Park. The hotels are full. I just needed a place to sleep. Remembered passing this place earlier today, and thought I might hole up in your barn."

"What is it, Russ?" came a deep voice from the front porch of the house.

"Got a young feller here needs a place to sleep, boss," answered Pittman.

"Well, bring him over to the house and let's get out of this cold air," said the boss.

"I'll bed your horse down, son," Ned Sears said to Jimmy. "Russ, you take him to the house."

Jimmy eyed the double-barreled shotgun in Russ Pittman's hand as they walked side by side toward the big two-story ranch house.

The boss was a tall man in his late sixties, with a square jaw and deep-set eyes. His full head of hair was solid white. A coal-oil lantern illuminated the parlor as the old man ushered Jimmy and Russ Pittman through the front door. He picked up the lantern and said, "Let's go back in the kitchen."

The warm air inside the house felt good to Jimmy. They passed through a long hallway and entered the high-ceilinged kitchen. The boss placed the lantern on the table. Extending a hand, he said, "I'm Britt Claiborne."

Jimmy shoved his cold hand into Claiborne's. "I'm Jimmy Blackburn, sir."

"What's this about you needing a place to sleep?"

"Well, sir, I—"

Suddenly a soft, feminine voice called from upstairs. "Daddy, what's going on?"

"Nothing wrong, honey!" Claiborne hollered in that direction. "Just a traveler needing shelter. You go on back to bed." The old man's eyes swung back to Jimmy, whose teeth were chattering. Seeming to have second thoughts, he walked to the foot of the staircase and called, "Joanna!"

"Yes, Daddy?" came the soft reply.

"Send Jezebel down here. I need her to make some hot coffee. This young fellow's got a chill."

"Yes, Daddy."

"Where you from, son?" asked Claiborne, fixing his eyes on the youth.

"Fort Collins, sir."

"You got folks there?"

Jimmy's face stiffened. "No, sir. They're dead."

"Oh, I'm sorry." Claiborne cleared his throat. "You hungry?"

"Uh, no. No, sir. I had a good meal in town."

"What you doing out here? Why didn't you stay in town?"

"The hotels are full, Mr. Claiborne. I noticed your ranch as I rode into Estes Park this afternoon. Thought maybe I could sleep in your barn, out of the cold."

"Hotels are full, eh?"

"Yes, sir."

"You sure it isn't that you're just financially embarrassed?"

"Oh, no, sir," answered the boy. "My pa left me plenty enough to live on."

"I don't understand why all three hotels would be full," said Britt Caliborne.

"It's the shoot-out tomorrow, boss," offered Russ Pittman.

The old man's face darkened. "Oh, yes. I'd forgotten. Another one of those fool gunfights." His mouth pulled into a thin line. "Nothing lower on this earth than a gunhawk."

Jimmy felt his stomach tighten.

"I'll be glad when we get these parts civilized," continued the old man. "It'll be good when men can live here without having to pack guns." He looked young Blackburn up and down. "You don't wear a gun, do you, son?"

"Uh, no, sir. No, I don't."

"Don't ever put one on," said Claiborne doggedly. "If you ain't wearing it, you don't have to use it."

Jimmy heard shuffling footsteps in the hallway. Presently a portly black woman entered the room. "Miz Joanna said you wanted me, Mr. Claiborne."

"Yes, Jezebel," said the old man. "This is Jimmy Blackburn. He's been out in that night air without proper attire. I think his blood has some icicles in it. Some of your coffee might warm him up."

"Yes, suh!" replied Jezebel. After scrutinizing him for a moment, she flashed Jimmy a smile and said, "Glad to meet you, Mr. Burntblack."

"Blackburn," Claiborne corrected her.

"Oh, I'm sorry. Blackburn. My head is still foggy from bein' waked up. I'll fix the coffee right away, suh!"

"I'm glad to meet you, ma'am," said Jimmy.

While Jezebel quickly built a fire and busied herself, Russ Pittman said, "Might as well let this boy sleep in the bunkhouse, boss. There's an extra bed out there."

"I was thinking the same thing," said Claiborne.

"The barn would be fine, sir," said Jimmy.

"No reason to do that." The old man smiled. "We'll see that you get a good night's sleep and a healthy breakfast in the morning. Then you can be on your way."

Chapter Five

The first glimmer of daylight was on the western horizon when Jimmy Blackburn was awakened by the B-Slash-C crew climbing out of their beds. He raised up on his elbow, blinking sleepily.

The dozen or so men paid him no mind as they laughed, hollered, and poked fun at one another while dressing. One of them said, "Boy, I sure would like to ride into town and see that gunfight today."

"If you don't mind losin' your job, go ahead," chided another. "You know how the boss feels about gunfights and them what does the gunfightin'."

Hoarse laughter made the rounds.

"I hear Spence Landford is ten feet tall," said a redheaded cowhand. "They say he can look a man to death with his eyes when he gets really mad."

Several men laughed again.

"All kiddin' aside, boys," put in another, "I had a friend told me he saw this with his own eyes. Down in Lawton, Oklahoma, Landford took on four gunhawks at the same time. Nobody'd stand with him, so he lit into 'em by his lonesome. Fanned the hammer from a crouched position and dead-centered every one of 'em in the chest. Then you know what Spence did with the one bullet that was left?"

"Naw, what'd he do, George?" said one.

"He punched it outta the cylinder and gave it to my friend for a souvenir."

The group laughed unbelievingly and left the bunkhouse. Jimmy swung his legs over the edge of the bed and touched his feet to the floor. He gasped when he felt the cold surface, and he lifted his feet just as Russ Pittman came through the door.

"Mornin'," said Pittman cheerfully. "Mr. Claiborne said to

tell you breakfast will be ready at the house in twenty minutes. Sure wish I could eat some of Jezebel's cookin'! I have to eat poor man's food with the crew."

"Are you the foreman here?" Jimmy asked.

"That's what they tell me," Russ said, laughing. "However, I wonder if sometimes the real foreman of this spread ain't Miss Joanna!"

"Oh, really?" said Jimmy, wincing as his bare feet once again made contact with the cold floor.

As the boy began to slip into his clothing, Russ Pittman chuckled and said, "Yeah. She kinda has all us men wrapped around her little finger."

"How's that?" asked Jimmy, buttoning his skirt.

"Wait'll you see her, my boy! Then you won't have to ask." Pittman cocked his big head and squinted one eye. "Come to think of it, you two are mighty close to the same age. You about sixteen?"

Jimmy squared his shoulders. "*Seventeen*," he said crustily.

Russ laughed. "Oh, pardon me, granddad! Well, Miss Joanna is sixteen. Looks nineteen. Purtiest little filly you ever set your peepers on! Her ma was a full-blooded Cherokee Indian. You just wait. If you don't fall all over yourself, I'm a suck-egg mule!"

Jimmy put his hand to his head. "I'll have to get my comb from my saddlebag."

"No need, son," said big Russ, pointing to a corner table. "There's a comb over there and some water to wash up in." Turning to leave, he said, "See you later."

When his face was washed and his hair combed, Jimmy walked to the front door of the large, stately white house. He held his hat in one hand as he knocked with the other.

Presently the door opened. "Good mornin', Mr. Burntblack," Jezebel said pleasantly. "Ya'll come in here. Breakfast is almost ready."

As Jimmy followed her into the kitchen, Britt Claiborne was coming in off the back porch. He was a strikingly handsome man and carried his years well, Jimmy thought.

"Morning, son," he said with a smile. "Sleep well?"

Jimmy was enjoying the enticing aroma of breakfast cooking. "Oh, just fine, sir," he replied, returning the smile. "I certainly appreciate your kind hospitality."

Gesturing toward the table, the owner of the B-Slash-C said, "Sit down, Jimmy. Take that place over there."

Jimmy noticed that there were three places set. He was sure Jezebel would do her eating later, so the third place had to be for Joanna. As the two men scraped their chairs forward, Claiborne spoke to the black woman. "Jezebel, will you call Joanna?" Looking back at Jimmy, he shook his white bushy head. "Females! Jezebel told her last night that a tall, handsome young stranger was staying the night and having breakfast with us this morning. She's spending a little extra time on herself."

Jimmy forced a little chuckle.

"Miz Joanna!" came Jezebel's voice from the hallway. "Yo' papa says to get yo' little self down here right now!"

"I'm coming!" came a soft voice, followed by rapid footsteps descending the stairs.

Jimmy fastened his eyes on the door, waiting in curious suspense. He had not been overly taken with girls up to this point in his life, although there were a couple who had touched his fancy. Betty Lou Hanson, a neighboring farmer's daughter, had gained his attention once or twice of late. And then there was Paula Templeton. Her father owned the feed and grain store in Fort Collins. Paula was short and pretty and had a pleasant personality. However, she wore men's clothes a lot and could handle hundred-pound feed sacks too well. Jimmy liked girls to be feminine, ladylike . . . as his mother had been.

Suddenly, like a fluttering dove, the graceful Joanna floated through the door. She paused and fixed her eyes on the table. "Looks good, Jezebel," she said softly.

Jimmy found himself instantly spellbound by Joanna's wholesome, dark-haired beauty. He could immediately detect the Cherokee characteristics—prominent cheekbones highlighted by slender temples, a slight bend to her perfectly shaped nose. Yet she had the strikingly fair skin and green eyes of her father. Of course, her eyes were more like emeralds with the sparkle of twinkling stars, he thought. Her velvet-brown hair framed the beautiful face in gentle waves, then swirled past her temples and lay on her shoulders like the finest dark silk.

The simple yellow dress she wore, the high neck and long sleeves decorated with white lace, complemented her well-developed figure. The only word that presented itself in Jimmy's confused thoughts was *princess*. She looked like a fairy-book princess.

"Joanna, this is Jimmy Blackburn," said Claiborne.

Their eyes met, and Jimmy's heart pounded hard against his ribs. He struggled to his feet, knocking his chair backward to the floor. Jezebel was passing behind him with a small tray bearing three glasses of tomato juice. She stumbled against the chair, spilling the tray. Glasses and tomato juice shattered and splattered to the floor.

It took the enchanted young man a few seconds to tear his eyes from the beautiful girl. Regaining his senses, he knelt to help Jezebel pick up the pieces of glass. "I—I'm sorry, ma'am. I didn't mean to—"

"It's all right, Mr. Burntblack. It was all my fault. I shoulda knowed better than to be walkin' behind you. You just sit back down. Ol' Jezebel will clean up this here mess. G'wan now."

Jimmy picked up the chair, apologized again, and waited for Joanna to take her seat. Sitting back down, he looked at Claiborne, smiled weakly, and cleared his throat.

Claiborne offered thanks for the food and took time to ask God to have mercy on the two men who were going to shoot it out in town at noon. Jimmy silently hoped that he would not be asked what his business was in Estes Park.

As he started eating, his eyes wandered to the face of Joanna, who sat across the table from him. Her features flushed slightly red, but then her father broke the spell.

"What's your business about in Estes, son?"

Jimmy was glad he had just shoveled a forkful of scrambled eggs into his mouth. He would have a few seconds to think. A moment later he touched a napkin to his lips and said, "I need to hire a man to do a little work for me."

"You running your own outfit?" asked Claiborne.

"Uh . . . well, yes, sir."

"How long your folks been dead, son?"

"Just . . . just about a month, sir." Jimmy's face pinched.

"Oh, I'm sorry, son. Forgive a foolish old man."

"That's all right, sir. You would have no way of knowing."

"Some kind of tragedy?" Claiborne asked tenderly.

"Yes, sir." Pain appeared in the boy's face. "My father, mother, and two sisters were . . . murdered."

Claiborne's face blanched.

Trying to ease the situation, Joanna said, "Where's your ranch, Jimmy?"

"Over by Fort Collins, Miss Joanna," Jimmy answered eagerly. "Only it's more a farm than a ranch."

"Son, if you're in a financial pinch," said Claiborne, trying to smooth things, "I could help—"

"Oh, no. Not at all, sir," Jimmy said quickly. "Everything's fine. Like I told you last night, my pa left me with plenty."

Breakfast was finished in relative silence. Jimmy thought once of Spence Landford. The repugnant Heglers followed Landford into his mind, and the familiar fury began to rise within him. Quickly he forced his thoughts to Joanna and realized he was staring at her. Their eyes met, and she flushed again. Then her graceful chin lifted and she spoke to Jezebel. "The breakfast was delicious, Jezebel, as usual."

"Thank you, Miz Joanna," said the big woman, beaming.

"Sure was, ma'am," added Jimmy. Turning to Claiborne, he said, "Well, sir, I'd better be heading for town."

Claiborne and his daughter stood up. Joanna said to her father, "Daddy, would it be all right if I rode as far as Beaver Creek with Jimmy? Chief needs a good riding."

Jimmy felt his heart jump. The lovely girl wanted to ride with him!

"That'd be all right, honey," replied the old man. "But you head right back, won't you?"

"Mmm-hmm," she hummed. Turning to the tall, lanky youth, she said, "I'll be just a few minutes, Jimmy. I'll meet you at the barn."

"Okay." He nodded.

"I'll have Russ saddle Chief for you," said Claiborne.

"Oh, thank you, Daddy," she said, standing on her tiptoes and planting a kiss on his cheek. With that she moved through the hall and bounded up the stairs.

"Come see us again, Mr. Burntblack," said Jezebel, smiling broadly.

"It's *Blackburn*, Jezebel," said Britt Claiborne.

"Oh, yes, suh, I keep forgettin'," she said, laughing heartily at her own mistake.

Joanna Claiborne dazzled Jimmy again when she approached the barn wearing a black split riding skirt with jacket to match. Beneath the jacket was a fluffy white blouse. Tilted properly on her head was a black, flat-crowned hat with a black-and-white neck cord. She wore black leather boots with two-inch heels. Jimmy drank her in with his eyes. He figured that without the boots she would stand about five feet three inches and would have to eat six meals a day to weigh a hundred and ten pounds.

He took his eyes off the girl long enough to finish cinching his saddle. Russ Pittman came around the barn leading a huge Appaloosa stallion, followed by Britt Claiborne. The ebony markings on the massive white animal blended perfectly with the black bridle and saddle, which were trimmed with silver studs. This obviously wealthy rancher had spared no expense on his beautiful daughter.

Joanna's face brightened as the big horse came into view. The moment the stallion saw her, it whinnied and bobbed its head.

"Chief!" she exclaimed, hastening to embrace the neck of the magnificent beast, which nuzzled her affectionately.

So she's charmed the big horse around her little finger too, thought Jimmy.

The girl thanked the foreman and adeptly swung into the saddle. Jimmy felt more than ever like an awkward youth as he beheld the regal mien of Joanna Claiborne as she sat proudly on the splendid Appaloosa. She was a princess, indeed.

"Ready to ride, Jimmy?" she asked, setting her eyes on the enraptured youth's face.

It took him a moment to find his voice. "Uh . . . yes!" Clearing his throat, he said, "I'm ready." Turning to Britt Claiborne, he shook his hand and said, "Thank you for your kindness, sir."

"My pleasure, son," responded the white-haired man. "How long will your business take in Estes?"

"I, uh, hope to settle it before the day's out," replied Jimmy.

"If you need a place to stay on the way back, you're welcome to the same bed you had last night."

"Thank you, sir." Jimmy smiled. "If it isn't too late at night, I'll do it." Nodding to the B-Slash-C foreman, he said, "Nice to have met you, Mr. Russ."

Pittman smiled. "Same here."

As the horses pulled away, Claiborne called, "Turn back at the creek, honey."

"I will," said Joanna.

Moving past the house, Jimmy saw Sonny Boy, the sheepdog, eyeing him from the porch with evident misgiving. *Looks like the dog is jealous,* he thought. *This girl's got them all dancing on her string.*

When the young couple reached the gate and turned onto the road, Russ Pittman mounted his own horse and cut across the pasture into the tall timber. Under orders from Britt Claiborne, the foreman would ride unseen, watching the girl every moment. Unknown to Joanna, she was never alone, even on her daily rides aboard the Appaloosa. Her father guarded the girl's well-being with the utmost vigilance.

The sun was high in the morning sky as Joanna and Jimmy rode slowly up the dusty trail. Jimmy was trying to think of something to say when Joanna asked, "Do you come to Estes Park often?"

"No, miss . . . I—"

"Please call me Joanna."

"Yes, miss . . . I mean Joanna. No, I don't."

"Why did you come here to hire a farmhand?"

"Well, he's not a farmhand. The man I'm hiring is a specialist. I'll only need his services for a short time."

"I hope you're not going to watch that awful gunfight," she said with a note of disgust.

Jimmy didn't know what to reply, so he remained mute.

Turning to look at him, Joanna said, "You *aren't*, are you?"

To evade giving an answer, he said quickly, "It's kind of hard to live in this part of the country and never see a gunfight." A tinge of guilt touched him. He had lived on the frontier all his life and had never seen one.

"I suppose so," replied Joanna, taking the bait. "But it's a horrible thing. Men wearing guns. Spilling blood. Killing each other like savage heathen."

"Yes, miss," the boy said quietly.

The conversation was chafing Jimmy's conscience. He felt a new subject had to be introduced immediately. "I understand you're part Indian," he said quickly.

A lofty smile took shape on the girl's lovely mouth. "Yes, and mighty proud of it. My mother was a full-blooded Cherokee. That makes me half Indian. Daddy met her when he was still back east—well, actually down south. He was traveling across Georgia in the winter and came across my mother half frozen to death in a forest. She'd been marching in the great Cherokee exodus."

"Is that what they called the Trail of Tears?"

"Yes. Mother had grown weary and fallen. She was only twenty-two, but her strength had given out. She fell behind and collapsed. No one knew it. Daddy found her and saved her life. Even though he was much older, they fell in love and were married. I wasn't born until quite a while later." Joanna's eyes dimmed. "She died giving birth to me. I never knew her."

"She must have been a beautiful woman," offered Jimmy.

Their eyes met, and Joanna blushed. Setting her gaze straight forward, between Chief's ears, she said, "Daddy says she was very beautiful. He often called her his Indian pr—"

Joanna's words were cut short as a large bald eagle swooped out of the sky, sunk its talons into a small, furry animal, then soared away and disappeared over the forest.

"Poor little fellow," she whined. "He didn't have a chance."

"Balance of nature," said Jimmy.

"That's what my brother Bob used to say," Joanna said.

"Your brother? How—"

"Actually, I had two. Bob and Sam.

"You speak in the past tense."

"Yes." Joanna paused. "Bob joined the Union Army in the war. He was killed at Roanoke."

"Oh."

"And Sam . . ." Joanna's words fell off as her lips pulled tight. Lifting her chin, she said coldly, "Sam Claiborne went bad, Jimmy. He became a . . . a gunfighter." The last word sounded as if it stung her mouth. "He broke Daddy's heart. Daddy had already borne the tragedies of burying his wife and losing Bob in the war. Sam learned the fast-draw. Against all of Daddy's pleadings, he left the ranch to make a name for himself."

Jimmy looked at Joanna out of the corner of his eye.

"Sam outdrew and killed four men," Joanna continued. "The fifth man he challenged left him lying dead in a Utah street."

Jimmy was searching for something else to say when the

gurgling of Beaver Creek broke the silence. Approaching the bridge, Joanna pulled the Appaloosa to a halt.

"Well, here's where Chief and I turn around," she said reluctantly. "I'm glad you stopped at our place, Jimmy. Please stop on your way back to Fort Collins if you can."

"I will, Joanna." A grateful smile touched his lips. "Thank you for riding this far with me."

"It's been nice," she said, reflecting his smile. Turning Chief slowly, she added, "Please do come back."

Jimmy's heart raced. He had to let Joanna know how he felt. As she started to ride away, he said, "Joanna . . ."

Drawing rein, she looked back over her shoulder.

"You started to tell me earlier what your father often called your mother. You were interrupted by the eagle."

"Oh, yes. He—"

"Let me guess," cut in Jimmy.

"All right," said Joanna, a quizzical look in her eyes.

"It's the same thing I thought of when I saw you come into the kitchen this morning."

"Yes?"

"Princess."

Joanna's face crimsoned. She looked at him for a long moment. "Yes. That was it," she said softly.

The youth felt his own face grow warm. "That's what you are, Joanna. A princess."

Still blushing, Joanna Claiborne smiled and kicked the stallion's sides. Jimmy watched her gallop away. When a bend in the road took her from sight, he crossed the bridge and rode toward Estes Park.

Chapter Six

A carnival atmosphere dominated the main street of Estes Park as Jimmy Blackburn rode in. Local merchants, taking advantage of the boost in population, were barking on the boardwalks, advertising their wares. Laughter and music came from the saloons. Men were making bets along the street, some casting their lots with Spence Landford, others confident that Chuck Farley would walk away the victor.

Though Farley was not the seasoned professional, word was out that Landford's draw had slowed. After all, he was over forty. Farley was in his early twenties, and it was said that of the six men he had killed so far, four were top-ranking gunmen.

It appeared to the majority that Chuck Farley was destined to become a legend. The heavy money was on him. The opposition argued that since Chad Farley had been overrated, so was his brother.

By the position of the sun Jimmy estimated the time to be about eleven-thirty. As he dismounted in front of the Water Wheel Hotel, a heavyset man was standing on the board sidewalk, eyeing his pocket watch.

"What time is it, sir?" asked the youth.

"Eleven-twenty," replied the man, without expression.

"Thank you," said Jimmy. He stepped past the man and entered the hotel lobby. The place was packed with jovial people, and a cloud of tobacco smoke hung heavy in the room.

Jimmy threw a glance at the old clerk behind the desk, who was intently listening to two businessmen discuss the outcome of the duel. He swung his gaze up the stairs. The shadowed corridor was dark and still. Outside, the crowd thickened as two men began to argue heatedly. Jimmy moved to the foot of the stairs, stationing himself where Landford would see him when he came down.

The two men outside were now exchanging blows in the middle of the street, and the crowd was working up to a fever pitch. "Kill 'im, Harry!" someone shouted.

"Put his blood in the street, Elwood!" screamed another.

They were becoming a frenzied mob, impatient to see blood. A fistfight would pacify them until the main event.

Jimmy ascended a couple of stairs and looked over the heads of the crowd in the lobby. Through the dusty, flyspecked windows he watched the fight. It went on for about five minutes before the town marshal and his deputy appeared. Amid the jeers of the crowd, they pulled the brawlers apart.

Finding his place next to the bottom step again, Jimmy had fixed his gaze on the top of the stairs when a cold, forbidding thought formed in his brain. What if Spence Landford's draw *had* slowed? What if *he* were the one to die out there in the street today?

Jimmy shook his head, as if to dislodge this notion. He would not allow himself to think that way. Spence Landford must emerge the victor . . . and somehow be persuaded to instruct him in the skills of gunfighting. The ugly faces of the Hegler brothers, as seen on the posters, came to mind. A fresh surge of hatred followed. The killers must die. They must die at the hands of James William Blackburn. Anything else would be a thwarting of justice.

Suddenly he thought of Joanna Claiborne. What was this strange, unfamiliar sensation she caused within him? The feeling seemed to originate in the middle of his chest and spread warmly through his entire body. He was sorry that she felt the same about gunfighters as her father did.

Jimmy's attention was drawn to the clock on the wall of the lobby. Six minutes to twelve. Still no movement upstairs.

His mind flashed back to the last moment he had seen Joanna . . . her fascinating profile outlined against the shade of the forest as she looked over her shoulder.

Abruptly a chorus of voices in the street united in one word: "*Farley.*" Apparently Chuck Farley had put in an appearance somewhere up the street. The voices became a muddled buzz.

The clock on the wall now indicated three minutes to twelve. A door opened and the corridor upstairs brightened with a sudden spray of light, then darkened again. Shortly, a tall, formidable figure appeared at the top of the stairs. Everyone in the lobby grew quiet.

Spence Landford slowly descended, his face stolid. The only sounds were the squeak of the stairs. As he reached the bottom his dark eyes settled on Jimmy's watchful features. "Wish you'd gone home, boy," he said evenly.

A path was cleared as the lean frame of the seasoned gunfighter moved toward the door, Jimmy close on his heels.

Landford emerged into the noonday sun. The hum of the crowd dwindled and died. A dog could be heard barking somewhere in the town. Landford stepped off the boardwalk, his wooden gaze scouring the street. To his right the crowd began to divide, moving to the sides.

Presently one man was left alone in the middle of the street—a solitary form, shoulders sloped, face drawn in cruel lines. Without changing expression or posture, Chuck Farley moved forward several steps. Stopping about ten yards from Landford, he stood spread-legged, his hand hovering over the gun on his hip. Spence Landford squared himself, easing his hand just above the well-worn grips of the Colt .45.

The chill of death penetrated the warm summer air and hung like a menacing pall over the town.

Spence Landford's voice cut the silence. "You don't have to go through with this, Farley," he said with a rasp. "You can turn around, climb on your horse, and ride out. Live to bounce your grandchildren on your knee."

Every eye glided toward Chuck Farley. "You wantin' to back out, Landford?" he asked dramatically.

"I don't cotton to killing you," said Landford flatly.

"You killed my brother right on this spot, mister," hissed Farley. "Now you're going to die in the same place." His hand darted downward.

In a smooth blinding flash, Spence Landford drew and fired. Farley's body jerked as the hot lead tore into his chest. His gun, having cleared leather, tilted forward and roared, the slug spurting dust as it dug into the street. Farley hovered for a brief moment, then fell headfirst.

Spence Landford quietly holstered his gun, wheeled, and left the blood-hungry crowd to feast their eyes on Chuck Farley's lifeless form. Jimmy, relief washing over him, hastened to Landford's side. "I guess there's no doubt who's fastest now, Mr. Landford," he said, keeping up with the gunfighter's pace.

Landford did not comment. Turning in at the livery stable,

he saddled his horse, tossed money in a tin pan on a bench, and led the animal toward the street.

"Mr. Landford," said Jimmy pleadingly, "you've got to teach me the fast-draw."

"Go home, kid," Landford said, mounting his horse. Spurring the animal, he headed east out of town.

Jimmy ran down the street, leaped into the saddle of his chestnut gelding, and galloped after him. Soon the youth pulled alongside the gunfighter. "You've got to help me, Mr. Landford!" he hollered.

Landford veered his horse off the road and stopped under some tall pines. His horse blew as Jimmy drew up beside him. "Look, Jimmy," said the gunman sharply, "do you want to end up like Chuck Farley?"

"No, sir, but—"

"Then get this fool notion out of your head."

"Mr. Landford, the Hegler brothers have got to pay for what they did."

"I agree, kid, but let it be handled by a man who wears a badge."

Ignoring the statement, Jimmy said, "You know, I *could* just sneak up on them with my rifle and shoot them in the back one at a time."

"But that'd be murder." Landford fished in his shirt pocket and pulled out a cigarillo.

"Right," agreed the youth. "I don't hanker to be a murderer. I'm willing to give them a fair chance, face me head-on. All I want is for you to teach me so I can take them. I'll pick the places and catch them so it's one-on-one each time."

Thumbing a match into flame, Landford held it to the cigarillo. "That'd be a long shot, kid. But let's say I did teach you. Let's say you did take out the Hegler gang. What then?"

"Then I'm going to finish school and go to college back east. I want to become a lawyer. I want to come back to the West and do my part to civilize the frontier."

"Jimmy, that's really good." Landford smiled. "The thing for you to do is forget the Heglers and pursue your education in law."

Jimmy's face hardened. "Can't you understand? I've got to settle with the Heglers *first*!"

"Son," said the gunfighter, "if you strap on a gun and draw

it fast enough and shoot it straight enough to kill the Hegler brothers, you'll never become a lawyer."

Jimmy shook his head. "You're wrong. I don't want to shoot anyone else. Just the men who murdered my family."

"Get off the horse, boy," said Landford, dismounting. "Let's sit down over here and talk a few minutes."

Jimmy slipped out of the saddle and followed. Landford moved next to a towering pine and eased himself down on a large rock. Pointing to a tree stump he said, "You take the comfortable spot."

As Jimmy took his place on the stump Landford said, "Let me tell you about gunfighters."

"I already know," snapped the youth. "Sheriff Cashman in Fort Collins told me. The irreversible law, right? Once you strap on a gun and live through a duel, you can't take it off, right?"

Landford's jaw squared. "That's right. The sheriff's been talking some good sense to you."

"Sooner or later there's always somebody faster than you, right?"

"That's right, Jimmy."

"It won't be that way with me," the boy said with confidence. "As soon as the last of the Hegler gang is dead I'll drop my gun in a river somewhere. The irreversible law won't hold for me."

"That's what I thought years ago, kid," said Landford, fixing his gaze on the youth. "But it didn't work that way. I learned the fast-draw just for fun. Never intended to use it. Made the mistake of wearing the gun into a town down in east Texas one day. A gunslick prodded me. I should've had enough sense to back off. Lost my temper and called him some choice names. He went for his gun. I killed him."

Jimmy listened, watching Landford's face.

"I thought it was all over. Told myself I'd never even wear the gun again. Ten days later a brother of the man I'd killed came riding onto our ranch. Challenged me. I told him I wouldn't put on a gun. He had some men with him and said if I didn't face him, they'd kill my ma and pa. I couldn't let that happen, so I went into the house and buckled on my gun. When the men led his horse away with his body draped over the saddle, I knew I would live with the gun until the day I died."

"But Mr. Landford," said Jimmy, "it won't be that way with me. I—"

"The worst part, Jimmy," Landford butted in, "you don't just live with the gun. You live with the faceless man."

A quizzical expression formed on Jimmy's face. Cocking his head, he said, "The faceless man?"

Landford's eyes grew icy. "You mentioned him a few minutes ago. He's the one sooner or later who's faster."

"Oh." Jimmy nodded, fixing his gaze on the ground.

"He's out there, son. He's waiting for Spence Landford. Like a ghost you can't touch, he waits. Somewhere in the dismal future, he waits."

The youth saw a haunting glaze come over the gunman's eyes. His skin prickled.

"The faceless man can afford to be patient," continued Landford. "It's written in destiny's book. At a certain time, in a certain place, he'll get me. Maybe on a dusty street, maybe in a saloon, or perhaps along the trail somewhere a cold voice will call from the shadows and tell me to turn around and draw."

Jimmy ran his tongue around his mouth, moistening his lips.

"He's out there, Jimmy," said Spence Landford, his voice dry. "Though I've lived with him for many years, I don't know his name and don't know what he looks like. I've looked for him, but he could be anyone. He could even be you. Sometimes I've glanced over my shoulder, expecting to see him standing there. One day I'll meet him, and when I do, he won't be a ghost. He'll be as real as the bullets in his gun . . . as real as the grave where they'll drop my breathless body."

Jimmy stood up to shake off the effect of Landford's words.

"I don't want the faceless man to haunt you, son. That's why I won't help you become a gunhawk." Landford stood up, dropped the cigarillo butt on the ground, and mashed it with his boot. "Besides," he added, "I've got to head for Oklahoma. Got an appointment in Tulsa."

"With the faceless man?" Jimmy asked pointedly.

The furrows in Landford's brow disappeared as his face tightened. He waited a moment, then said, "Could be. Man forced one of my best friends into a gunfight, knowing my friend had an injured hand. Was nothing short of murder."

"How'd you learn about it?" asked the boy.

"Letter came to my hotel in Denver, just before I rode up here."

"Couldn't it wait until you teach me the fast-draw?"

"Don't you ever listen? I told you, kid. I'm not going to teach you!"

Temper flared inside of Jimmy. "You really care what happens to me?" he asked heatedly.

"Yeah, kid. That's why I'm not going to do it."

"Well, then I'll just have to get somebody else to teach me, because I'm going after the Heglers!"

"Yeah, and if they don't teach you right, you'll get slaughtered too!"

"Then *you'd* better teach me."

The boy's words seemed to have an effect on Landford. He studied the determination fixed on Jimmy's face. Swinging his fist through the air, he swore. "Why don't you just let the law handle it?"

Jimmy's eyes widened. "That man in Tulsa . . ."

"Yeah?"

"Why don't you just let the law handle it?"

"Because the law—"

"Won't handle it," Jimmy finished the statement for him. He saw a weakening in Landford's eyes. "Why don't you just forget it?" the youth pushed him further.

"'Cause it was my friend he murdered, that's why."

"You're telling me to forget the Heglers," said Jimmy.

"That's different!" bit back Landford. Before those two words had died in the air, the gunman knew that the stubborn young man had him in the corner.

Jimmy's eyes narrowed. "You bet it's different, Mr. Landford. The man you're after only murdered a friend. The Heglers murdered my family . . . and blood is thicker than water, Mr. Landford!"

Landford lifted himself to his full height, took a deep breath, and let it out slowly. "Okay, kid," he said resignedly. "I'm going to teach you. I'll give you ten days. After you get the mechanics, the rest is practice. If you don't have it in ten days, you'll never get it. If you've got a lick of natural ability, when I get through you'll have everything but experience. I can't give you that."

A broad smile crept over Jimmy's face. "Thanks, Mr.

Landford," he said with elation. "We'll go to my place. There's plenty of room, and nobody'll bother us there."

The gunfighter laid his hand on Jimmy's shoulder. "Could we dispense with the 'mister' stuff, kid? You call me Spence, okay?"

"Sure, Spence," agreed Jimmy. "I'd like that." Turning toward his horse, he said, "Let's get riding."

Landford mounted. As Jimmy placed his foot in the stirrup he turned and looked up at his new companion. "I've got to stop at a ranch on the way home. It'll only take a minute. It's about five miles from here." Swinging into the saddle, he said, "Then we can hightail it to Fort Collins. We can be there before midnight if we hurry."

As they crossed the bridge at Beaver Creek Jimmy remembered the scene earlier in the day when Joanna rode away on the big Appaloosa.

The B-Slash-C soon came into view. Briefly Jimmy told Spence about spending the night there, explaining that he wanted to stop as a courtesy to his newfound friends.

"You told me last night that you had a place to stay," scolded Landford.

"Just didn't want to be a bother to you," said Jimmy defensively. Eyeing the gunfighter closely, he said, "Spence . . ."

"Yeah."

"I need to explain something before we reach the ranch."

"I'm listening."

"Mr. Claiborne had a son who was a gunfighter. He . . . he met his faceless man."

"Yeah?"

"The old man has a very strong dislike for gunfighters. His daughter feels the same way."

"You want I should tell 'em that I shoe horses for a living or something?"

"If you took off your gun, they might not even ask about your occupation. And . . . and if they did, you could say you're a teacher. You know, a sort of private tutor. That wouldn't be lying. Right now that's what you are."

"Anything you say, kid," said Landford, pulling his horse to a halt. He untied the leather cord that encircled his thigh, unbuckled his gun belt, and slipped it into one of his saddlebags. Prodding his horse forward again, he smiled and ran a finger across his heavy mustache, saying, "Okay, kid. Just call me Professor Spencer. Somebody there might know the name Spence Landford."

Joanna Claiborne was the first to greet the two riders as they approached the house. She was sitting on the front porch shelling peas. Spying Jimmy, she bounded off the steps with a big smile.

"Hello!" Jimmy called out.

"Hello, Jimmy," she responded. "I'm glad you could come by again." Her eyes moved to Spence Landford.

"Joanna Claiborne, this is Mr. Spencer," said Jimmy.

Landford touched the brim of his hat. "It's a pleasure, Miss Joanna," he said, smiling.

"This is the man I told you about, Joanna," said Jimmy advisedly.

"Oh, your hired man?"

Jimmy knew if he corrected her thinking and reminded Joanna that he had told her the man he would hire was a specialist, the conversation could get sticky. "Yes," he replied, eyeing Landford briefly.

The girl looked back at Landford. "I'm happy to meet you, Mr. Spencer."

Jimmy's eye caught movement over the barn. A quick glance revealed the approaching figure of Russ Pittman. Looking back at the girl, he asked, "Is your father around?"

"Not right now," said Joanna. "He's up in the timber with the men. He'll be back about sundown."

"Oh. Guess I'll miss him this time. Mr. Spencer and I have to keep moving. We've got a big day ahead of us tomorrow at the farm."

Russ Pittman drew near. "Howdy, Jimmy," he said in a friendly tone.

"Hello, Mr. Russ," replied the youth.

Pittman's gaze lingered on the rugged face of the gunfighter.

"This is Mr. Spencer," Jimmy said. "Mr. Spencer, this is Mr. Russ Pittman."

"Howdy." Landford nodded.

"Howdy," replied Pittman, sober-faced.

"Mr. Spencer just hired on to work for Jimmy," said Joanna to the foreman.

"Why don't you fellas climb off them horses and we'll have

Jezebel heat up the coffeepot," said Pittman, ignoring the girl's statement.

A high-pitched voice came from an upstairs window of the house. " 'Scuse me, Mr. Russ," hollered Jezebel. "You have Mr. Burntblack and his friend come on in!"

"Don't have time, Miss Jezebel," called back Jimmy. "But thanks anyway!" Turning to Pittman, he said, "Thanks to you, too, Mr. Russ."

Pittman smiled at Jimmy, then gave a cold look toward Landford. "Maybe next time," he said evenly.

"Okay," replied Jimmy. Fixing his eyes on the captivating features of the girl, he said, "I *do* plan to come back."

Joanna's face reddened.

Speaking to both, Jimmy said, "Thanks again for your hospitality." Glancing sideways, he spoke to his companion. "We better be moving, Mr. Spencer."

The two horses turned a tight circle. Jimmy twisted around in the saddle. " 'Bye, Princess."

A smile tugged at the corners of Joanna's mouth. Her face flushed again. "'Bye."

The strange, warm sensation spread through Jimmy's breast once again.

The same type of feeling was running through Joanna Claiborne's heart as she watched the two horses gallop away. She waited a long moment, then spoke to the foreman without taking her eyes from the diminishing figures. "Russ, Jimmy's such a nice boy. But I have a funny feeling about Mr. Spencer."

Pittman said nothing, his gaze fixed on the two riders.

"Did you notice," asked Joanna, "in the introductions, both of your names were used? And it was so with me. But Jimmy only called him Mr. Spencer. Do you suppose his name is really Spencer?"

"Yes, honey," replied Russ with gravel in his voice. "His name is Spencer, all right. Spencer Landford."

Joanna turned and looked at Pittman, her face losing its color.

Chapter Seven

Jimmy Blackburn woke up at the crack of dawn. His thoughts dwelt pleasantly on the daughter of Britt Claiborne. Slowly they were replaced with the business at hand. This was the first day of his private tutoring by the famous Spence Landford.

By six-thirty teacher and pupil had eaten breakfast and were ready for lesson number one. As they stepped out of the house and crossed the porch, Jimmy paused and looked down at the deep-brown spots on the porch floor. A fresh hatred for the Hegler gang flamed inside him.

"What's that?" asked Landford.

"My pa's blood," said Jimmy through his teeth.

Stepping off the porch, the youth adjusted Lonnie Hegler's gun belt on his slender waist. He walked to the spot where Hegler had died, between the house and barn, and said, "Okay, Spence, it's time for school to begin."

"I assume," said Landford, "that you've already done some drawing practice."

"Yep."

"Unload the gun and let me see you do it."

Jimmy broke the action of the Colt .45 and punched out the cartridges. He slipped them into his pants pocket and dropped the gun in the holster.

"Now draw it over and over again," said Landford, "while I walk around you and get a look from every angle."

Jimmy responded eagerly. Again and again the revolver was whipped from its sheath. Landford circled slowly, cocking his head, bending over, straightening up. After watching for a while he said, "You seem to have a natural knack for it, boy. There are many ways to draw a gun. Every man has to find the method and stance of his body that works best for him."

The youth continued drawing without cocking the hammer.

"Wait a minute," said Landford. "The holster needs to be a little lower. Some gunfighters have learned to draw fast with the gun butt almost even with their waist, but usually it's a short man with short arms. You're built almost exactly like me. You'll draw faster if the gun is lower."

Jimmy worked the belt lower on his slim waist, then adjusted the leather thong on his thigh.

"That's better, said Landford. "See, you've got to draw the gun thinking of your arm as a pendulum—like on a clock. You don't want to bend your elbow. It takes a fraction of a second to bend your elbow. That fraction can mean the difference between living or dying. The gun needs to come out of the holster in a smooth upswing, so that it's instantly in firing position."

"Like this?" asked the youth, drawing the gun as had just been explained.

"That's it," said Landford, pleased. "You do have a natural ability for it. Now do that for a while, and then we'll work on cocking the hammer."

When Jimmy had done it seven or eight times, Landford said, "Hold it. Let me see that holster." Examining the leather inside the holster, he said, "Go ahead and draw some more. I'll be right back."

The gunfighter passed through the corral gate and entered the barn. He fumbled momentarily in his saddlebags in the semidarkness of the building, then emerged carrying a bottle of oil. "You need to keep some of this with you, son," he said. "Keeps the leather soft. The gun will come out easier."

Landford's experienced hands soon had Jimmy's holster well oiled. "Strap it back on and practice some more draws," he said.

When the boy had whipped the gun out another fifty or sixty times, Landford said, "Now let's work on cocking the hammer as you draw."

The experienced gunfighter showed the determined youth how the cocking of the hammer required a perfect synchronizing of thumb and fingers. When the hand swung forward, the thumb had to slip over the hammer and lever it back in the exact instant that the fingers secured a full grip on the handle. By the time the muzzle cleared leather, the hammer had to be in its firing position.

Landford watched with amazement as Jimmy responded adeptly to his instructions. On the outside he showed mild satisfaction at his pupil's progess; inside, he was astounded. Jimmy displayed more proficiency with the Colt .45 than any beginner he had ever seen, including himself.

For five full days Landford drilled his student from sunrise to sunset. With each draw Jimmy seemed to gain speed and confidence.

On day six they loaded the gun. Tin cans were procured from the Blackburn dump. Landford lined the corral fence with cans, eight inches apart, then gave the boy one brief demonstration. Six times he drew and fired. Six cans flipped from the fence. Jimmy's mouth hung open in awe at the speed of Landford's hand.

Lining the cans on the fence again, he said, "Okay, son. You try it."

The youth's swiftness in drawing the gun was excellent, but his accuracy needed attention. Drawing and firing six times, he hit only one can. A look of discouragement pinched his face. As Jimmy thumbed fresh cartridges into the cylinder, Landford said, "The key to accuracy, my boy, is concentration. Before you draw, you pick your target. Then you concentrate on that target. Right now it's a tin can. Later it'll be the center of a man's chest. If you want him to die fast, just put that .45 slug dead center. It will explode his heart."

"If I want him to die hard and slow, where do I aim?"

Reading the pent-up vengeance in Jimmy's eyes, Landford said slowly, "You put it in his gut. It will mess up his innards something fierce, but he'll die slow."

Jimmy turned toward the row of tin cans. The Colt zipped from its holster and roared. The can to the far right sailed off the fence. He dropped the weapon into the holster, paused a moment, drew and fired again. The second can disappeared.

"That's it, boy," said Landford. "Concentrate."

The Poudre Valley echoed for the next four days, as Jimmy shot up tin cans, tree limbs, and paper targets. The only break in the incessant roaring of the gun came on the eighth day, when Jimmy left Landford long enough to ride into town and buy more ammunition.

At noon on the tenth day Spence Landford said, "All right, Jimmy. You've mastered the mechanics of it. Your stance is right. Your concentration is excellent."

A broad smile crept its way across Jimmy's mouth.

Landford continued. "You're already faster and more accurate than most gunfighters ever become. Most of them die before they ever attain that plateau."

"That's because they didn't have you to teach them," said Jimmy with a note of deep appreciation.

A tight smile tugged at the gunfighter's lips. "I tell you these things, son, because you need self-confidence. But don't get overconfident. You have a natural dexterity with a gun. You have good eyes and keen senses. What you don't have . . . is experience."

"The only experience I want is killing four men, Spence," said Jimmy. "Then my gunfighting will be over."

Landford's features stiffened. "I hope so, boy." He lifted his own gun from its holster and emptied the cylinder. "Empty yours too," he said to the youth. "For your last lesson you're going to draw against me."

Jimmy felt his Adam's apple stick in his throat. "I—I'm sure glad it's with empty guns," he said nervously.

Landford turned and walked a dozen paces, then wheeled. Positioning himself in his natural stance, he eased his hand to a hovering position over the gun. "Now, Jimmy, you've just challenged me. I've accepted, telling you to draw first. Do it."

Bringing everything Landford had taught him to the forefront of his mind, Jimmy took his stance, concentrating deeply. His hand darted down.

Landford's gun was out and the hammer snapped before the boy had fully palmed his gun. His mouth slacked as his eyes bulged. He looked down at the gun, still in its holster, swung his gaze back to Landford, and blinked.

"That's what I meant about overconfidence," said the gunfighter dryly.

"But . . ." Worry crowded the boy's features.

"It's okay, Jimmy. Don't let it discourage you. The draw you just saw is the reason I'm still alive."

Jimmy Blackburn shook his head. "But that's just it, Spence. I *didn't* see it!" He blinked and shook his head again. "You've got to be the fastest in the whole world!"

"No, son," said Landford soberly. "There's one that I know that's faster for sure."

Jimmy's brow furrowed. "Who?"

"The faceless man."

Landford's eyes were cold when he spoke. Silence prevailed. After a long moment Jimmy broke the spell by saying, "Spence, you had your gun out and fired almost before I even touched mine. Yet I moved first. How—"

"Very observant, kid," said the seasoned gunman with a half smile. "You're absolutely correct."

"But how?"

"Your eyes," said Landford.

"My eyes?"

"Yep. You told me you were going to draw a split second before you did it. That gave me an extra edge. In this business you don't deal in seconds of time, son. You deal in *tenths* of seconds. A tenth of a second can mean the difference of life or death. You've got to beat your opponent by enough margin to keep two things from occuring."

"What's that?"

"You've got to keep him from lining the muzzle on you. If he gets that far, he can be dead on his feet and the second thing can still happen. The hammer can drop and the gun fire. No man can move faster than a bullet."

"I understand," said Jimmy. "But how did you read my eyes?"

"It's a thing you can't explain with words," replied Landford. "You just have to see it to know what I'm talking about. The only time you don't see it is when you're up against a man who's learned to control it."

"I guess that takes time and experience, too, huh?"

"Yep."

"But what if a fellow like me goes up against one of the sharpies first thing?"

"Then a fellow like you is dead," said Landford flatly.

For the first time in setting out on his course of vengeance, Jimmy had a touch of fear overwhelm his hatred for the Hegler brothers. He felt his lean frame shiver. Instantly he controlled himself. "Then a fellow like me has got to practice," he said confidently.

"That's right," agreed the seasoned gunfighter. "I've shown you all I can show you. From here on out it's up to you. Your ten days of tutoring are up. I'll be pulling out for Tulsa in the morning."

Jimmy practiced the quick-draw until darkness forced him

to stop. After supper he and Landford sat on the front porch
of the house, enjoying the cool summer evening. There was
no moon. Other than the twinkling stars overhead, all that
was clearly visible to Jimmy's eyes was the red-hot tip of
Landford's cigarillo.

Both sat in silence for a long while. Jimmy thought of
Joanna Claiborne. The memory of her beautiful face warmed
his heart. He wondered when he'd see her again. Thinking
through his situation, he figured to return home after settling
with the Heglers. He would finish his last year of schooling,
then seek out a good college in the East for his education in
law. Certainly there would be time before then to make a few
trips to the B-Slash-C. Maybe, if things developed, one day
he could ask Joanna to—

Jimmy's thoughts were interrupted by Landford's words.
"How soon you plan to head for Missouri?"

"Right soon. Figure to practice a lot on the way." Jimmy
paused and said, "I was thinking this afternoon, Spence.
You're going to Tulsa. I'm heading for Joplin. We could travel
most of the way together."

"Hadn't thought about that, kid. If you can pull out tomorrow, guess we could."

"Well," said Jimmy hesitatingly, "it will take me just about
one day to get everything in order. I'll have to see Mr. Hoffer
and arrange for him to watch the place and keep an eye on
the stock till I get back. A few other loose ends tied up and
I'll be ready to go. You couldn't wait one more day, could
you?"

Landford flipped the cigarillo stub over the porch rail and
swatted a mosquito that brushed his face. Standing up and
stretching, he said, "Well, I guess it'd be worth one more day
to have such good company."

It was barely daylight when Jimmy Blackburn and Spence
Landford rode away from the Blackburn farm. At sunset the
previous day Jimmy had visited the graves of his parents and
sisters, renewing his vow to take vengeance on the Heglers
for their brutal crime.

The two riders angled across Colorado, heading southeast.
As the lowering sun touched the western horizon they found
a spot next to a small creek and set up camp. While Landford
opened and heated a can of beans, Jimmy found some sticks

and stood them upright in the soft earth of the creek bank.
One by one he shattered them as he practiced the fast draw.
He missed occasionally, but his accuracy was steadily improving.

After supper the travelers emptied their guns and drew
against each other. The exercise was repeated again and again
until it was so dark neither man could see the other.

At dawn the next day they were on the trail again. As the
altitude dropped, the heat became more noticeable. About an
hour before sundown Landford spotted a thick stand of cottonwood trees surrounding a bubbling spring. "Let's pull
over early, Jimmy," he said. "I've got an idea."

Jimmy watched as the gunfighter climbed one of the cottonwoods with an empty bean can he had saved. "What I'm
going to do," he said, crawling out on a large, low-hanging
limb, "is hang the can on this string." From his shirt pocket
Landford produced a piece of string about five feet long. As
he tied the string around the top rim of the can, then tied the
other end to the limb, he explained, "I'll swing the can, and
you draw and fire. It'll improve the speed of your draw and
tone up your reflexes."

Back on the ground the gunfighter stood just behind the
trunk, holding the can with the string taut. Jimmy stood
poised and ready. Landford released the can, which swung
downward in a full arc. Jimmy drew and fired, missing the
can. The operation was repeated over and over. Jimmy had
emptied his gun four times without hitting the target.

As he was reloading he asked, "What's my problem,
Spence?"

"Lack of concentration," answered his companion. "You're
not concentrating hard enough."

"I suppose you could get it with the first shot," chided the
youth.

"Mmm-hmm," hummed Landford idly.

"Let's see it," challenged Jimmy.

"Okay," said Landford, walking to where Jimmy stood.
"You swing the can."

Jimmy stood behind the trunk and released the tin target.
Landford's hand whipped out the Colt .45. It roared and the
string snapped just above the can. Jimmy stepped over and
picked up the untouched bean can, the string dangling. His
unbelieving eyes met those of the gunfighter.

Blowing the smoke from the gun's muzzle, Landford said casually, "Concentration."

Before darkness forced him to stop, Jimmy had hit the can three times. Each time there was less metal at which to shoot.

At breakfast two days later Landford said, "We oughta reach Cheyenne Wells by midafternoon, Jimmy. What do you say we get us each a room at the hotel and sleep in a bed tonight? I'll pay for yours."

"Sounds great, Spence," agreed Jimmy, "but I can pay for my own room. I brought some cash with me, plus a bank draft if I run low." Cocking his head sideways, he said, "How do you make a living? Where do you get your money?"

"Hire out my gun when the cash runs low," replied Landford quietly. "Seems nearly everywhere I go, somebody needs a bodyguard . . . or wants a legitimate score settled. Every once in a while I see a chance to collect a bounty. One way or another I seem to keep myself and my horse in food and other necessities."

Jimmy thought a minute. "Don't you ever get tired of drifting?"

"Not really," replied Landford. "Sometimes, though, I stay in one place a whole month."

"Ever think of settling down . . . getting married?"

The gunfighter's face stiffened. "Yeah, I've thought about it. But it can't be. A man that lives by the gun can't settle down. No woman in her right mind wants to be saddled to a gunslinger."

Jimmy thought of Joanna. He wondered if she would consider being the wife of a lawyer.

As they finished breakfast Jimmy said, "Since we're not in any big hurry, could we practice some more?"

"Sure." Landford smiled.

For nearly two hours the two men faced each other with empty guns. Jimmy was now learning to "deadpan" his eyes, and Landford was not reading the signal. The determined youth was now getting his gun all the way out before Landford's hammer hit the empty chamber.

As they mounted up, Landford said, "You're coming along fine, boy. You're a natural."

Cheyenne Wells came into view late in the afternoon. The sun was hot on their backs as the two riders moved across the flat land into the town. Little dust devils skipped across the wide street, bouncing against the sun-bleached frame buildings. A large gray cat darted across the street from under the porch of the general store, followed by a yapping dog.

Jimmy noticed two men standing in front of the bank. They broke off their conversation as their eyes focused on Spence Landford's face.

"You been here before, Spence?" the youth asked from the side of his mouth.

"Yep."

"Those two men seemed to know you."

"Possible."

Landford drew rein at the Plains Hotel. "We'll check in, then stable the animals," he said to the youth.

Jimmy followed the gunfighter across the lobby to the desk. The clerk was slouched in an easy chair, reading the newspaper. He was tall and thin, not much older than Jimmy. An elderly man watched them from a chair in the lobby.

Landford stood at the desk, ignored by the preoccupied clerk. He waited for a long moment while the clerk continued reading. The gunfighter cleared his throat, his patience wearing thin. The clerk looked up and said, "Be with you in a minute."

"It's already been more than a minute," said Landford.

The young man closed the newspaper, folded it, and slapped it to the floor. Moving stiffly, he approached the desk with a sour look. "Two rooms?" he asked, his tone abrupt.

A touch of temper flashed through Landford. "Business so good you can afford to be nasty?"

Ignoring the question, the clerk repeated his own. "Two rooms?"

"Yeah, two rooms."

Spinning the register, the clerk said, "Sign it."

"Maybe you oughta go back to bed and climb out of the other side," said Landford, scratching his name on the register. "Here, Jimmy." He handed the pen to his companion and stepped aside.

Jimmy dipped the pen in the inkwell and wrote his name under Landford's. The clerk pulled two keys from the cubbyholes behind him and palmed them on the desk. Turning the register back, he spoke as his eyes fell on the page. "Rooms five and seven, Mr. Land—" His face blanched. He lifted his widened eyes to meet those of the gunfighter. "R-rooms f-five and seven, s-sir. Ad-adjoining rooms."

"You want your money in advance, don't you?" asked Landford, pulling a gold eagle from his vest.

"H-however you w-want, sir," answered the changed young man. "How l-long will you and y-your friend be s-s-staying?"

"One night," replied the gunfighter, laying the edge of the coin on the desk, then snapping it down hard.

The clerk jumped, ran a nervous hand over his mouth, and said, "That'll be t-two dollars." Hurriedly he fumbled in a drawer and handed Landford eight dollars.

The quiet man scooped up the keys. "Let's get the saddle-bags, boy," he said to Jimmy.

As the pair stepped out into the fading sunlight, the old gentleman seated in the lobby was heard to say, "Yer dadblamed lucky you didn't gitcher head blowed off, kid. Spence Landford don't put up with a lotta nonsense!"

As darkness settled over the Colorado plains, the tall, slender partners crossed the street from the hotel and entered the Dutch Oven Café. Finding an empty table in the busy place, they sat down. Jimmy saw the eyes of the crowd roam to Spence Landford amid furtive whispers.

"Is it this way everywhere you go?" Jimmy asked his friend.

"Just about," answered Landford. "If it's a place I've never been, there's usually someone there who knows me from elsewhere."

They were about midway through the meal when the door opened and a medium-built, blond-haired young man came into the room, his eyes scanning the tables. There was a silver deputy's badge pinned to his vest. His gaze fell on Landford; then he wove his way across the room. There was urgent concern on his face as he approached.

Without any greeting, the lawman said, "Landford, you've got to get out of town right now." Beads of sweat glistened on his brow.

Landford laid his fork on the table. Swallowing a mouthful of food, he said, "Where's Sheriff Turner?"

"He's out of town on business," the nervous deputy explained.

"Well, I'm not breaking any laws, Galloway."

"I know that," said Deputy Sheriff Hank Galloway, "but there's going to be bloodshed if you don't go."

Jimmy could read the worry in the lawman's eyes.

"What're you talking about?" asked the gunfighter.

"Upton Young and his bunch rode into town about an hour ago. Somebody at the Antelope Saloon told them you were in town. They're tankin' up on whiskey right now. Soon's they get enough they'll be looking you up."

Landford sighed and shook his head.

"Who's Upton Young, Spence?" asked Jimmy.

"Piece of trash that crawled out from under a rock," replied Landford. "He put his kid brother up to shooting me in the back over in Lamar. The young whelp missed, and I killed him. Word soon spread that Young vowed he'd get me if I ever showed up in Lamar again. Looks like he'd just as soon my blood flowed in Cheyenne Wells."

"Look, Landford," said Galloway, "we've got a nice, peaceful town. If you'd just take your friend here and ride out, the Young bunch'll be gone tomorrow. Things'll settle down, and we won't have any killing."

Landford wiped his mouth with a napkin and rose from his chair. He unsheathed the Colt .45 and spun the cylinder, checking the loads. "How many's he got with him?" he said to Galloway, dropping the gun back in the holster.

"Two. Young makes three."

Turning to Jimmy, who was now on his feet, Landford said, "You go on back to the hotel."

"Listen to me, Landford," said the deputy. "We haven't had a gunfight in Cheyenne Wells for nearly a year. New people have been moving in because it's a peaceful town."

"It'll be peaceful again," said Landford evenly, "just as soon as I get this over with."

"Spence, you can't go up against three men by yourself," argued Jimmy.

"If you're suggesting that you jump in with me, kid, forget it. Save yourself for the one thing you got to do. Get it done and throw that gun in the river you were talking about. Now go lock yourself in your room until I get back."

Galloway took off his hat and wiped sweat from his forehead. "Why do you have to do this, Landford? If you just ride out—"

"You're wrong, Deputy," cut in Landford. "If I just ride out, it's not going to settle it. Young knows I'm here. He's not going to let me get this close without trying to kill me.

Trouble is, I've got this kid with me. If I don't handle it now, they'll bushwhack me along the trail and kill the kid too."

Galloway's growing concern was nearly to the point of anger. "Well, at least it wouldn't be in our town!" he blurted. "And none of our citizens will be struck by a stray bullet."

Landford's face turned to granite. His dark eyes bolted Galloway with a cold stare.

The tall gunfighter opened the café door as the customers sat in fear. The streetlamps had been lit, and people were milling about. He threw a glance up the street toward the Antelope Saloon. Music and laughter filtered through the swinging doors.

Without looking behind, Landford said, "Deputy, you go tell the gang I'm out here in the street. That way nobody'll get shot up in the saloon."

The young lawman angrily stepped around the gunslinger and headed up the street.

Without turning around, Landford said, "Kid, you still there?"

"Yes, sir," came the voice from behind.

"Do like I told you, Jimmy. I want you off the street. Go lock yourself in your hotel room."

Reluctantly, Jimmy lumbered across the street and stepped onto the porch of the hotel. Before entering he turned and set his eyes on the back of Landford, who stood in the middle of the street.

People were coming like bugs out of the woodwork, lining up on the board sidewalks. Stealthily, Jimmy slipped down the street and mingled with the crowd. His height allowed him a clear view of the makeshift battleground.

Suddenly the music from the saloon stopped and died in the air. "Go on! All of yuh! Clear out!" came a big, bellowing voice from within.

First through the doors was the deputy, followed by cowboys, trail hands, saloon girls, sharply dressed gamblers, and finally the bartender. All of them found places in the crowd.

Spence Landford was in his stance, shoulders slightly hunched, feet spread.

All eyes were on the saloon door as a giant form emerged onto the wooden walk. Upton Young was a big, thick-bodied man. His dark eyes and full black beard made an awesome impression on the wide-eyed crowd.

Flanking Young as he stepped into the street were a pair of rowdy-looking men, one on each side. All three wore big six-guns on their hips. They lined up abreast and stopped about forty feet from Spence Landford.

Jimmy adjusted his position until he was parallel with the famous gunfighter. The side view of the man accentuated the cut of his jaw, the determination in his face.

"I understand you're looking for me, Young," said Landford.

"Got a score to settle," growled Young.

"Your brother would still be alive if you hadn't sent him to blow a hole in my back." Landford's voice was amazingly calm.

Hatred pulled at Upton Young's dark features. His hand swooped downward. The other two followed suit.

Landford's .45 was out quicker than the eye could see. At the same time he lowered his crouch, the gun hand bracing oddly against his thigh. The left hand was fanning the hammer with blinding speed.

Big Upton grunted heavily as the slug tore into his chest. His gun hand had not cleared leather. The second to fall was the man to Young's right. The third man was mortally struck, but not before he got off one shot.

A lance of fear shot through Jimmy's body as he saw Landford go down. The saloon girls and a couple of women in the crowd were screaming as Jimmy shoved his way clear. Kneeling beside the fallen Landford, he saw a hole seared in the gunfighter's pants on the right thigh. Blood was soaking through.

Wincing as he tried to pull his leg under him, Landford swore. "This isn't your hotel room, boy! I told you—" A spasm of pain cut off his words.

Jimmy shot a glance at the three fallen gunhawks. None moved as men from the crowd began to gather around them. "You stay right here, Spence," gasped Jimmy. "I'll find a doctor."

"I'm right here, son," came a welcome voice. The physician of Cheyenne Wells knelt beside Landford and examined the wound in the dim light of the streetlamps. "Can't tell for sure, but it doesn't look too bad," said the silver-haired doctor. Looking at Jimmy, he said, "You with Landford, son?"

"Yes, sir," replied the youth.

"Let's get him over to my office. Need to get that bleeding stopped."

In less than an hour the doctor had cleaned the wound and stitched it up, pronouncing it superficial. The bullet had passed clean through, just under the surface of the skin.

"Will I be able to ride, Doc?" asked Landford as the physician finished wrapping a bandage on the leg.

"As long as you keep the horse to a moderate walk," came the answer. "You won't be able to put your weight completely on it for several days."

"Hey, Spence," chuckled Jimmy, "maybe I could outdraw you now."

Landford shook his head. "The way you're going, kid, it won't be long before you can do it anyway. All you need is experience. A little of that goes a long way." Standing up and putting the bulk of his weight on the left leg, the gunfighter said, "Thanks, Doc. How much do I owe you?"

"Three dollars will cover it," said the physician.

Jimmy helped his friend back to the hotel and into his room. "I'll have to get myself another pair of pants," said Landford, easing down on the bed. The right leg of his pants had been slit from top to bottom by the doctor.

"I want to know something," said Jimmy.

"What's that?" asked the gunfighter, laying his head on the pillow.

"Why'd you tie into all of those gunmen alone?"

"Was my fight. Couldn't ask anybody else in on it."

"I heard one of the punchers at the B-Slash-C talking about how you could fan a gun. He wasn't kidding!"

"I was a little slow tonight," said Landford grimly, "or I wouldn't have a hole in my leg."

"You sure didn't look slow to me," said the youth.

"I made a mistake." Landford stared at the ceiling, thinking. "I wasn't watching Young's eyes. I let him get a little too much start on me. When you're fanning on that many men, you need to be able to start at one end and do it in a sweep. I had to take out Young first, because he went for his gun first. The man on his right went next. Having to come all the way back to the man on Young's left took time; that's why he got off his shot."

"But how could you know Young was going to draw first?"

asked Jimmy. "You couldn't watch the eyes of all three. Any one of them might have gone for his gun first."

"True, but not likely," said Landford. "In most cases when you've got a bunch like that, their leader will make the first move."

Jimmy was quiet for a moment. Then he said, "Maybe I better have you teach me how to fan. Then I could take out all four Heglers at once."

"Forget it, kid," snorted Landford. "Fanning is for graduates. You're still in primary school."

"But what if I ride into Joplin and run into all of them at once?"

Landford's voice rasped hard. "Just see that you don't."

Chapter Eight

The two riders crossed the Kansas border at sundown the day they rode out of Cheyenne Wells. Travel was slow for a few days, and they had to stop periodically to rest Landford's leg. Jimmy took advantage of the time to practice drawing and firing.

Within a week the gunfighter's leg was much improved. At dusk on the eighth day out of Cheyenne Wells, the weary travelers camped in the grassy draw some twenty miles west of Wichita. After supper Landford threw tin cans in the air from behind a large mound. Jimmy could not see him, therefore could not anticipate when a can would suddenly pop into the air. He had to operate completely on his reflexes. Of a dozen shots, drawing and firing as each can flew into the air, he missed only one.

"Kid, you're a thousand percent over what you were when we left Fort Collins," said Landford. "My leg's feeling better. We'll have a go at it in the morning. We'll square off and see how you do against me."

The night passed with Joanna Claiborne floating through Jimmy's dreams.

After breakfast Landford said, "Okay, kid. Let's unload the guns and see if you've picked up as much speed as I think."

With ten yards between them both men went into their stances. Briefly they studied each other's eyes. With lightning speed, Jimmy drew. Landford winced as his gun came up. Jimmy's hammer snapped a split-second ahead of Landford's. His young face went white. "That leg has really slowed you," he said shakily.

"Yeah, a little," said Landford, squeezing his leg just above the wound. "It's got some healing to do yet." Squinting his eyes and shaking his head, he said, "But Mr. Blackburn, sir . . . you are getting good. I'm mighty glad to see it."

Jimmy smiled and loaded his gun.

Late afternoon brought Jimmy and his tutor into Wichita. Turning onto Kellogg Street, they rode slowly toward the center of town. Jimmy thought he saw recognition register on faces as people eyed Landford. "I suppose you've been here too," said the youth quietly.

"Few times," came the reply.

The Sunflower Hotel was situated a few yards from the bank of the Arkansas River. They checked into the hotel, procuring rooms that overlooked the lazy stream. While Landford rested, Jimmy practiced drawing the Colt .45 on his hip. Then, for a few moments, he sat down at the window and watched the setting sun change the color of the river.

Landford and Jimmy had dinner together in the hotel dining room. By the time they finished night had darkened the land. As they stepped out into the humid air, the gunfighter said, "I'm going to get me a drink, kid. You can tag along or go back up to your room. Whichever you want."

"I'll tag along," said the youth. "Might have to keep you out of trouble."

Landford laughed and headed down the street. Jimmy noticed that his friend was trying hard not to limp. "Probably ought to have a doctor take a look at your leg before we leave town," he suggested.

Landford acknowledged the suggestion weakly and proceeded toward his destination.

Jimmy followed the gunfighter through the doors of the Rusty Gun Saloon. The big smoke-filled room was gaudy, with a green tapestry on one wall and purple drapes over the windows. The heavy odor of whiskey and beer hung in the close air. On the far wall was a picture of a herd of wild horses. Hanging on a weathered board just above the center of the bar was a rusty old revolver, and behind the bar a long mirror reflected the light of flickering lanterns suspended from a wagon wheel hanging from the ceiling.

The gambling tables were busy, and the bar was lined with men. Off in a corner a fat man in a sweaty shirt was pounding a piano. A few women moved aimlessly through the crowd, stopping momentarily to talk or drop into a customer's lap. The heavy murmur of voices was broken now and then by a loud, boisterous laugh.

Landford elbowed his way to the bar, also making room for Jimmy.

"What'll it be?" asked the bartender. He was a bald man with a handlebar mustache.

"Whiskey," responded Landford. "Sarsaparilla for my partner here." He caught Jimmy's eye in the mirror. "That okay, kid?"

"Uh . . . yeah." Jimmy smiled.

Unseen by Spence Landford, a pair of dark eyes was watching from a faro table. The man studied Landford with a look of pure hatred.

The gunslinger had ordered a second shot when his eye was drawn in the mirror to the face of the man, now approaching him from behind. Two other men left the faro table, following. Slowly Landford set down his glass and turned around. Jimmy sensed trouble and fixed his gaze on the face of the dark-eyed man.

"When did you get out, Rocky?" asked Landford coldly.

Ignoring the question, Rocky Dyer bared his teeth. "You're gonna face me on the street this time, Landford. You won't get the drop on me again."

The piano stopped playing. The laughter died out. Silence moved across the room like an unseen hand as faces swung around curiously. Landford took in the whole crowd in a single glance.

Jimmy let his line of sight drop to the low-slung gun on Dyer's hip. The man had the cut of a gunhawk, all right.

Unnoticed, a small man slipped through the swinging doors and darted up the street.

"I got the drop on you so I wouldn't have to kill you," said Landford evenly.

Someone mumbled something at the end of the bar.

"The only place for a bounty hunter is six feet in the dirt," grumbled Dyer.

"There wouldn't be bounty hunters if there weren't outlaws," replied Landford.

Rocky Dyer swore. "Well, there's about to be one less bounty hunter in this world."

The two men behind Dyer stepped to the side. Chairs scraped as the crowd began filing toward the walls. Jimmy thought of his friend's leg, and the scene earlier in the day when he had outdrawn Landford flashed into his mind. Panic swept over him.

"Six long years I rotted in that prison, bounty hunter," said Dyer, his lips drawn thin. "All I could think about was spittin' on your dead carcass."

"You do it, then talk about it," said Landford.

"He's fast, Rocky," came a voice from the crowd. "Better back off and fergit it!"

Jimmy's mind was spinning. What could he do to stop it? Landford's bad leg could get him killed.

"Make your play," said Landford. "I got things to do."

"All you gotta do tonight is die," growled Dyer.

Suddenly the swinging doors banged against the walls. Three men with badges pinned to their vests burst through, guns drawn. "*Hold it!*" bellowed the sheriff.

Dyer checked his hand and swung his gaze toward the door.

The little man who had left earlier slipped back into the crowd. The two deputies flanked the sheriff closely.

"I told you when you came into town, Dyer," barked the sheriff. "No gunplay! You agreed."

"That was before I knew you allowed bounty hunters in Wichita, Sheriff," said Dyer coolly.

Sheriff Todd Baxter's gaze shifted to the craggy face of Spence Landford, then swept back to Dyer. "You picked a good way to commit suicide, Dyer," he said. "Landford can draw and kill you and have time to clean his fingernails before you hit the floor."

Dyer swore. "I got a feelin' he ain't as fast as everybody thinks he is."

"Well, you ain't finding out in my town," rasped Baxter. "Now you can either go to jail till Landford leaves town, or give me your word that you'll go back to what you were doing and forget it."

Rocky Dyer looked at Landford a long moment. With his eyes still on him, he spoke to the sheriff. "Okay, Baxter. You have my word."

"Good," breathed the sheriff with relief. "Now go back and take up where you left off." Baxter waited until Dyer and his two cohorts had made their way back to their tables. "All right, everybody, trouble's over," he said in a loud voice. "Back to whatever you were doing!"

The piano rang out and the crowd began to move about. As Jimmy pursed his lips and let out a silent sigh, the sheriff turned to Landford. "Thanks for not killing him, Spence."

"I'm afraid it's only temporary, Bax," said the gunfighter. "I doubt if he'll stick to his word."

Todd Baxter hunched his shoulders, took a deep breath, and released it slowly. Speaking to his deputies, he said, "Let's go, boys."

As the three lawmen passed through the door, Landford looked at his youthful partner's pallid face. "What's the matter, kid?" He chuckled. "You scared?"

"Yeah," nodded Jimmy. "Scared you'd draw against him and forget you have a bum leg. Slow as you were this morning, he'd have killed you."

Spence laid a hand on Jimmy's shoulder. "I wasn't slow this morning, kid," he said with a wide smile. "You were just fast!"

"You can smile right through a lie better than anybody I've ever met," said Jimmy. "Why don't we head back to the hotel and get you off that leg?"

"Okay, boy," agreed the gunfighter, "let's go." Landford turned back to the bar and tossed off the whiskey left in his glass. As he set the glass down the bald-headed bartender handed him a folded piece of paper.

"What's this?" asked Landford.

"Message from Mr. Dyer, sir."

Landford glanced toward the table where Rocky Dyer sat with his cronies. Dyer's hard eyes were fixed on him.

Unfolding the paper, he read the hastily written note.

> I'll meet you in the street in front of the hotel at one o'clock. Streetlamps stay on all night. My pards have orders not to interfere. Fail to show up, I'll kill your young friend.
>
> R.D.

Landford folded the note, shot Dyer a cold stare, and nodded. Dyer nodded back. Forcing himself not to limp, the lean-bodied gunfighter sauntered through the swinging doors, his young companion on his heels.

"You're not going to do it, Spence," snapped Jimmy, guessing the contents of the note. "It'll be suicide with your leg like that. You saw how it was this morning."

"He's got to be slower than a three-legged stool," said Landford evenly.

"How do you know?"

"Gut feeling."

"I'm not going to let you do it, Spence."

"How do you know what the note said, anyhow, kid?"

"By the look you gave him."

As they entered the hotel lobby and headed upstairs, Jimmy said, "You'll have to fight all three of them."

"No, I won't," Landford said as they topped the stairs.

"What makes you think so?"

"He gave his word."

Landford unlocked his room, entered, and lit a lantern. Passing through the door the gunfighter had left open, Jimmy said, "He broke his word to the sheriff. What makes you think he'll keep it with you?"

"He will. It's sort of like honor among thieves. Don't ask me to explain it. That's just the way it is. You wear that gun very long, you'll know what I mean."

Jimmy was convinced—Landford would not be deterred. "When do you face him?" he asked.

"At one o'clock on the street outside."

"What time is it now?"

Slipping the watch from his vest pocket, Landford said, "Nine twenty-two."

"Can I stay here with you until it's time to go?"

"Sure, kid, but you're not going down there with me."

"Aw, Spence—"

"You heard me, kid. That's final." The gunfighter tossed his hat onto the dresser and stretched out on the bed. He pulled the watch from his vest and extended it to Jimmy. "I'm going to see if I can snooze a little. Will you wake me up at twelve-thirty?"

"Uh huh," answered the youth. "Twelve-thirty."

Landford squirmed for a few minutes and sat up. "Since I've got three hours, I might just as well get comfortable," he said, slipping out of his buckskin vest. Flattening back down, he said, "Want to pull my boots off me, boy? Go easy with the right one."

Jimmy complied, placing the boots at the foot of the bed.

Then he turned the lantern low and carried a chair to the window. He watched the dark river for a few minutes, then the people on the street moving slowly toward their homes. Time seemed to pass rapidly. A strange coldness settled in Jimmy's stomach. He had grown fond of Spence Landford and he simply couldn't let him die.

At midnight the noise from the saloons died out and the last stragglers abandoned the street. Jimmy watched the three lawmen walk past the hotel, followed by an old man, who doused every other streetlamp. He noticed that, with this done, there was a pronounced dark area between the remaining lanterns.

Twelve-thirty came. Landford was sleeping soundly. A warm breeze played with the curtains at the window.

Jimmy was glad that he and Landford were the same height and were built so much alike. The buckskin vest was a little loose, but not so it would be noticeable. He thought about changing boots, but if he could stay in the shadows enough, Dyer couldn't tell.

The main thing would be the hat. His own was flat-crowned and black. Landford's was high-crowned and light gray. The brim was broad, and the streetlamps were tall. His face would be well shadowed. He sat silently in the dark, listening to his friend's even breathing. At five to one he stood up.

Wearing Landford's hat and vest, Jimmy eased through the door and closed it quietly behind him. He stopped under the lantern in the corridor and checked the loads in his .45. As he passed through the lobby his knees felt like water. His stomach knotted.

Stepping outside, he was suddenly aware of his heavy, strained breathing. His heart was pounding like a sledgehammer against his ribs.

The tall, slender youth stepped off the boardwalk and peered down the street. Something cold gripped his spine as Rocky Dyer appeared in the middle of the street to his right. The man stood spread-legged, ready to draw. Jimmy could see the outlines of two other men under the streetlamp.

Spence Landford's star pupil moved to the center of the street, his hat low. He repeated one word under his breath as he halted at the edge of a pool of light. *Concentrate.*

Jimmy was making a mental note of the exact position where Rocky Dyer's chest was centered when Dyer said,

"Well, Landford, at least you're not yellow. They'll say you died brave anyhow."

Every faculty in Jimmy Blackburn was now calling on the long hours of practice. As he forced himself to concentrate, his heart settled down and his hands relaxed. Then suddenly the other man's boots grated on the hard surface of the street as his hand darted downward.

Jimmy's reflexes went into action at the first movement of Dyer's feet. He drew and fired. A bullet whirled past his head as Rocky's body lurched backward and slammed the ground. Dyer groaned once, then lay still, his chest motionless beneath the rising haze of smoke.

Spence Landford jerked awake at the sound of the two shots cutting the silence of the night air. The sharp noise clattered and reverberated among the false-fronted buildings as he sat up and looked around the dimly lit room. The absence of the kid struck fear into his heart. His gaze fell on Jimmy's hat and vest. The instant he realized his own were missing, the situation was clear.

Glancing at his watch, he dashed to the open window, wincing from the pain in his leg. There were voices in the shadowy street, but the view allowed by the window showed him nothing. One name filtered out of the growing din of voices and became clear: "Dyer."

Wheeling and checking his gun in the vague light of the lantern, Spence Landford swore. Quickly he sat down and pulled on his boots, saying audibly, "Fool kid went and got himself killed." The gunfighter limped to the door and jerked it open.

A dull numbness filled Jimmy Blackburn's mind and body as he watched the dead man's partners rush to his lifeless form. Doors were opening along the street. Lights began to appear in windows, followed by the show of sleepy faces. As the youth holstered his gun and turned toward the hotel, the fast-growing crowd set up a din of voices. Eyes darted in Jimmy's direction as he passed through the lobby door.

At this point the lobby was still empty. Halfway up the stairs he heard one name shouted clearly above the noise of the crowd. "Dyer."

Jimmy's legs were feeling stronger as he made his way

down the gloomy corridor. At the instant he reached Spence Landford's door, it flew open. Landford stood glued to the spot, his hand frozen to the doorknob. The gunfighter's eyes focused on Jimmy's face in disbelief.

Jimmy said calmly, "Looks like I was Rocky Dyer's faceless man."

Landford shook his head, half in anger. "Kid . . . what did you do that for?"

A look of deep affection came into Jimmy's eyes. "You're my friend," he said, his voice breaking. "I couldn't let him kill you."

Landford still was shaking his head. "Yes, but kid, you could've—"

The gunfighter's words were cut short by the sound of voices and footsteps downstairs in the lobby. Landford pulled Jimmy through the door and closed it. "Did anybody recognize you?" he asked hastily.

"Don't think so. Dyer sure thought I was you."

The footsteps were now at the top of the stairs. "Gimme the vest, quick!" snapped Landford.

"What?"

The gunfighter whipped his high-crowned hat off the youth's head, placing it on his own. "Hurry! The vest!"

Jimmy wriggled out of the buckskin vest. Landford snatched it from his fingers, saying, "Get your own on, quick! Let me do the talking, you hear?"

As Jimmy complied, a heavy knock shook the door. Landford waited a few seconds, then pulled it open. Sheriff Todd Baxter stood there, his face lined with anger. Behind him stood one of his deputies. "You gave me your word, Spence!" hissed Baxter.

Throwing up both palms, Landford said, "Hold on, Bax. Dyer gave you his word. You didn't ask for mine."

"Well, I figured—"

"He forced it," Landford interrupted, turning to the dresser. Picking up Dyer's note, he handed it to the lawman, then commanded Jimmy to turn up the lantern flame.

Baxter read it and immediately calmed down.

"I'm sure you wouldn't want to see any innocent people murdered," said Landford.

"Why didn't you bring this note to me?" complained the sheriff. "I could've—"

Nobody writes adventures like

Take "FLINT" for
10 DAYS FREE!

DETACH AND MAIL • POSTAGE PAID

"It would only have delayed the inevitable," said Landford.

"I know but—"

"Look at it this way," cut in the gunfighter. "Wichita has one less troublemaker now."

Baxter smiled weakly. "Can't argue with that." He lifted his hat and scratched his head. "I can't figure how Dyer thought he could outdraw the likes of you anyway. Everybody knows you've got an invisible gun hand."

"Guess he didn't believe it," said Landford dryly.

"Wherever he is now," said the sheriff, "he knows it."

Landford shot Jimmy a furtive wink. "Yes, Bax. He sure does."

Chapter Nine

Spence Landford had his leg examined by a Wichita doctor before he and Jimmy again hit the trail. As they rode he explained to Jimmy why it was best that everybody thought Rocky Dyer had been killed by him. Dyer was a notorious gunfighter. If it were known that a young novice like Jimmy had taken him out, Jimmy would be plagued with glory seekers standing in line to challenge him. The youth told Landford he understood, and thanked him.

Three days later they rode into Sedan, Kansas. They had stopped at two other towns along the way, without incident. Sedan was where the two friends would part. Landford would take a straight line south to Tulsa. Jimmy would head due east to Joplin.

At dawn the next day they saddled up and rode to the eastern edge of town.

"Kid, I've been thinking," said Landford, a cautious look in his eyes. "You just might not be able to single out those Heglers and face them one at a time. My leg's feeling lots better now. Why don't I go on to Joplin with you? Two guns'll be better than one."

A resolute look formed in Jimmy's eyes. "I want all four of the Heglers dead, Spence, but I've got to be the one to do it. Thanks, but that's the way it's got to be."

Landford nodded. "All right, Jimmy. I understand."

"Thanks for teaching me how to handle a gun," said the youth, struggling to keep his voice steady. He cleared his throat and added, "Who's the man you're after in Tulsa?"

"Fellow named Dick Elston."

"He supposed to be fast?"

"Yeah."

"You're sure the leg's better?"

"Positive. Should be perfect by the time I get to Tulsa."

Landford's saddle squeaked as he leaned over and extended his hand. Jimmy took it and squeezed tightly. "Thanks for standing in for me against Dyer, kid."

"If you hadn't trained me right, you would've had to fight him anyhow . . . with my corpse lying in the street," said Jimmy, his eyes misting.

" 'Bye, kid."

The lump returned to Jimmy's throat. He nodded and forced a smile, blinking against the tears.

Landford spun his horse quickly and galloped away. He did not want his former pupil to see the moisture collecting in his own eyes.

Jimmy watched him until the horse and rider became a black dot and dissolved into the southern horizon. Touching spurs to the gelding's sides, he headed east. It was a hundred miles to Joplin.

Holding the horse to a steady pace, the young man was determined to reach Joplin inside three days. At first his thoughts centered on lovely Joanna. As he drew nearer to the Missouri border, however, the ugly faces of the Hegler brothers took preeminence in his mind, and the bloody scene on that black day at the farm came sharply into focus.

Jimmy lived it over again. Vividly he saw his father die on the porch in a pool of his own blood. There was the crumpled body of his mother, lying twisted against the cupboard. Daisy's lifeless head and arm hung over the edge of the loft. There were Myra's sightless eyes, glassy in death, staring toward the ceiling.

Blazing, uncontrollable fury seared through Jimmy, until the vivid scene blurred, leaving his face rigid.

He rode into Joplin close to midnight on the second day, woke the local hostler, and boarded his horse for the night. Finding the nearest hotel, he got the clerk out of bed, then slept till six-thirty the next morning.

With a healthy breakfast under his belt, Jimmy headed for the general store. Since everyone in the surrounding area would do business there, it was the most logical place to inquire for the location of the Hegler home.

A little bell rang above his head as he entered the store. A middle-aged man was busy stocking a shelf behind the counter. He looked at Jimmy and smiled. "Morning," he said warmly.

"Good morning, sir," Jimmy responded. "I'm needing some information."

"I'll try," said the man, returning to his task.

"Do you know a family named Hegler . . . lives around these parts?"

The man's jaw slacked, and his face took on a bleached look. He scrutinized Jimmy. "You're too young to be a lawman," he observed aloud. "And you don't look like their kind. What do you want with them?"

"Just need to see them," replied the youth evenly.

"They friends of your'n?"

"Nope."

The man looked around suspiciously and lowered his voice. "Then, son, whatever direction you came from, you'd best forget that wild bunch and retrace your tracks. They're wicked and mean. Clannish as a nest of rattlesnakes and twice as deadly. That big greasy Luke would as soon kill you as look at you. The other four are pert' near as bad."

Jimmy's eyes widened. "Other *four*?"

"Yep. There's Les, Lonnie, Larry, and Lyle."

"Lonnie's dead," said Jimmy flatly. He didn't mention that he was wearing Lonnie's gun.

The storekeeper's eyebrows arched. "He die in prison?"

"Nope."

"Well, they came ridin' in some time after they got out of Leavenworth, but I never bothered countin' them."

"Do you know where they live?"

"Uh-huh. 'Bout five miles north o' town. You take the road to Carthage out 'bout four miles. You'll see a farm just off the road to the left. Has a white picket fence around the house. Just past that place you'll see a road veer off to the right. Follow it 'bout a mile back in the woods. Can't miss it. Filthy place. House and barn near to collapsin'. Boys' ma and pa died while they was in prison. No-good sons don't do a thing to fix it up."

"Just the four of them live there?"

"Yeah. They got no other kin. Folks in these parts were mighty sad to see them get out o' prison."

"How often do they come into town?"

"Can't rightly say. Once is too often. They been comin' into the store 'bout once a week. Usually it's Les and Larry. Bartender over at the Lagoon Saloon could tell you more'n I can 'bout that."

Jimmy thanked the man and stepped out into the muggy morning heat. He wished for the cool air of Colorado. Cutting across the street, the lanky youth moved through the dark doorway of the tavern. The only customers in the place were two men who sat facing each other at a table. The bartender, a big, thick-bodied man, was hoisting a beer keg into place behind the bar.

The men at the table gave Jimmy a casual look as he moved toward the bar. "Morning," he said to the man adjusting the keg.

"Suppose it is." The bartender nodded.

"You acquainted with Luke Hegler and his brothers?"

"Guess you could say that," said the big man, picking up an empty keg.

"They come in here often?"

"Two, three times a week, when they ain't out raisin' devilment somewheres else."

A voice from behind the tall youth cut in. "Which one you wantin' to see?"

Turning, Jimmy saw it was one of the men at the table. "Any of them," he said. "Doesn't make any difference."

"Les will be along any minute," said the man. "He's planning to meet us here for a game of cards."

Jimmy's heart skipped a beat. This was a stroke of luck. He wondered if Les would be alone. He hoped so, but would face him no matter what. The men here already knew he was looking for a Hegler.

Checking the layout of the room, Jimmy eyed a table next to the back wall. "I'll just sit back here and wait," he told the man, who nodded.

Jimmy moved to the table and sat down. Ten minutes later he recognized the face of Les Hegler as the man appeared in the bright light just outside the saloon door. *Just like the picture in Cashman's office*, Jimmy thought, his heart quickening. The same feeling had come over him the moment he had faced Rocky Dyer.

Les Hegler entered the dark room and moved to the two men at the table. After he greeted them, one of the men said. "There's a kid back there who wants to see you."

Les Hegler squinted through the gloom as Jimmy stood up, a mixture of hatred, fear, and relief running through him. Relief that Les was alone. Fear that the man might be fast with the gun on his hip. Hatred . . . The bloody scene at the farm flashed before him. The hatred overrode the fear.

Hegler recognized the gunfighter's stance as Jimmy positioned himself. He came to a quick halt. "Hey, what's this?" he asked, trying to see the youth's face clearly.

Jimmy's voice was steady, cold as ice. "I've come to kill you, Hegler." The two men shoved back their chairs and joined the bartender behind the bar.

"Who are you?" asked Les, lowering his hand over his gun belt.

"Name's Blackburn. From Colorado."

Hegler shook his head slowly. "Look, I—"

"You murdered my pa, my mother, and my sisters," Jimmy said levelly. All fear was gone; he was in perfect control.

Les Hegler knew there was only one thing to do. His hand plunged downward. As naturally as a bird takes flight, Jimmy palmed the Colt .45 and the gun roared. Hegler's revolver slipped from his fingers as the impact of Jimmy's bullet slammed him against the wall next to the door. As the gun hit the floor it discharged, sending a slug into the bar. The three men behind the bar jumped, eyes wide.

The room was heavy with blue smoke. The acrid smell of burnt gunpowder hung in the air.

Jimmy looked down at the body of Les Hegler, and a sense of satisfaction washed over him. *One down, three to go*, he thought, holstering the Colt.

Heavy footsteps suddenly thundered on the boardwalk. An alarmed voice shouted, "Les! Les!" Larry Hegler bolted through the door. Peering through the blue haze, he spied the young man from Colorado, then dropped his gaze to the corpse of his brother. Fire filled his eyes as he looked back at Jimmy.

"Why you—" Hegler swiftly clawed for his gun.

The son of Will and Sarah Blackburn wanted each Hegler to know why he was dying and who was doing the killing, but it was evident he would have to forgo the pleasure with this one. Jimmy drew and shot him dead center in the chest. Larry went down without clearing leather.

Calmly, Jimmy punched out the spent cartridges and replaced them with fresh ones.

The bartender swore lustily and came out from behind the bar. Jimmy was looking out the door to see if any more

Heglers were coming. Some men were hurrying toward the saloon, but there were no Heglers among them.

The barkeep studied Jimmy's grave countenance and swore again. "Hey, you're just a kid. How'd you learn to handle a gun like that?"

"Had a good teacher," said the youth tightly.

Several men elbowed their way in, gasping, cursing as they spied the dead men on the floor. "Sheriff's out of town," said one.

Jimmy pushed past them and headed out the door. No one made a move to stop him.

Jimmy Blackburn silently agreed with the Joplin store-keeper. The Hegler place *was* filthy. He had seen cleaner pigpens. Having dismounted and tied his horse in the deep shade of a dense thicket of trees, Jimmy concealed himself behind a big oak. The weather-worn house stood some thirty yards away. There were a few tumbledown sheds between the house and the barn.

The youth slowly swept the area with his eyes. A slight breeze stirred the trees, and birds were chirping happily in the branches. There was no other sign of movement.

After a few minutes Jimmy heard a door slam. It had come from the back of the house. Presently a large figure came into view, heading for the privy, which stood some twenty yards behind the house. The privy leaned backward dangerously, apparently because the ground to the rear had eroded. It looked as though a stiff wind would easily topple it. The man wore a gun slung low and thonged to his thigh. As he disappeared inside, Jimmy wished he knew where the other one was.

A moment later he saw a rider coming across the meadow to his left. The man was too far away to identify, but he had the burly body of a Hegler. The rider reined his horse and dismounted. He was looking at something on the ground, moving about casually.

Jimmy threw his glance back to the leaning outhouse. If he caught the man when he came out, the one in the meadow would not be able to see it. The buildings would block his view. By the time the one in the meadow arrived, he would be the only one left for Jimmy to deal with.

Looking back to the meadow, he saw that the rider was still

studying the ground and had moved farther in the other
direction. Stealthily Jimmy darted toward the privy. He stationed himself on the path, thirty feet away. *Hurry up!* he
said in his mind. *Hurry up!*

Abruptly the sagging door came open. It was Big Luke. He
was buckling the gun belt as his dark eyes landed on the
lean-bodied youth, standing spread-legged in the path. "Whatta
you want?" his heavy voice bellowed.

"You!" snapped Jimmy. "My name's Blackburn. Will Blackburn was my father."

Luke's eyes widened. He squared his massive shoulders as
a wide grin exposed his dirty yellow teeth. "So his little boy
has come to get even." He chuckled humorlessly.

Jimmy wondered if one bullet could kill a man Luke's size.
He estimated him at close to three hundred pounds. He
figured the brute would probably be slow on the draw but
knew it was best not to count on it.

"Tell me, Blackburn," said Big Luke, standing with his
broad back to the outhouse, "did you give Lonnie a decent
burial?"

"Sheriff did. After I put a pitchfork through his throat." He
paused for effect. "Your brother was still alive when you left
him."

Luke looked momentarily unsettled. Then he seemed to
shake it off as he said, "You plannin' to gun me, kid?"

"Yep."

"Lyle's out in the field."

"I'll get him next."

"Les 'n' Larry'll be comin' home."

"That's right. In a hearse."

The huge man swore. "What you talking about?"

"I killed them."

"You're lyin'."

"You'll find out the truth in hell." Jimmy's eyes were
steady, dark, cold. He concentrated on Luke's massive chest
without taking his gaze from the hairy face. Suddenly he saw
it in the big man's eyes. The inexpressible signal that Spence
Landford had talked about. Big Luke was going for his gun.

Jimmy's hand flashed downward. The Colt .45 came out of
the holster and roared in a blur of timeless motion. Luke
Hegler's revolver was still in the holster, his hand frozen to
the handle as the slug ripped into his meaty chest. A heavy

grunt escaped his lips as the impact drove him against the privy. The small structure rocked backward from the weight of Luke's body, then settled again.

The monstrous man straightened up and staggered, blinking in disbelief, trying to draw his gun. Jimmy's weapon roared again. And again. The double impact slammed Luke into the privy with tremendous force. It rocked again . . . and this time toppled over backward.

Like a giant grizzly bear Luke somehow gained his balance and reared to full height. Jimmy held the Colt in both hands, took aim, and put a bullet through his forehead. Luke's head snapped back from the violent force. His body flipped into the hole where the outhouse had stood.

Jimmy ran to the side of the house and peered around the corner toward the meadow. Lyle was astride the horse, galloping hard toward the sounds he had just heard. Jimmy flattened himself against the house and reloaded his gun. He could hear Lyle skidding the horse to a stop by the barn.

As Jimmy came around the house, Lyle was off the horse, swinging his head back and forth, trying to pinpoint the spot where the shots had been fired. He was positioned directly in front of the open barn door, gun in hand.

Jimmy held his revolver loosely at his side, ready to bring it up.

Lyle's gaze found the lanky youth. Eyes wide, he said, "Where's Luke?"

"Exactly where he belongs."

"Who are you?" asked Lyle, not grasping Jimmy's answer.

"James William Blackburn."

The name did not register in the big man's brain. "Where's Luke?" he asked again.

"He's dead," said Jimmy, a jagged edge in his voice. "So are Les and Larry." While the words filtered into Lyle's consciousness, he rasped, "I said my name is *Blackburn*."

It all struck home at once. Lyle dived for the open barn door as Jimmy raised his gun and fired. The man yelled as the bullet ripped through his leg. He managed to stand and stick his head out the door to see Jimmy run toward the barn. The youth plunged behind a rain barrel as Lyle's gun roared. The bullet kicked up dirt beside the barrel.

Taking a quick look, Jimmy saw that Lyle had left the door. Fixing his eyes on the dark opening, he ran full speed toward it. He flattened against the wall beside the door and glanced inside. He saw a trail of blood leading across the floor to a crude ladder that led to the hayloft.

Jimmy swung around the door's edge and flattened against the dark inside wall. Hay crackled at the top of the ladder. The youth saw the muzzle in time to dodge as Lyle's gun roared. He crouched behind a stack of wooden boxes, listening, as Lyle worked his way toward the upper hayloft door at the front of the barn.

The wary youth eased his way around the boxes, watching as dust and hay particles dropped from the cracks between the boards. Suddenly Jimmy saw blood coming between the boards, a few feet from the upper opening. Looking down, he spotted a small board at his feet. He picked it up slowly with his left hand and tossed it outside through the door.

Lyle's gun roared as he impulsively fired at the clattering board. Jimmy ran under the spot, thinking of how his sisters had died . . . and fired upward, through the floorboards. A thumping sound came from overhead. Jimmy fired at the same spot again.

Lyle Hegler let out a small cry and rolled out of the loft headfirst, cracking the ground with a sickening sound. Jimmy stepped out of the smoky barn and looked down at Lyle's sprawled form. The head was tipped at an unnatural angle, the neck broken. One bullet had ripped through Lyle's neck, severing a vein. Blood oozed thickly from the wound, soaking the dirt beneath the body. The dry earth absorbed it quickly, turning a dull brown.

The son of Will and Sarah Blackburn stood over the crumpled form of Lyle Hegler. Suddenly it came to him that it was all over. The last of the Heglers was dead. The flame of vengeance that had so possessed him slowly flickered out.

Tears welled in the youth's eyes. As he stared blankly at Lyle Hegler's corpse, he spoke. "Pa . . . Mama . . . Daisy . . . Myra . . . I killed them." Jimmy's face contorted. "I killed them," he said again, his voice rising, "I killed them! *I killed them!*" The floodgates broke. He wept and sobbed for ten minutes like a little child, then dried his tears and rode away.

Chapter Ten

Jimmy stopped in Joplin long enough to buy ammunition and trail supplies. The proprietor of the general store informed the youth that the town looked on him as a hero. The Heglers were feared and hated in Joplin, and the store owner was delighted to learn that the other two were also dead. As Jimmy stepped out onto the street he was surprised to see that a crowd had gathered, waiting for him to appear. Trying to ignore them, he crammed the items into his saddlebags.

"Say, Mr. Black," said one of the men, "that was some shootin' you did this mornin'."

Cinching the leather straps, Jimmy looked over his shoulder and said, "Where'd you get that name?"

"Everybody in town knows it, son," replied the man. "You told Les Hegler your name was Black before you slapped leather like greased lightning and blowed him outta this ol' world. Bartender at the Lagoon told us."

"Yes, sir, young feller," put in another, "you really got a fast hand there. Hegler was no slouch with a gun!"

"Two less Heglers in these parts will sure make it more livable, kid," voiced another.

"He killed Luke 'n' Lyle, too!" came a voice from the door of the general store.

The gaze of the crowd fell upon the owner of the general store, then moved back to Jimmy. "That true, son?" asked the man who had spoken first.

"Yes, sir," replied Jimmy, casting his eyes downward.

The crowd instantly voiced approval.

"My name's Elmer Simpson," said the same man, extending his hand. "I think the folks in this town would like to throw a little celebration in your honor."

The growing crowd cheered. Jimmy noticed that the bartender from the Lagoon Saloon had joined the crowd.

"Mr. Simpson," said the disconcerted youth, "I really don't have time. I've got to head for Colorado."

"Gunfighters never stay in one place very long, Elmer," came a voice from the crowd. "He's probably got somebody up in Colorado that's just itchin' to square off with him."

"I'm not a gunfighter," said Jimmy. "I just had a score to settle with the Heglers. Now I'm going home."

"Who do you think you're kiddin'?" said the bartender, stepping out of the throng. "I watched you draw on Les. You're a professional. What's your full name, Black?"

Jimmy's mind was spinning. Spence Landford had warned him that something like this would happen. The best thing to do was to let this town think his name *was* Black. Then the whole matter could stop right here. "Uh . . . Jim," he answered the bartender. "Name's Jim."

Lifting his voice, the bartender shouted, "Free drinks at the Lagoon for everybody! In honor of the gunfighter who finally rid Joplin of the Heglers . . . *Jim Black!*"

The crowd hooted its approval and pushed toward the saloon. Several men took time to pause and shake Jim Black's hand, or pat him on the back.

Suddenly Jimmy wondered if perhaps they weren't right— perhaps he *was* a gunfighter now, like it or not. His mind flashed back to the words of Sheriff Floyd Cashman. *"If you take out the Hegler brothers, your life will never be the same. You will never be the same. Once you strap on that gun and use it, there's an irreversible law that goes into effect. You can't take it off. You'll have to use it again—either as a gunfighter or as a lawman."*

As the crowd dispersed, Jimmy thought of a gunfighter's phantom nemesis—the one Spence Landford called the faceless man.

Jimmy owned up to one cold, hard fact. Like it or not, he had killed five men with the big iron on his hip. He *was* now a gunfighter. He had lived through five confrontations with death. A cold chill tapped his backbone as the gray thought threaded through his mind: *Maybe somewhere out there is my faceless man.*

Wanting nothing but to leave town quickly, he mounted his horse, reined it in a tight circle, and rode off without looking back.

*   *   *

Jimmy halted the chestnut gelding just outside Sedan, at the spot where he had last seen Spence Landford. He wondered if Landford had found . . . what was his name? Elston. Dick Elston. Had Landford's leg healed sufficiently? Had he been able to outdraw Elston? Jimmy wished he knew.

The hours passed into days. It was midafternoon when he rode into Wichita, bone tired and needing a bath. Leaving the gelding at a nearby stable, he draped the saddlebags over his shoulder and walked to the Sunflower Hotel. Requesting the same room he had stayed in before, he paused a moment, then signed the register *Jim Black*, figuring he would change back to his real name as soon as he crossed the Colorado border. He asked for hot water to be sent up, and mounted the stairs.

After a leisurely bath the exhausted young man stretched out on the bed and fell asleep.

The evening breeze was teasing the curtains when Jimmy awoke in the nearly dark room. The sleep had refreshed him. He rolled off the bed and looked out the window. The final glow of the sunset reflected on the warm waters of the Arkansas. His stomach growled, reminding him that he had not eaten since breakfast.

After lighting a lantern and combing his hair, he descended the stairs and crossed the lobby toward the dining room. As he nodded and smiled at the clerk the elderly man said, "Hey, young feller . . ."

Stopping, Jimmy said, "Yes, sir?"

"Weren't you in here a week ago with Spence Landford?"

"Uh . . . yēs, I was," the youth said tentatively.

"Well, is your name Blackburn or Black? Last week you signed the register Jimmy Blackburn. Today you signed it Jim Black."

Angry at himself for not anticipating that something like this would happen, he bluffed and said, "It's Black." He could have kicked himself for not using his real name.

"Well, why did you—"

"Just one of those foolish things a fellow does," he cut in, forcing a laugh.

The clerk laughed hollowly and turned to greet a man coming through the door. Jimmy heard the man say something to the clerk about relieving him so he could eat supper.

Jimmy entered the dining room and picked a table in the

far corner. The place was fairly crowded. Eight or nine men were eating together at a large table across the room. He recognized Sheriff Todd Baxter in the group. Baxter's gaze touched the youth's face lightly, passed on, then returned. The lawman nodded in recognition, then turned his attention to a big red-faced man who was dominating the conversation at the table.

The waitress took Jimmy's order. As she walked away he noticed the hotel clerk come in and take a table next to the group of men, then heard the big red-faced man say, "That's the way they're telling it in Joplin." Jimmy's ears immediately perked up. He missed the next few words, but got enough to learn that the man speaking had been on a stagecoach that had passed through Joplin. Again Jimmy grew angry at himself for not having dropped his false name right away.

"That's the way it is for gunfighters," said one of the men. "There's always one somewhere else down the trail that's faster."

"Yeah, but that's hard to swallow," said another. "Four guys bein' blowed out by a wet-nose kid."

Two or three at the table spoke at once. A question was asked that Jimmy could not distinguish. Then came a clearcut answer: "Called himself Jim Black. They said he wasn't more'n eighteen or nineteen years old. Had a draw faster'n a lizard's tongue."

The clerk threw a glance at Jimmy, shifted it to the redfaced man, then back to Jimmy. The latter fixed his gaze on the white tablecloth in front of him, pretending not to hear the conversation. He could feel the clerk's eyes on him as talk continued at the large table.

The man with the florid face enlarged on the Joplin news, filling the group in on how this Jim Black had waded through the Hegler gang. With a flourish of color he told of the deaths of Les and Larry Hegler at the Lagoon Saloon. The way the man described it, Jimmy hardly recognized the incident. Of course, this was the usual course of hearsay. With each telling, the tale changed and enlarged. To hear the man talk, the youthful gunfighter could draw and fire as fast as a man could blink his eyes.

Then the story turned to Black's killing of Lyle and Luke. The waitress brought Jimmy's dinner. While he ate in silence he heard of the gunfight with Lyle at the barn. This, too, was embellished almost beyond recognition. From time to time Jim could sense the gaze of the clerk.

The red-faced man had purposely saved Big Luke's finish for the climax. The group roared with laughter when they heard that Luke Hegler had ended up in the outhouse hole.

As the laughter subsided one man commented that young Jim Black would soon have his tracks dogged by challengers. The stories would travel like prairie fire in a high wind, and green envy would push gunhawks to track him down and face him.

Jimmy remembered once again the warning of Sheriff Floyd Cashman, then the conversation under the tall pine trees with Spence Landford. He could almost hear Landford's voice. And his own . . .

"Let me tell you about gunfighters."

"I already know. The irreversible law, right? Once you strap on a gun and live through a duel, you can't take it off, right? Sooner or later there's always somebody faster than you, right?"

"That's right, Jimmy."

"It won't be that way with me. As soon as the last of the Hegler gang is dead, I'll drop my gun in a river somewhere. The irreversible law won't hold for me."

Jimmy was brought back to the present by the waitress. "More coffee, sir?" she asked pleasantly.

"Uh . . . no. No, thanks," he replied, forcing a smile.

Jimmy decided the best thing for him to do was to leave town at first light and go back to being Jimmy Blackburn. On the way home he would take the back trails and stay out of towns as much as possible. Five men were already dead by his gun hand, he reminded himself. Although he felt no compunction concerning the four Heglers, the death of Rocky Dyer did not rest so easily on his conscience.

The men around the table were still talking about gunfighters when, abruptly, the hotel clerk left his own table and stepped to the large one. Bending low, he said something to Sheriff Todd Baxter. The lawman twisted in his chair and eyed Jimmy across the room. Conversation around the table trailed off to nothing as Baxter stood and approached Jimmy, who had just pushed back his chair, preparing to leave.

Standing over him, the sheriff said, "You're the young fellow that was traveling with Spence Landford?"

Looking up, Jimmy said, "Yes, sir."

"Where'd you two part company?"

Jimmy wondered how the lawman knew for a fact that they *had* split up. "Uh . . . just outside of Sedan."

Baxter's eyes narrowed. "You *did* go to Joplin, right?"

Jimmy nodded.

"Your name Jim Black?"

Jimmy shot a glance past the sheriff to the hotel clerk, who was watching carefully.

"Yes, sir, Mr. Baxter," he answered reluctantly.

A heavy murmuring broke out among the men at the table.

"You here to start trouble?" asked the sheriff.

"No, sir," said the youth. "Just passing through on my way home."

"Where's that?"

The eyes and ears of the group were welded on the young gunfighter. "Colorado."

"When you leaving?"

"Dawn."

"Good," said Baxter, relief showing in his face. He turned to leave, paused, then wheeled around. "Too bad about your partner."

Puzzlement pinched Jimmy's face. "Partner?"

"Spence Landford."

His throat went dry. "What do you mean?"

"Buyin' a piece of real estate in Tulsa."

Jim Black stood up. "Are you telling me he's . . . he's *dead*?"

"Sorry," said Baxter. "I figured you probably knew."

Cold gripped Jimmy's heart. "Was it Dick Elston?"

"Nope. Landford killed Elston. Story is, a young upstart gunnie named Duncan Wheeler saw the shoot-out. Challenged Landford. Flat outdrew him."

Jim shook his head, as if to dislodge the words that had just registered in his brain.

"That's why I asked when you were leaving," said Baxter. "Report is that Wheeler is headed this way. All I need is for him to ride in here and find you. He'd be challenging you right here on one of our streets. We don't cotton to bloodletting in Wichita, Black. Savvy?"

Jimmy felt numb all over. *Spence . . . dead. He finally met his faceless man. Duncan Wheeler. Must've been a fair fight. Sheriff said Wheeler flat outdrew him.*

The only word of Baxter's that filtered through Jimmy's thoughts was "Savvy?"

Blankly, he looked at the lawman. "Huh?"

"I said we don't want no gunfighting in this town."

"Uh . . . yeah. Yeah, Sheriff," he said. "Don't worry. I'm leaving at dawn."

The long trip home was filled with memories, sweet and bitter. Jimmy found the farm as he had left it. Neighbors had pooled their efforts and put up the hay. The grass was showing patches of brown as summer faded into autumn and the frosty nights took their toll.

As usual winter came early to Colorado. Jimmy set his mind to spending the long, cold months finishing school. For some reason he felt uncomfortable sitting in the schoolhouse at LaPorte, a small nearby town. Money was in sufficient supply, so the youth hired a special tutor from Fort Collins, who came twice a week, giving lessons and leaving assignments.

As the days turned into weeks, Jimmy paused in his studies at times to look out the window and watch the falling snow. Often his thoughts would drift to Joanna Claiborne. He wanted to see her again but knew he could not simply ride up to the ranch. Her father would consider the girl too young as yet for suitors. He would have to have a reason for being in the area.

Amid the farm chores and his lessons, Jimmy took time daily to practice his fast-draw. Although he was intent on going east to law school, there was an unexplainable need somewhere deep inside him, a voice that said, *You must never grow rusty with the gun. Practice. Discipline yourself to it. Practice and improve. Never let up.*

Neighbors grew accustomed to hearing gunfire daily from the Blackburn place. Jimmy did practice, and his fast-draw improved.

With the spring rains and warm breezes came the day when Jimmy's tutor handed him his diploma. It wasn't until he looked it over, after the tutor had left, that the date struck him. May 27, 1873. The next day was his birthday! He would be eighteen. A cold wave of sorrow broke over him. One

year. It would be one year since the Hegler gang rode in
and . . .

He thought about his family, about his mother and father.
What would they think about the road he had taken? Surely
they would understand why he'd killed the Heglers, but what
about the other man he'd gunned down?

His gunfighting days were over, he again resolved. He
wanted to uphold the law, but not as a gunfighter or a
lawman—not with a gun. He would be an attorney, a man his
folks would approve of. As soon as he hung his shingle in
front of his law office, he'd retire his gun for good.

Jimmy laid down the diploma and stood up. Quickly he put
his mind to other things. Tomorrow he would ride to Fort
Collins and see if the stage lines had brought him any mail
from back east. He had sent for application papers from three
schools. It was time they were arriving.

While in Fort Collins the next day Jimmy found the mail
he was expecting and learned of a ranchers' stock sale that
was being held in Estes Park the following week. He would
have to sell the beef cattle and the horses. Neighbors had
offered to buy them at a fair price, but Jimmy resolved that
Will Blackburn's horse would be bought by a rancher, not a
farmer.

Jimmy made the quick decision to take his father's horse to
Estes Park for the sale. Of course, the B-Slash-C Ranch was
right on the way.

Joanna Claiborne thrilled as the big Appaloosa carried her
like a feather across rolling pasture. She loved the feeling of
the magnificent animal beneath her and the sting of the wind
in her face.

Under the cautious eye of Russ Pittman the lovely girl rode
from corner to corner of the rolling south pasture. Her daz-
zling Cherokee features seemed to come to life as horse and
girl blended into one smooth body of motion.

Thundering past Pittman, who sat his horse in front of the
barn, she shouted, "One more time to the gate and we'll be
through!"

The big man waved, his eyes adoring the graceful young
woman astride the Appaloosa.

As the majestic stallion carried Joanna toward the ranch
gate, Pittman's gaze was drawn past the galloping Appaloosa

to the road. A rider approached astride a chestnut gelding, followed by a red roan. Pittman saw Joanna draw rein as she became aware of the rider and horses. The gate was too far away for the B-Slash-C foreman to distinguish the rider's features, but he carefully studied Joanna's reaction. Apparently she knew the rider, for she had nudged the big stallion toward the gate.

Across the way Jimmy Blackburn felt a warm rush as the dark-haired Joanna rode slowly toward him. Her lovely form was accentuated by the orange glow of the setting sun behind her. She seemed more mature and looked more beautiful than before, if that was possible.

"Hello, Princess," said the infatuated youth, smiling broadly.

Chief snorted and blew as he drew alongside the chestnut. Joanna studied Jimmy's features for a moment before she spoke. "Jimmy? It *is* Jimmy Blackburn?"

Clearing his throat, he said, "Yes, it's me. Guess it's been almost a year, hasn't it?"

The young woman smiled warmly. "It will be a year in exactly nineteen days."

Jimmy's heart thumped against his ribs. Their meeting a year ago must have been important to her if she had it that precisely in her mind.

Joanna spoke again. "You've put on weight."

"Yeah," said the youth, nodding. "I weighed myself at the feed store in Fort Collins a few days ago. Tipped the scales at one eighty-three. That's nearly twenty-five pounds since last year."

"I hardly knew you," she said, emerald eyes shining. "You taking the roan somewhere?"

"Uh-huh. To the sale at Estes tomorrow."

"Oh, that's nice. My father is taking me."

"Good!" Jimmy smiled. "Maybe I'll see you there." Jimmy was hoping for an invitation to sleep in the bunkhouse as before. Instead he saw the girl's countenance darken. Her eyes dulled as she said with hesitation, "I . . . I hope so. That would be nice."

The coldness that suddenly came between them was as real as the warmth Jimmy had been feeling in his heart. With furrowed brow he said, "Princess, is something wrong?"

Joanna bit her lips. "Well . . ." She cleared her throat.

"Well, you know when you stopped by with your hired man last year?"

The memory of Claiborne's feeling toward gunfighters popped into Jimmy's mind. He sensed what was coming. "Yes," he replied cautiously.

"Russ said you lied to us, Jimmy." Her green eyes met his own. "He was a *gunfighter*. You told us he was a man you'd hired. You said his name was Mr. Spencer."

Jimmy's face flushed at the scorn in the young woman's eyes. "I . . . well, I . . . didn't exactly lie, Joanna," he stammered. "I really did hire him. And . . . well, his name *was* Spencer."

"Yes," she said bitingly, "Spencer Landford." He could not meet her accusing gaze. "What did you hire him for? To do what?"

Jimmy's mind went numb, to match his tongue. While she waited for an answer Joanna said, "Russ told my father that you were with Spence Landford. Daddy said if you ever came back, Russ was to run you off." The lovely face pinched. "Not only because you were keeping company with a . . . a gunslinger, but because you lied."

Over Joanna's shoulder Jimmy could see Russ Pittman riding toward them. "But, Joanna," he said hastily, "there's a reasonable explanation for what I did. Would you give me a chance to explain it?"

Her deep-green eyes softened. She managed a weak smile. "Of course I will, Jimmy. I—"

"Miss Joanna!" cut in Pittman's heavy voice as he rode up. "I don't think your father would approve of you talkin' with the likes of him!"

Jimmy felt his face turn hot as anger rose within him. "What have I done that's so terrible?" he snapped, staring down Pittman.

"You run with the wrong crowd," grumbled the big man.

"I had a good reason for being with Spence Landford," said Jimmy.

"Ain't no reason for runnin' with a gunnie."

"If you'll allow me to explain—"

"Don't need any explainin'," Pittman butted in. "You—"

"That's enough!" Joanna glared at Pittman. "I think we at least should hear what he's got to say, Russ. Jimmy's entitled to that much."

"Beggin' your pardon, Miss Joanna," said Pittman, "but he ain't entitled to nothin'. We don't owe him a thing. He can run with a gun packer if he chooses, but he can stay away from the B-Slash-C."

Jimmy eyed the revolver on the big man's hip. "You got a gun on," he said crisply. "That makes *you* a gun packer."

Pittman's eyes flashed. "You done some growin', son, but you ain't growed big enough to talk like that to me. You watch your mouth. It so happens that Mr. Claiborne wants me to wear this gun any time I'm lookin' out for Miss Joanna. But I ain't no fast-draw gunfighter."

"This kind of talk will accomplish nothing," said the young woman. "Russ, you ride on to the house, and I'll be right behind you."

Pittman shook his head, straightening in the saddle. "I'm not leavin' you here with this—"

"You heard me, Russ!"

He started to speak again, then saw the fury in Joanna's green eyes. Reining the horse in a circle, he said, "Don't be too long."

"I'm not a child," she snapped back. "Don't bark orders at me!"

Pittman's face darkened. He spurred his horse and rode away.

"Joanna," said Jimmy softly, "I didn't mean to cause trouble. I . . . I just stopped by so I could see you."

"It's all right," she said with a smile. "Russ will get over it. He watches me like an old mother hen. Sometimes I think Daddy hired him to be my bodyguard, rather than to boss the men." Joanna's eyes softened. "I would like to hear your explanation about Spence Landford, Jimmy. Maybe I can persuade Daddy to let you talk to both of us in Estes after the sale tomorrow."

Jimmy's face lit up. "That'd be great, Princess," he said, eagerness in his voice.

"What will you do about a place to stay tonight?" she asked. "The hotels will be filled."

"Oh, that's nothing. I've done a lot of camping since I saw you last. One more night won't be a problem."

"Then I'll see you in town tomorrow," said Joanna warmly.

Jimmy felt helpless in the sweet gaze of her eyes. "Okay. Tomorrow."

Swinging Chief around, she looked over her shoulder, exposing the captivating profile of her Indian features. Jimmy was transfixed.

"I hope you won't think me brazen," she said, "but I want you to know I've thought about you many times in this past year. I like you a lot."

Jimmy's throat tightened. Working his tongue loose, he said, "I . . . I've thought about you too. And I like *you* a lot." He paused, smiled, and added one word: "Princess."

Joanna blushed and put the big Appaloosa in a gallop.

At Fort Collins Duncan Wheeler, slim and clad in black from hat to boots, rode into the yard of the Blackburn farm, reined in, and slid from his silver-studded black saddle. The pearl-handled pistols slung low on his hips stood out in contrast to the black belt and holsters. He was a baby-faced man of twenty-five, his features almost unnaturally handsome. His eyes were cold and narrow, however, and the lid of his left eye drooped, giving him a sinister appearance.

Wheeler had already killed seven men in cold blood. Several well-known gunhawks had gone down under his guns. Recently he had gained considerable stature by outdrawing the famed Spence Landford. Wheeler had been unaware that Landford was suffering from a leg wound that wasn't healing properly, slowing his draw.

The slim gunfighter walked past the two horses and buckboard that stood next to the corral gate and knocked on the door of the house. He was eager to challenge and kill the youthful gunfighter who had outdrawn the Hegler gang. He had come to goad him into a shoot-out on the crowded main street in Fort Collins.

Getting no answer at the door, Wheeler swaggered to the corral gate. Just as he started to unlatch it, the barn door squeaked open and an elderly man emerged into the light of the lowering sun.

"Howdy, stranger," the old man said. "Kin I help yuh?"

Duncan Wheeler looked at the man without smiling. "Is this the Blackburn place?" he asked.

"Yes, it is," said the elderly farmer, "but ain't nobody home. I'm Dan Hoffer, neighbor over thataway." He pointed past the barn.

"I'm tryin' to find a dude name Jim Black," said Wheeler.

"Folks in Fort Collins said they'd never heard of him, but the description I gave matched that of a farm kid named Jimmy Blackburn. Directed me out here. Tall, square-jawed kid. Dark hair. Sorta handsome."

"Don't know anything about a Jim Black, but sounds like you're lookin' fer Jimmy Blackburn, all right. The two names are a lot alike, though, eh?"

"Yeah," said Wheeler without expression. "Know where I can find him?"

Chapter Eleven

Estes Park was thronged with people as Jimmy glanced at the midmorning sun above the saw-toothed mountains to the east. The sale would begin at ten o'clock. Having deposited and registered the roan with the auctioneer, he folded the receipt and stuffed it in his shirt pocket.

The sale yard and corrals were located next to the river on the south end of town. Jimmy led the chestnut under the shade of the tall pines lining the bank of the river. Leaving his horse, he headed for the corrals. As he moved through the crowd his eyes roamed the area, searching for the face of Joanna Claiborne.

Jimmy was idly looking over the split-rail fence at some of the horses when his attention was drawn to a surrey circling the sales area. In it were Joanna Claiborne and Russ Pittman.

Jimmy climbed up on the bottom rail of the fence, lifting himself above the crowd. Raising his hand, he waved, and she smiled and waved back. She said something to Pittman as the surrey drew to a stop in the parking area. The big man was obviously in disagreement with what she was saying, but to no avail. Dressed in her riding clothes with flat-crowned hat, Joanna alighted and headed for Jimmy. Pittman was soon on her heels.

"Good morning, Jimmy."

"It sure is now." Jimmy smiled, overwhelmed with her beauty.

A group of four or five cowboys strolled by, openly admiring the young woman. One said something Jimmy could not distinguish, and the others laughed. Jimmy felt a stab of temper. It quickly eased as Joanna stepped close and tilted her head back, saying, "You've grown taller, Jimmy. How tall are you now?"

"I guess I'm six-two without my boots on," he said hastily. "Where's your father?"

Pittman arrived, looking sour, as Joanna said, "He's got a cold coming on. He was going to look for a good saddle horse to buy, so he sent Russ. I begged to come along. Daddy said I could as long as Russ kept me with him."

Jimmy noticed the gun on Pittman's hip.

Turning to the big man, who had not bothered to greet him, he said, "Howdy, Mr. Pittman."

Pittman grunted, his mouth turned down.

"Russ, can Jimmy sit with us in the stands?" Joanna asked sweetly.

"If I say no, you'll throw a fit. 'Spect he can."

Speaking to Pittman, Jimmy said, "If you want a good saddle horse for the ranch, Mr. Pittman, buy the roan gelding I brought over. He was my dad's horse. A mighty fine one."

Russ mumbled something inaudible, then said, "We'd better get us a seat."

As the trio blended with the crowd and entered the arena, a black horse came into town from the north. Astride it was a slim, baby-faced man with one droopy eyelid. A pair of pearl-handled Colts were thonged to his thighs.

During the course of the stock sale Joanna informed Jimmy that her father refused to see him and that Jimmy was not welcome at the B-Slash-C. She hastened to assure him that she felt Britt Claiborne was being unfair, but that she was powerless at this point to change his mind.

The heavy-hearted young man trailed Russ Pittman and Joanna from the arena. The B-Slash-C foreman had bid on a buckskin gelding and bought it. The young couple stood a few paces away while Pittman waited his turn in line at the cashier's table.

Lowering his voice, Jimmy said, "Princess, I mean no disrespect for your father, but I want to see you again. For one thing, I want to tell you about Spence Landford. For another . . ." He swallowed hard. "I just want to be with you."

Joanna reached down and squeezed his hand. "I feel the same way, Jimmy. I really do."

Jimmy's heart pounded hard in his chest.

"It will take a little time," said Joanna, "but I think I can crack Daddy's shell. If we can show him that you—"

Joanna's words were cut short by a piercing male voice shouting, "Anybody here know Jim Black?"

Jimmy's blood ran cold. Turning, he saw a slim, baby-faced man dressed in black, with a pair of low-slung guns on his hips. The young man was stopping people as they milled about, repeating his question about Jim Black.

The last thing Jimmy needed right now was for Joanna to learn of his gunfighting. He would tell her the whole story at the first opportunity, but for her to learn this way would destroy everything between them. He knew he had to evade this gunfighter, whoever he was.

The baby-faced man carefully scrutinized every tall, slender male that passed him. "You Jim Black?" he asked one after another.

Jimmy was trying to think of a way to get away quickly when Joanna said with hot disgust, "That man is contemptible . . . a typical cocky gunfighter. He has a sneer built on his face."

Suddenly Duncan Wheeler's gaze fell on Joanna. Russ Pittman bristled as Wheeler ambled toward her. Jimmy shoved his hat forward, throwing more shade on his face. The gunfighter had not seen Jim Black before, but Jimmy did not know how much of a description he might have been given.

Wheeler fixed his narrow-set eyes on Joanna, removed his hat, and said, "Well, hello there, girlie."

Joanna gave him a freezing glare.

Jimmy's face flamed. He held himself in check. Big Russ Pittman squared his broad shoulders and said, "Move along, sonny. The lady is not interested in the likes of you."

Ignoring Pittman with an air of insolence, Wheeler said to Joanna, "What's your name, girlie? Mine's Duncan Wheeler. Certainly you've heard of me."

Jimmy's blood took on the chill of ice at the mention of the name. *Spence Landford's faceless man!* Quickly the heat of savage passion turned his blood hot. He wanted to kill Wheeler in the worst way. . . .

"No, I've never heard of you," Joanna was saying with a tone of contempt. "Are you supposed to be somebody special?"

The odious smile that curled Wheeler's lips disappeared.

"You're lyin', girlie," he snapped. "You've heard of me all right."

Russ Pittman's face hardened. "You watch your mouth, scum," he hissed, "or I'll put my fist to it."

Wheeler jumped back and planted his feet, dropping his hands and holding them just over the butts of his guns. "Okay, big fish," he prodded, "I'm callin' you!"

A large crowd was gathering. They began to push away from the line of fire as Pittman, in anger, responded, "You're on, scum!"

Joanna's face blanched. "No, Russ," she pleaded. "You're no gunfighter. He'll kill you!"

"I won't stand for that piece of hog meat callin' you a liar, Miss Joanna," said Pittman.

Wheeler waited like a vulture about to pounce on a prairie dog. Jimmy knew that if Pittman went against the man who outdrew Spence Landford, he would be killed. Russ had no liking for Jimmy, but he was totally loyal and devoted to Joanna Claiborne. Jimmy couldn't let him die.

Pittman, not listening to Joanna's pleadings, turned and walked away from her. Just as he prepared to square off with Wheeler, Jimmy's voice cut the air. *"Wheeler!"*

The impudent gunslinger swung his gaze to the tall youth as Jimmy said heavily, "I'm Jim Black."

Pittman's jowls sagged. Joanna gasped and put a hand to her mouth. An excited hum swept through the crowd. Duncan Wheeler sneered, looking Jimmy up and down. "You? You're the man who took out the Heglers down in Joplin?"

"Yes, I am."

Wheeler guffawed and spat. "You ain't even wearin' a gun. You ain't no gunfighter." Turning back to Pittman, he said, "Draw, big boy!"

"Wheeler!" bellowed Jimmy. The baby-faced man looked at him again. "I'm calling *you*! My gun's in my saddlebag." Jimmy threw Pittman a glance. "Russ, you get over there with the crowd. Take Joanna with you."

Joanna sank her fingers into Russ Pittman's muscular arm as he moved beside her. She was pale white.

Jimmy returned quickly from the shade of the tall pines, buckling on his gun. He paused at the edge of the crowd to thong down the holster and check the loads. Duncan Wheeler was thinking how lucky he was to take out Jim Black in front of a crowd like this. Word would spread fast. He would be more famous than ever.

Joanna stood watching as Jimmy Blackburn, alias Jim Black, planted his feet where Russ Pittman had stood a few moments before. Unconsciously, she was biting down hard on an index finger, her eyes glazed with tears. As Jimmy faced the vicious young gunfighter, the truth came home to Joanna's heart. She was in love with the boy who affectionately called her Princess. Only he was no longer a boy. He was a man. And in order to save Russ Pittman from a violent death, he was laying his own life on the line.

The crowd stood in awe, breathless. Joanna tried to look away but could not tear her eyes away from the scene of impending violence.

Jimmy thought of Spence Landford as he fixed his gaze on Wheeler's obnoxious face. Hatred burned through him. Not only had this man killed Landford, but he had openly insulted Joanna.

"It's the end of the trail for you, Black," sneered Duncan Wheeler, attempting intimidation. "You want me to pray for you before I send you to meet your Maker?"

"Pray for yourself," Jimmy said, concentrating on the third button from the top of Wheeler's shirt.

As Jimmy spoke, Duncan Wheeler, like a springing cat, went for both his guns. The .45s roared, but Jimmy had drawn and fired a split second faster. One of Wheeler's slugs plowed into a nearby wagon. The other cut a furrow along Jimmy's left side.

Wheeler let out a grunt. Jimmy's bullet had torn into his chest. He staggered, dropped both guns, and clutched the wound. Blood spurted between his fingers as he looked down, a curious, surprised expression on his face. He seemed to hang a moment in the thin afternoon air, then collapsed in a heap, dead.

Jimmy waited until he saw Wheeler drop, then lowered himself to one knee. His left side felt on fire.

Joanna rushed to him, kneeling to examine the wound. Blood was spreading from the rip in his shirt. Pain registered in his face.

"Oh, Jimmy," Joanna gasped, looking into his eyes through her tears, "is it bad?"

"Just a crease, I think," breathed the youth.

Pittman dropped down on Jimmy's other side. As the crowd moved in and talk resumed, Pittman said, "Don't let him move, Miss Joanna. I'll get the doc." With that he barged through the crowd, jostling people out of his way.

Jimmy remained on one knee, pressing his hands against the bleeding wound.

"Jimmy," said Joanna, wiping tears from her cheeks, "you did it to save Russ. Oh, Jimmy . . ." She sniffed, wiped more tears, and it came out before she realized it had left her tongue: "Jimmy, I love you. I—"

"Kid, do you realize who you just killed?" interrupted a middle-aged man. "That's Duncan Wheeler! He's one of the top guns in the whole country. Uh . . . that is, he *was*. He's the man who killed Spence Landford!"

A woman in her early thirties bent down and said, "Mr. Black, why don't you lie down on your right side? It will slow the bleeding until your friend brings the doctor."

Jimmy eyed the woman with appreciation and nodded. He was digesting what Joanna had just said. Somehow the pain seemed suddenly to diminish. The kind woman and the weeping girl helped him ease down onto his side.

Estes Park's marshal had arrived on the scene and was directing the removal of Duncan Wheeler's body. Abruptly Russ Pittman elbowed through the crowd, clearing a path for the doctor. The physician made a quick appraisal of the wound and said to Pittman, "It's not bad, but I'll need to stitch it up." Lifting his eyes to the crowd, he said, "Couple of you men carry this boy over to my office."

"I'll take care of it, Doc," said Russ. Kneeling, he grasped Jimmy tenderly and stood up, cradling him in his arms. The Colt .45 lay in the dust. "Bring his gun, please, Miss Joanna," he said softly.

Joanna picked up the gun, holding it with distaste, as if it were a dead snake.

Within an hour the doctor had cleaned, stitched, and bandaged the wound. "Now, son," he said advisedly, "I want to look at you again in three days. You live around here?"

"No, sir," replied Jimmy. "I live about thirty-five, forty miles away. Over by—"

"He's going to stay at the B-Slash-C," blurted Joanna. "Until . . . until he's able to ride."

"Then have him back in three days," said the physician.

Russ Pittman drove the surrey very carefully as the trio rode toward the ranch. Jimmy's chestnut was tied behind. His father's roan gelding had fetched a good price at the auction, which had resumed after the gunfight.

"Jimmy," said Russ, "I don't know how to thank you for what you did." The big man choked up, then swallowed hard. "I'm no fast gun. Wheeler would have killed me."

Joanna, who sat between them, looked at Jimmy with adoring eyes. "That was a very brave thing you did."

Looking down, the man who killed Duncan Wheeler said, "I couldn't just stand there and let you die, Russ."

"What's this Jim Black business?" asked Pittman. "And how did you get so all-fired fast with a gun?"

"I'm sure that's what Jimmy wanted to explain to us," suggested Joanna. "I'm sure Daddy will be willing to listen now that Jimmy has saved your life. Let's hold off till we get home. Then he'll only have to tell it once."

Britt Claiborne, when he learned of the incident at Estes Park, consented to listen to Jimmy's story. He sat in the parlor huddled in a blanket, sniffling and wiping his red nose. Russ and Joanna flanked the old man, eager to hear what Jimmy had to say.

He reminded them that during his first visit he had told them that his parents had been murdered. Backing up to the Heglers' trial in Topeka, when his father had testified against the brothers, Jimmy gave his listeners all the details he could remember or piece together. He brought them up to his meeting with Spence Landford in Estes Park, then covered the events of the past year.

"So that's why I was able to outdraw Duncan Wheeler today," he said, closing off. "I tried to avoid a fight, but he left me no choice."

Britt Claiborne blew his nose, looked at the young man through bloodshot eyes, and said, "I appreciate your saving Russ's life, Jimmy. I mean that sincerely. In gratitude, this ranch will always grant you a warm welcome."

Joanna's face brightened as she eyed her father. Jimmy smiled at her, then spoke up. "Thank you, Mr. Claiborne. I appreciate that."

"I musk ask one more thing," said Claiborne. "Are you through wearing that gun now?"

Jimmy's face stiffened. "I wish I could tell you that I am, sir," he said with strained voice, "but I'm afraid there are going to be more challengers dogging my tracks."

"But, Jimmy," put in Joanna, "what about when you go back east to college?"

"Once I get there," he answered, "I can hang up the gun. When I come back, I hope I won't have to wear it again. But it might not work that way. Spence Landford told me that a gunfighter can never shed his image until he lies dead at the feet of the faceless man."

"The faceless man?" asked Joanna.

"Yes," said Jim. "The one man who lurks out there in the shadows of the future . . . who is faster."

"You mean like you were to Duncan Wheeler?" asked Russ.

"Yes." Jimmy nodded grimly.

"But when you're a respected lawyer, all that will change," argued Joanna.

"I hope so," said Jim.

"But you *are* going to try, aren't you?" asked the young woman, her emerald eyes searching his. "You're going to *try* to give up the gun."

"Yes, Joanna," replied Jimmy. "I sure am."

After two weeks and three trips to the physician, Jimmy was ready to ride. Jezebel had prepared a special going away meal for the young man's supper on the last night. Jimmy planned to rise early the next morning and head for home. It was now mid-June. There was much to do if he was going to enroll in college and be there by September.

Britt Claiborne shook hands with him in the parlor and bid him good-bye, then retired upstairs to his room. Russ Pittman, who had been spared mess-hall food for the occasion, told Jimmy he would see him in the bunkhouse later, then disappeared through the door. Jezebel busied herself in the kitchen while humming an old spiritual.

Jimmy and Joanna strolled out to the front porch and sat in the swing. Sonny Boy wagged his tail at Joanna, eyed the young man with suspicion, then curled up.

The stars twinkled as crickets filled the cool night air with music. The pair sat in silence for a long moment. As Jimmy set his eyes on the half-breed girl, a tingling sensation spread through his chest like a thousand tiny needles. He could not think of a diplomatic way to approach the subject he had in mind. He'd been thinking about it for two weeks, and this was the first time they had been alone since the day he'd killed Duncan Wheeler. It was now or never.

Taking a deep breath, Jimmy said, "Princess . . ."

Her eyes met his. "Yes?"

"Did you mean what you said in Estes Park?"

"What was that?" she asked innocently.

"You know. When I was shot."

The pale light exposed a touch of crimson in her face. "You mean when I said I love you?"

Jimmy nodded, his throat tight.

Almost in a whisper she breathed, "Yes, Jimmy, I meant it. I love you."

Every fiber in the young man's body seemed to catch fire, disconnect, then connect back again. Twisting in the swing to face her squarely, he started to put his arms around her, then checked himself.

Wordlessly Joanna leaned into his arms. He pulled her close and whispered, "I love you, too, Princess. I have since the first moment I saw you. There hasn't been a single day that I haven't thought of you. I—"

Jim was interrupted by Jezebel calling from the kitchen. "Miz Joanna! It's time fo' you to be comin' in!"

"In a minute, Jezebel," she answered.

Jim released his hold on her. Joanna stood up and walked to the porch rail. As he stepped up behind her she said, "When will I see you again?" She kept her back to him, waiting for his answer.

"Well," he said, clearing his throat, "there's about enough money in Pa's account to see me through law school. I can graduate in two years if I work straight through."

"You mean you won't be coming back at all for two years?" There was a quiver in her voice.

"I . . . I don't think so. I'm going to try to rent out the farm, but it won't bring in too much. I plan to sell it when I come back after graduation. I'll need the money to open up my law office and buy a house in Fort Collins."

Joanna slowly turned, her face glistening with tears. "Then I'll wait for you, Jimmy . . . if you want me to."

He folded her into his arms. "If? There's no *if* about it. Of course I want you to."

Inside the house Jezebel had not heard Joanna's reply moments before, and she started toward the front door. Meanwhile, Jimmy looked down into Joanna's eyes. She tilted her head back, and he found her lips.

Bursting through the screen door without really looking, Jezebel said, "Miz Joanna, it's time fo'—"

The young couple held the kiss in spite of the awkward interruption. Pulling slowly apart, they looked at the embarrassed woman, who gulped and said, "Oh . . . I'm sorry. I didn't mean . . . I mean . . . uh . . ."

"It's all right, Jezebel," said Joanna calmly. "Jimmy is going away for a long time. We were saying good-bye."

Trying to ease the awkwardness of the moment, the large black woman chuckled and said, "I didn't hear no *sayin'*. Looked to me like it was just plain *kissin'* good-bye."

"Why, Jezebel," said Jimmy, "I do believe you're blushing!"

She poked him lightly and said, "Mr. Jimmy, you is funnin' me now. You know good and well this here face can't turn red!" Turning to Joanna, she said, "Honey, you better get on inside. Yo' daddy will be gettin' upset."

"All right, Jezebel," Joanna said, smiling. "Just three minutes, okay?"

"Okay, darlin'," responded Jezebel. Looking up at the tall young man, she said with a tremor, "You come back, Mr. Jimmy. Ol' Jezebel loves you too." With that she gave him a quick embrace and went back into the house.

Joanna spoke first. "Will you write me often?"

"Sure will," Jimmy said, taking both of her hands in his. "I won't know which school I'll be going to until I pick up the mail, but it will be in New York or Boston. You'll hear from me soon, I promise. You will answer, won't you?"

"Of course," she said softly. "That will help the time pass more quickly."

"Yes," Jimmy said, a catch in his voice. "And as soon as I can set up my office and get a few clients, you'll become Mrs. Jim Blackburn."

"Mrs. James William Blackburn," she said, moving close. "We'll let Jim Black fade away as of now. I would never want to be Mrs. Jim Black."

A coldness crawled up Jimmy's spine. He hoped with all

his heart that the time away from this raw country would erase its memory of Jim Black, the gunfighter, so he could be accepted back as James W. Blackburn, attorney-at-law.

After a long, tender kiss, Joanna turned her tear-stained face toward the door and disappeared inside. Jimmy stepped off the porch and walked in the darkness toward the bunk-house. The cool night air emphasized the presence of Joanna's tears on his face. The sweetness of her lips lingered on his own.

The first hint of dawn found James Blackburn astride the chestnut gelding, moving slowly past the big white house. He looked up at Joanna's window. It was too dark for him to see the lovely face pressed against the glass as Joanna watched his shadowed form through a veil of tears.

Chapter Twelve

The steady clicking of the train's steel wheels blended with the beat of Jim Blackburn's heart. It had been almost two years since he had seen Joanna Claiborne, and he looked and felt much older. His friends at school no longer called him Jimmy, but James or simply Jim, yet his heart had not changed. He still loved Joanna, and in the last two years many letters had passed between them. Jim would travel by stagecoach from Denver, and she would be waiting for him at the Wells Fargo office in Estes Park.

Jim had left Boston by rail three days earlier. It was seven-thirty in the morning, and the train was one hour out of Kansas City. The rolling autumn hills outside the window were gradually tapering into flat land as the big engine thundered westward, spewing black smoke. Behind the coal car and the baggage coach there were four passenger cars, followed by the caboose.

In the second passenger car Jim sat alone next to the window on the left side of the aisle. The man just ahead was reading a Kansas City newspaper. Directly across the aisle a young mother was trying to quiet her baby.

Jim looked down at the black leather valise by his feet. Inside was his diploma. He was now qualified to hang up a shingle and practice law. He thought grimly of the Colt .45 that lay next to the diploma. Would he have to strap it on again? Or would the West have forgotten the lanky kid who had outdrawn and killed some of its famous gunfighters? Had the world seen the last of Jim Black?

One thing was in Jim's favor. His appearance had changed. He now stood six feet three inches before stepping into his boots. Heavy labor on the Boston docks during his spare time had thickened his large frame with solid muscle. He now weighed two hundred twenty pounds. The heavy mustache that matched his dark hair had a dual purpose. It not only changed his appearance, but also covered a ragged scar on the upper lip. The scar was the result of one of many fights in which he had been involved on the docks. While working among the longshoremen, he had learned to fight with his fists as a matter of survival.

He truly hoped that Jim Black would be forgotten, but the reality of what Spence Landford had said kept him wary. Consequently, he had disciplined himself to practice the fast-draw during the past two years. If anything, he was faster than ever. Jim hoped he would never have to use it again. He had not forgotten Joanna's words two years ago: *"We'll let Jim Black fade away as of now. I would never want to be Mrs. Jim Black."*

Jim's attention was drawn to a man standing in the aisle, complaining to the young mother about her crying baby.

"I'm sorry, sir," she was saying, "he has colic. There's nothing I can do to quiet him."

"Well, stuff something in his mouth," the man growled.

Jim felt a rush of temper at the ill manners of the man. He unfolded, standing over six feet five in his boots. Towering above the man, he tapped his shoulder. The man swung his face around and up, his mouth drawn in a thin, petulant line. His countenance quickly changed as he took in Jim Blackburn's size.

"You never cried when you were a baby, I suppose," said Jim sharply.

"Well, I, uh . . . I, uh, suppose I—" the man stammered, his mouth sagging.

"Now, why don't you apologize to the lady and find a seat in another car?" The look in Jim's eyes made it clear that the rude man had better follow his suggestion.

Clearing his throat nervously, the man turned to the young mother and said, "I, er . . . I'm sorry, ma'am." He wheeled, spoke to his wife two seats back, and led her toward the rear door.

The conductor was just coming through the same door. He stepped aside, taking note of the sour look on the man's face. Moving to Jim, who still stood in the aisle, he said, "Some kind of problem?"

"Slight one," responded Jim. "It's all right now."

As the conductor moved on, the young mother spoke to the big man. "Thank you."

"My pleasure, ma'am," Jim answered, touching the brim of his hat.

Turning toward his seat, Jim noticed a small, thin man sitting across the aisle near the front of the car. Dressed in a black suit, he was half turned in the seat, studying Jim's angular face. Their eyes met, and the little man looked quickly away and spun around.

Jim returned to his seat, slumped down, and pulled his hat low over his eyes. The steady, monotonous clicking of the wheels, along with the rocking motion of the car, soon lulled him to sleep. Waking up once as the train rounded a sharp bend, he opened his eyes and lifted his hat to find the little man in the black suit staring at him. Jim clapped the Stetson over his face and went back to sleep.

The morning wore on. The train gave up several passengers at Topeka and was taking on a few more. Awake now, Jim looked out the window. Several armed guards surrounded a cart on the platform. A number of heavy wooden boxes were being loaded into the baggage coach. Two of the guards remained on board as the train lurched and, amid hissing steam, pulled out of the station. Jim figured the boxes probably contained gold.

The big man's legs needed stretching as the train reached top speed. He stood up stiffly and walked forward. As he passed through the door, the thin man in the black suit studied his broad back.

The air was cooler outside. Jim stood between the cars, observing the grassy fields that flanked the tracks. Two men stopped and chatted with him as they passed from car to car. Later, the conductor joined him. It turned out that Boston had been his boyhood home, and the two of them had something in common to talk about.

Jim returned to his seat after about an hour. The curious little man in the black suit was pretending to be engrossed in a newspaper. The young mother and her baby were both asleep.

As the train began to slow down, the conductor passed through, announcing Junction City as the next stop. Passengers who wished to eat lunch in one of the town's eating places would have an hour layover to do so.

Junction City was a quiet town, and the passengers took their repast without incident. Jim threw a glance at the baggage car as he returned to the depot. The guards stood in the open door, rifles cradled in their arms.

Jim reboarded the train and took his previous seat. A few moments later some of the other passengers returned, followed by two new men who caught Jim's attention. They were dressed in range clothes and were unshaven. Both were wearing guns.

The two newcomers scanned the car, then sat side by side in the front seat to the right of the aisle. Outside, the conductor shouted, "All aboard!" The whistle blew and the train pitched forward. Jim had just noticed that the little man in the black suit was gone when the man came through the door and started down the aisle. Panting for breath, he dropped into the seat beside Jim.

The little man produced a handkerchief, removed his derby hat, and mopped his brow. Jim tossed him a casual glance, wondering why he had chosen to sit there when several other seats were available.

After catching his breath, the little man turned to Jim and said in a low voice, "You're Jim Black, aren't you?"

Jim furrowed his brow. "Do I know you?"

"My name is Stanley Dent. I'm the undertaker in Estes Park. I buried Duncan Wheeler after you killed him. You've changed, but I never forget a face."

Jim nodded. "I've been in Massachusetts. You've got a knack for names too."

"Wasn't hard to remember yours. Since the day you killed Wheeler, a dozen gunhawks have come through Estes hunting you so they can make a name for themselves."

A heavy, sinking feeling settled over Jim. He could almost feel the weight of the Colt .45 on his hip again. Even after two years, would he still have to go on being dogged by every greenhorn gunfighter until age slowed his hand? Was there no way for him to live in the land he loved without being shadowed by a faceless man who would one day outdraw him?

"We've got a problem, Mr. Black," said Dent in a hushed tone.

"A problem?" echoed Jim.

"You see those two men up front? On the right."

"Yes."

"There are four others just like them on this train. I over-heard them talking at the depot. It's a miracle they didn't see me. There's a gold shipment aboard. From what I could put together, the rest of the gang is waiting about halfway be-tween here and Abilene. The six outlaws are supposed to take control—"

Dent's words were cut short as one of the gunmen stood up and casually made his way to the rear of the car. He opened the door and stepped out.

Suddenly, from one of the cars up ahead, a muffled volley of gunshots was heard. Jim leaned over to open the valise. Instantly the remaining outlaw leaped from the seat, gun in hand. Facing the passengers, he roared, "Everybody put their hands up!"

The young mother across the aisle let out a scream. The baby awakened with a start and began to cry. A woman toward the rear of the car called out her husband's name.

"We're takin' over this train!" bellowed the outlaw, his eyes raking the car to see if all hands were raised. For a moment his attention was on the woman with the baby. While he sharply commanded her to lay down the infant and raise her hands, Jim palmed his Colt. He lined the muzzle on the outlaw's chest, holding the gun between the two seats in front of him. It would be a clear shot. No passengers were in the way.

The outlaw's gaze swung to Jim, whose hands were not visible. "Hey, you!" he shouted, teeth bared. "Get your hands up!"

Jim's gun roared, and the slug tore into the man's chest. The impact flipped him backward. He bounced off the door and fell across the seat where he had sat earlier.

Jim bounded over Stanley Dent into the aisle. The coach was filled with blue smoke. Jim ran to the front, made sure the gunman was dead, and picked up his gun. Above the sounds of weeping women and the crying baby he said, "Any of you men got guns?"

One middle-aged man responded. "Got one right here," he said, pulling a revolver from his hand luggage.

"Good," said Jim. "Anyone else know how to use one?"

A tall, slender man in his late thirties stood up. "I can," he volunteered.

The woman seated next to him objected. "No, Art. Don't get involved," she pleaded.

"I'm already involved," retorted Art. "I'm on this train."

Jim adeptly flipped the outlaw's gun in his own hand, catching it by the barrel. He held it out to the slender man. "You two watch that back door," he said quickly. "There are five more outlaws on this train. It's my guess there are at least two to the rear. There's one back there for sure. The rest of the gang is waiting a few miles up the track. We've got to subdue the others before we get there. I'm going up front. I have a feeling those shots we heard were in the baggage coach. If the others try to come through that rear door, shoot them!"

The two armed men nodded.

Wheeling, Jim opened the forward door and stepped outside. Moving to the next car, he peered through the small window. One of the gang had his back to the door. He was holding a sawed-off shotgun on the frightened passengers, who were twisted in their seats, hands raised over their heads.

At first Jim thought of turning the knob and slamming the door into the man, but if the impact caused the shotgun to discharge, it could kill or wound several passengers. Quickly he returned to the coach behind. Stepping inside, he removed his hat and donned the one belonging to the dead outlaw. He paused momentarily to check on the two men waiting with guns aimed at the rear door.

Jim tipped the outlaw's hat low over his face and lowered himself to the man's approximate height as he stepped outside once again. He felt confident that the man with the shotgun would recognize the hat through the window. It was a rebel officer's hat from the Civil War and was considerably sweat-stained.

Gun in hand, Jim tilted his head down and tapped on the window. The man with the shotgun threw a quick glance over his shoulder at the familiar hat and opened the door. He kept his eyes on the passengers and said, "Did you have to shoot somebody back there, Rafe?"

The cold rim of Jim's muzzle touched the man on the nape of his neck. His back stiffened. Jim shut the door with his heel and spoke through clenched teeth, "Ease the hammer down slow, mister. Now."

The outlaw obeyed. Jim reached around and jerked the shotgun from his hands. "Bless you, mister," said a male passenger as they all lowered their aching arms.

Big Jim shoved the outlaw down on an empty seat. "How many in the cars up ahead?" he demanded, slipping the Colt under his belt.

The man scowled. "I ain't tellin' you nothin'!"

Jim shoved him against the window, placed the muzzle of the twelve-gauge over the end of his nose, and eased back the hammer. The man's eyes bulged. "I asked you a question," Jim hissed.

"There's two," replied the outlaw, visibly shaken.

Turning to the passengers, Jim said, "Any of you got a gun?"

They looked at one another, shaking their heads. Jim noticed a big man who appeared to be in his early forties. "Hey, friend," he said to him. "Come here, will you?"

The husky man slipped out of his seat. As he made his way down the aisle, Jim pulled the shotgun away from the outlaw's face and said, "Think you can handle this one?"

"Sure can," said the man.

"If he starts to move from that seat, punch him out."

"It'd be a pleasure," said the big man, popping his meaty right fist into his left palm.

The outlaw's face registered fear.

"I'm going after the two up ahead," said Jim. "See if you can find out from this buzzard just where his gang is waiting by the tracks up ahead."

"Will do," responded the husky man.

Jim charged up the aisle and out the door. He looked through the small, barred window of the baggage coach and saw an outlaw sitting on a stack of wooden crates, spinning the cylinder of his revolver. Jim lunged through the door, shotgun poised and cocked. "Drop it!" he shouted.

The outlaw was fast and foolish, and he whipped the gun around and fired. The bullet struck a lantern hanging by the door, shattering it and splashing kerosene into Jim's face. But Jim had already squeezed the trigger of the twelve-gauge. The muzzle had lifted slightly, sending the full charge square into the outlaw's face, almost decapitating him.

Jim's eyes burned like fire. The rocking coach seemed to whirl around him as he blinked against the kerosene. Through

his blurred vision he made out a canteen lying against the
coach wall near a small table. He stumbled toward it, laid
down the shotgun, and grasped the canteen. He splashed
water into his eyes repeatedly. After a minute or so the
burning eased some and his vision improved.

Within another few minutes Jim could see sufficiently,
though there was still some burning. Tears moistened his
eyes. Blinking and scanning the baggage coach, he saw blood
on the floor next to the side door. The guards were nowhere
to be seen. Apparently the outlaws had shot them and tossed
their bodies out the door.

It was easy to figure where the other gunman was. He
would be in the engine, making sure the train stopped when
it reached the place where the rest of the gang was waiting.

Moving out the front door, Jim discarded the empty shotgun and once again palmed his Colt. He glanced down both
sides of the coal car ahead but saw no one. He moved to his
left. There was a steel railing running around the car at about
chest height, and a six-inch ledge four feet below it. He
stepped onto the ledge, grasping the railing with his left hand
and hooking his right elbow over it for balance. Slowly he
inched toward the engine.

As Jim neared the front of the coal car he stopped and
glanced around the corner. He could see the body of the
fireman lying on the floor of the cab. The outlaw, his back
turned, stood by the body, holding a gun on the engineer.

Cautiously, Jim slipped up behind the outlaw. Just as he
planted his feet on the floor of the cab, the outlaw whirled,
but Jim's Colt, swung in a wide arc, connected violently with
the man's temple. He staggered sideways, then keeled over,
pitching headlong out of the cab. His body bounced, flipped,
and rolled on the ground, arms and legs thrashing like a rag
doll.

Jim looked at the engineer. "You all right?" he shouted
above the noise of the train.

"Am now!" replied the engineer, smiling.

"The rest of the gang is waiting up the track somewhere,"
shouted Jim. "I've got two more to dispose of in the last two
cars. If we reach the gang before I get back, don't slow down.
Keep it full speed ahead!"

"Will do," agreed the engineer, nodding.

Jim hurried back along the side of the coal car. Reaching

the baggage coach, he climbed up the ladder to the top and, moving along the roof, headed toward the rear of the train. His eyes still burned from the kerosene.

Joanna Claiborne appeared at the kitchen door, dressed for riding. "Good morning, Daddy," she said gaily, leaning over to kiss her father's cheek.

Britt Claiborne gave her an adoring look. "Good morning, honey. You're certainly in high spirits. Are you sure you'll be able to stand the next three days?"

"If her spirits get any higher," put in Jezebel, laying a platter of scrambled eggs on the table, "she's gonna bang her pretty little head on the ceilin'!"

"You've turned down a lot of fine young men these past two years, Joanna," said Claiborne. "I hope Jim Blackburn is going to be worth it."

"Oh, he is, Daddy, he is," she insisted, floating down onto her chair. "You'll see. He's going to make a fine lawyer. You'll be proud of him. And you'll be proud to have your grandchildren raised in a lawyer's home."

"Grandchildren?" said the silver-haired man, arching his bushy eyebrows. "That young man hasn't approached me about marrying you yet."

"He will, Daddy," Joanna said confidently. "And just think— since he's decided to open his office in Estes Park, you can see your grandchildren as often as you want."

"I didn't know he had decided that for sure."

"He has." Joanna smiled with assurance.

"When you wrote and told him about Fred Bennett's death, you told me he answered that he was only *interested* in taking over Fred's practice. I didn't know he'd decided on it for sure."

"Mmm-hmm. He's going to try to get Mr. Bennett's old office. At least that's what he said in the last letter."

Britt Claiborne's face darkened. "Joanna, I hope for your sake Jim has gotten gunfighting out of his system."

"He has, Daddy," the young woman said with confidence. "I'm sure law school has refined him considerably. Besides, he knows I would never marry a gunfighter."

Jim leaped across to the roof of the last passenger car and moved quickly to the rear. A glance at the left side of the caboose revealed the body of the trainman draped loosely through the window frame. Blood was streaked on the side of the car.

Warily, Jim eased himself over the edge and dropped to the platform between the cars. Squatting low, he removed the sweat-stained hat and peered into the caboose. There was no one inside. Still keeping low, he moved to the passenger car door and peeked through. The outlaw who had taken control of this car had made the occupants lean forward in their seats and grasp the seat backs in front of them with both hands. He stood at the front of the car holding a sawed-off single-barreled shotgun, exactly as his partner had done.

The outlaw's gaze fell on the rear window just before Jim ducked. Jim quickly moved aside. Footsteps rushed down the aisle and the shotgun roared. The door shattered, sending splinters and shards of glass over him. Instantly he jumped up and looked through the hole. The gunman was thumbing another shell into the smoking chamber. Screams and cries were coming from the passengers.

Jim's Colt bucked against his palm. The outlaw fell backward and lay still. The conductor, who had been held in the car, leaped up and shouted, "You got him, mister!"

Suddenly the forward door burst open. The last of the outlaws charged through, glancing down at his partner's corpse. Lifting his eyes, he looked past the conductor to Jim and raised his gun.

"Get down!" Jim bellowed at the conductor, his eyes still watering.

It was too late. The outlaw fired, dropping the conductor with a bullet in the back. Before the man could fire again, Jim shot him through the heart. Stepping over the two bodies and ignoring the praises of the passengers, Jim quickly darted to the next car. The occupants were in a frenzy. As he hurried through the coach, he said, "It's all right now, folks. Everything's under control."

Reaching the next car, he remembered the two men he had stationed in there with guns trained on the door. He knew that with all the shooting, they were bound to be edgy. Taking no chances, he stepped to the side and turned the knob. Pushing the door open slightly, he hollered, "Hey! Don't shoot! The gang's all dead except for one we're holding in the first car."

"Come on in," came a male voice.

As Jim entered and headed through the coach, the passengers began asking questions. "No time to talk now," he called out. "The rest of the gang is waiting up ahead."

Jim bolted through the door of the next car to find the remaining outlaw out cold in the aisle. The big, husky man stood over him. "What happened?" asked Jim.

"Thought he could get by me," said the man. "Had to hit him."

Kneeling down, Jim said, "Somebody get me some water. I've got to bring him to."

It took several minutes to rouse the outlaw. Bracing him up in a seat, Jim said, "Where's your gang waiting?"

A look of insolence spread across the outlaw's face. "Wouldn't you like to know?" He laughed wickedly. "My friends will stop this train no matter what you do."

One thought came into Jim's mind. *Barricade*. The gang could build a barricade that would derail the train.

Stanley Dent had followed Jim from the second car. Looking at the small man, Jim said, "Mr. Dent, would you make your way up to the engine and tell the engineer to slow down and watch for a barricade on the tracks?"

"Sure will, Jim," said Dent.

"Tell him to blow the whistle three times as soon as he sees anything. I'll be up there shortly."

Dent nodded and slipped through the forward door. As he passed through the baggage coach his gaze fell on the man whose face had been blown away, and the sight caused his stomach to roll. Hurriedly he made his way to the next car.

Jim lowered his angular face till he was almost nose to nose with the outlaw. "I want to know where your friends are and what they have planned."

The outlaw's lip curled over his teeth. "You go to the devil," he said impudently.

Jim put his right hand to the man's face, grasping his nose between thumb and index and middle fingers. Before the outlaw could flinch, Jim twisted the nose violently. The cartilage snapped. The man howled as blood spurted.

"I'll twist it clean off unless you tell me what I want to know," said Jim hotly.

"All right!" said the outlaw, cupping his hands over his

bleeding nose. "They're waitin' where the track bends just before it crosses the bridge over Wilson Lake River."

"Is there a barricade?"

"Yes. Just in case somethin' went wrong."

"It sure did!" laughed the husky man. The passengers laughed with him, mocking the bleeding outlaw.

"How many men?" asked Jim.

"Nine."

"What's the barricade made of?"

At that moment the whistle on the engine blew three times and the cars began slowing. A wicked gleam came into the outlaw's eyes.

"I asked you a question, mister," Jim rasped. "If I have to ask it again, your nose comes off."

Jim reached for the man's broken nose, but the outlaw jerked back. "No! I'll tell you." Wiping blood from his upper lip, he said, "It's not solid. It's just brush. Looks solid, but it ain't."

"You better be telling the truth," said Jim evenly. "You're on this train too. If it derails, you go with it."

"I ain't lyin'," the outlaw said defensively. "It's just there to make the engineer stop the train so's they can get the gold."

Jim left him and ran forward as the whistle blasted three times again and the train slowed further. Bolting through the baggage coach, he made his way alongside the coal car. As he reached the cab of the engine he stuck his head out the window and looked up the track. About three hundred yards ahead several men were standing beside a large dark mass heaped on the rails.

Looking at Stanley Dent's pallid face, then at the engineer, Jim said, "Full speed ahead!"

"But what about that barricade?" asked the engineer heatedly.

"It's only brush," said Jim. "Nothing solid. Ram it!"

Up ahead, waiting beside the barricade, Hench Barkley and eight of his men watched the train approach. It had slowed to half speed, a sure sign that their partners were in command.

"There it is, boss," said one of the outlaws. "A quarter of a million in gold!"

Barkley, a short, stocky man of fifty, nodded and smiled. "We'll live high on the hog now, boys."

Abruptly, billows of steam poured from the pistons as the train started accelerating to full speed. A heavy frown streaked Barkley's brow as one of the gang remarked that the train should be slowing down. The outlaw chief swore.

"Somethin's wrong, boss," put in another.

"I knew I should've handled it myself," said Barkley, swearing again. "If you want a thing done right, you gotta do it yourself."

The big engine was bearing down on the barricade. "We better get outta here, boys," hollered the gang leader. "There's gonna be stuff flyin' everywhere!"

The outlaws scattered as the engine bore down on the pile of brush on the tracks. The iron cowcatcher hit the barricade with a thunderous impact, strewing debris thirty yards in both directions.

At the moment of the impact the outlaw in the first passenger car slipped past the big man guarding him. He bolted to the door, stepped out between the cars, and leaped free of the train.

Hench Barkley saw the man hit the ground and roll. "Come on, fellas!" he shouted. "That looked like Roy Selman."

Selman lay still as the gang circled him. The sound of the train was dying out as Barkley knelt beside him. Selman's clothes were torn. His skin was scraped and bleeding. Blood was trickling from his broken nose.

"Is he dead, Hench?" asked one of the men.

"Naw, he's breathin'. Just out cold."

Within a few minutes Roy Selman began to stir and finally opened his eyes. He groaned, sniffed blood, spit it out, and looked up at the curious faces.

Hench Barkley swore and said, "What happened, Roy?"

Selman sat up and shook his head. "Some big dude waded through us like a bull elephant. Killed all of 'em, I guess, but me."

"One man?" boomed Barkley.

Selman nodded. "We'd have made it easy if it wasn't fer him."

Barkley's face mirrored the fury that was boiling inside him. "Do you know his name?"

"Heard a little skinny man talkin' who said he knew him. Said the big dude was Jim Black."

The name registered vaguely. Barkley repeated it several times audibly. Suddenly it struck him. "Jim Black! I know where I heard that name. He's the slick who killed Duncan Wheeler a couple years ago." Looking at Selman, he said, "You any idea where this Jim Black was headed?"

"Nope," replied Selman. "But they said the skinny little drip was from someplace called Estes Park. Since he knew Black, it could be that's where Black's from."

Hench Barkley's face went red, matching the fire in his eyes. The muscles in his jaws tightened. "Jim Black cheated me out of a fortune," he breathed furiously. "He don't know it, but he's a dead man."

Chapter Thirteen

When the engineer stopped the train in Salina, intending to report the incident, Jim Blackburn asked him for extra time so he could have the local doctor take a look at his eyes. He found Salina's physician at home, just finishing dinner. After examining Jim's eyes, the doctor told him he was lucky, that the kerosene could have damaged his vision permanently. By his washing the noxious fluid out quickly, he had saved his eyesight. However, he should have the eyes checked periodically by a doctor, just to make sure they remained all right.

A full report was made on the incident at the sheriff's office. The lawman identified the would-be train robbers as the Hench Barkley gang. A posse was quickly formed and headed east to track them down.

The engineer wired the railroad office in Kansas City, informing them in detail of the attempted robbery and reporting that the gold was safe. Stanley Dent had told the engineer that the man who foiled the robbery was named Jim Black, which was the name that went in the lengthy message to Kansas City.

Two days and dozens of stops later the train pulled into Denver. Jim Blackburn and Stanley Dent stood at the Wells Fargo office early the next morning, waiting to board the stagecoach bound for Estes Park. While the driver and shotgunner were loading luggage, a young man approached, bearing two neatly tied bundles of newspapers. He called to the driver, who was standing on top of the coach. "Here's the papers for Boulder and Estes Park, Mr. Nelson."

"Thanks, Arthur," replied the driver.

Jim's eyes drifted by chance to the top of the bundle. There, on the front page, were the bold, blaring headlines:

KANSAS TRAIN ROBBERY FOILED BY GUNHAWK

Gunfighter Jim Black comes out of seclusion
to save A.T. & S.F. Railroad loss of $250,000.

Jim's blood ran cold. If anyone from the B-Slash-C saw that
newspaper or heard of it . . .

During the long ride to Estes Park Jim sat quietly, ponder-
ing his predicament. There was no way this story was not
going to reach the Claiborne ranch. He might as well tell
Joanna about it immediately. After all, it wasn't as if he was
gunfighting. He had merely done what was right.

Stanley Dent squeezed enough conversation out of his
traveling companion to learn that Jim planned to open a law
office in Estes Park. Jim, with his mind totally fixed on
Joanna, and knowing it was too late now to hide his former
identity, did not bother explaining to Dent that his name was
Blackburn, not Black.

As the stagecoach topped the last sharp crest before the
road dropped into Estes Park, Jim's heart raced. *Two years,*
he thought. *I wonder if she's changed? Could the time possibly have made her more beautiful?*

The afternoon sun was touching the tips of the majestic
peaks to the west as the stagecoach crossed the bridge and
swung onto Main Street. Horses, buggies, and surreys were
parked along the dusty street in front of the Wells Fargo
office. Jim eagerly scanned the street and the faces along the
boardwalk. There was no sign of Joanna.

The stage pulled to a halt in a cloud of dust. Stanley Dent
jumped out of the coach and hollered, "Hey, everybody!
Gather 'round!" Pointing to the tall man emerging from the
stage, he said, "Remember Jim Black? The man who killed
Duncan Wheeler right here in our town?"

Widened eyes and curious faces closed in.

"Well, Jim Black is a hero again, folks! Gather 'round! Let
me tell you about the big train robbery!"

While Dent carried on, Jim, embarrassed, searched the
street for some sign of Joanna. Suddenly he spotted the
surrey coming up the street. Russ Pittman held the reins,
and beside the big foreman sat the most beautiful woman Jim
had ever seen. She wore a taffeta dress bedecked with deli-
cate lace. The high collar adorned her long, graceful neck,

which was circled by a black ribbon bearing an ivory cameo brooch.

Pittman halted short of the growing crowd. With long, impatient strides Jim made for the surrey. Joanna beamed at him as she stepped down. Russ Pittman, who loved her like a daughter, watched the tender scene with misty eyes.

Tears were on Joanna's cheeks as Jim stood before her. Neither one spoke. They just stood staring at each other, living a moment of rapture.

Finally Jim found his voice. "Hello, Princess."

"Jim! Oh, Jim!" she exclaimed as he bent down and kissed her.

Newspapers were passed out among the crowd. Jim held Joanna's hands and drank her in with his eyes. "You're more beautiful than ever." He shook his head in disbelief.

"And you're more handsome than ever too," she smiled. "Goodness! Have you quit growing yet? You must be two inches taller. And I like your mustache," she said. "It makes you look old and dignified. Just right for a prominent attorney."

Before Jim could comment, someone in the crowd shouted, *"Jim Black!"*

Joanna's face blanched. She turned toward the excited people waving newspapers.

"Hey, Jim!" shouted a man. "Glad you're back in these parts! We need a man like you!"

"The railroad give you a reward, Jim?" asked another.

"Jim, what's this all about?" asked Joanna. "They're calling you Jim Black."

"Let's head for the ranch, honey," he said. "I'll explain it on the way." Placing his valise on the floorboards of the surrey, he stretched his hand toward Russ Pittman. "Hello, Russ," he said in a friendly tone.

"Welcome home," responded Pittman as their hands met.

The lowering sun set the clouds aflame with a mixture of orange, red, and purple as the surrey turned off the road onto the B-Slash-C land.

"Certainly I understand, Jim," said Joanna. "I'm very proud that you saved the train. The only thing that bothers me is that the town is calling you Jim Black."

"Well, they'll just have to learn different," Jim said flatly.

"When I hang out my shingle, I'll make them forget Jim Black."

"Might not be so easy," spoke up Pittman. "Didn't you hear that fellow back there say this town needs a man like you? Well, he wasn't talkin' about no lawyer."

"Oh?"

Pittman shook his head. "Joanna didn't tell you in her letters, but you'll find out soon enough, I reckon."

Jim looked at Joanna, who averted her eyes.

"Yeah," said Pittman. "A bunch of killers murdered our last two marshals. They come into town from somewhere west every few weeks. Shoot the place up. Never know when they're gonna show up. That's why Miss Joanna and I were late. We got to the edge of town and we heard Stanley Dent shouting. I had to make sure it wasn't them killers actin' up before we drove on in."

Britt Claiborne and Jezebel were standing on the front porch of the large white house as Russ Pittman pulled the surrey to a stop.

"Look how that boy done growed!" exclaimed Jezebel as Jim jumped down from the surrey.

Claiborne stepped off the porch and gripped Jim's hand. "Welcome back, Jimmy," said the elderly man. "Er . . . I mean *Jim*. Joanna says it's not Jimmy anymore." Tilting his head back, he added, "From the size of you, I guess I should call you sir!"

Jezebel opened her arms and moved toward the smiling young man. "Welcome home, Mr. Burntblack," she said, embracing him.

Jim laughed. "Good to see you, Jezebel."

"I'll put your gear in the bunkhouse, Jim," said Pittman. "We've got your bed ready."

"Thanks, Russ," said Jim. "I'll be out later."

"Yeah," chuckled Jezebel, "he'll be out after he eats some of Jezebel's cookin' and does a little sparkin' with Miz Joanna."

"Jezebel!" said Joanna, her face flushing.

Laughing heartily, the big black woman stepped up on the porch. "Supper will be ready in about ten minutes. Y'all get yo' hands washed."

At the supper table Jim explained his plans to Britt Claiborne. He planned to ride into Estes Park the next day to talk to Fred Bennett's widow. As soon as he could arrange for the rental of her husband's old office and the purchase of his law books, he would hang out his shingle.

The owner of the B-Slash-C was deeply pleased by the young man's initiative and said he was certain Jim would make a successful lawyer.

When the meal was finished, Jim said, "Mr. Claiborne, could you and I step out on the front porch? Get a little fresh air?" He threw Joanna a quick glance. She smiled and looked at Jezebel.

"Sure, my boy," replied Claiborne.

The night air was clean and cool as the two men emerged from the house. The older man looked into the heavens and said, "God's got all His lamps lit tonight."

"Sure does," Jim agreed. Not much for hedging around, he immediately said, "Mr. Claiborne, I'd like your permission to marry Joanna."

Britt Claiborne studied the heavens quietly for a long moment. Then he turned to face the young man. Tears were visible in his eyes. He spoke softly, almost choking. "Every father who has a daughter knows that the inevitable hour will come. It is right and proper that she should marry and have her own family. It's . . . well, son, it's hard to believe she's of marrying age. I still think of her as a little girl. Guess I always will."

"I understand, sir," said Jim.

"Because of what you've done in getting your education, and because of the ambition you show, I'm pleased, Jim, to grant my permission."

"Thank you, sir," said Jim, smiling broadly.

"I would hope that you would give it some time, son," put in Claiborne. "The two of you need to get to know each other better."

"Well, actually, sir," Jim responded uneasily, "in our correspondence, we agreed on November twenty-fifth."

"November twenty-fifth?" echoed Claiborne. "That's—"

"Yes, sir," cut in Jim. "That's the same day you married Joanna's mother. But that will still give Joanna nearly three months to learn all my faults."

"That should be time enough." The silver-haired man chuckled. "You'll find that she has a few too. Stubborn. Has a mind of her own. Got it from her mother."

The two men laughed together.

"Three months will give me time to sell the farm," said Jim. "I want to buy Joanna a nice house in Estes."

"Good," agreed Claiborne. "One thing, son. Just for my peace of mind."

"Yes, sir?"

"You don't wear a gun anymore, do you?"

"No. No, I don't," replied Jim.

"Good, son. Good. I had a boy named Sam. He—"

"Yes, sir. Joanna told me. He was a gunfighter."

"I warned him," said the old man, shaking his head. "Live by the gun, die by the gun. There's always somebody faster. He wouldn't listen. Died in a pool of his own blood over in Utah."

Jim thought it best to clear the air by telling Britt Claiborne about the railroad incident. The old man was a bit disturbed but agreed that Jim had done the right thing.

Presently Jezebel appeared at the door. "Miz Joanna is wonderin' if you gentlemen is through with yo' business."

"Tell her to come out," replied Joanna's father.

In less than a minute the lovely young woman came through the door. She looked at Jim, then her father, in the pale light.

"I've given my wholehearted consent to your becoming Mrs. James Blackburn," said Claiborne.

"Oh, Daddy!" exclaimed Joanna, embracing him joyously, then stepping into Jim's arms.

As Claiborne looked on he said, "Joanna, it means a lot to me that you've set November twenty-fifth for your wedding day."

"Thank you, Daddy," she replied warmly. "I only wish Mother could know."

Suddenly the silver-haired man wheeled around and gazed eastward toward the road.

"What is it, sir?" asked Jim.

"Listen," whispered Claiborne.

From out of the darkness came the sound of hooves. A horse blew. Another nickered.

"Riders," said Joanna.

Claiborne peered hard, trying to see in the moonless night. "Joanna," he said firmly, "you go in the house."

Wordlessly the young woman squeezed Jim's hand, then slipped quietly inside.

Abruptly a voice came out of the dark. "Britt! It's Harry Coyle. I've got some other townsmen with me. Tom Sanders, Cliff Henderson, Stanley Dent, and Morris Wadley."

"What are you boys doing out here this time of night, Harry?" asked Claiborne as the horses approached the house. Turning toward the door momentarily, he said, "Joanna, light a lantern and bring it out."

"We want to see Jim Black," said Coyle, answering Claiborne's question.

"There's no one by the name of Jim Black here," replied the silver-haired man.

"Who you trying to kid, Britt?" asked Coyle. "The whole town saw him head out here this afternoon with Pittman and your daughter. Besides, I don't even need a light to see that's him standing next to you."

"I meant what I said, Harry," said Claiborne. "This young fellow is Jim Blackburn, my future son-in-law. He's an attorney."

"He may have changed his name, Britt," put in Stanley Dent, "but he's still one of the fastest men alive with a gun . . . and he sure knows how to handle himself against a gang of gunmen. I was with him on that train."

"What do you men want of me?" asked Jim as Joanna appeared with the lantern.

"We need your help, Jim," said Harry Coyle. "There's a gang of cutthroats been menacing our town. They've already killed two of our marshals and shot up the town bad. They'll be back any day now. More blood will be shed if they're not stopped."

Before Jim could speak, Joanna answered Coyle. "My father's already told you that Jim Black the gunfighter no longer exists, Mr. Coyle. Jim Blackburn doesn't wear a gun. He's going to open a law office in town."

"Meaning no disrespect, Miss Joanna," said Harry Coyle, "but right now our town needs a lawman more than it needs a lawyer. And as head of the town council, I've come to ask Jim to be that man."

"I thought you hired a new marshal, Harry," put in Britt Claiborne.

"We did, Britt, but he ain't no match for Del Wolfram and

his bunch. Sheb Meade is sixty-six years old. He was a good lawman in his day, but Wolfram's gang will kill him and hang his hide on a flagpole in front of the Fargo office. Least that's what they said they'd do to the next marshal when they killed the last one."

"I'm sorry, boys," said Claiborne, "but Jim here has hung up his gun. He's through with killing."

"Just a moment," Jim interjected. "How many men does Wolfram have in his bunch?"

"Six plus himself," answered Tom Sanders. "Seven of the meanest hombres you ever saw in your life. They'll end up burning the town to the ground if we don't stop them."

"Can you get enough men together to give them a show-down? Make them face an army of guns?" asked Jim.

"Never do it, Jim," answered Harry Coyle. "The men are scared to death. People are ready to pull up stakes and move out. Estes Park will become a ghost town."

"Wolfram and his bunch are savages," said Morris Wadley. "They get their fun watching a town quiver. What they need is to face a man who won't be bullied. We know Jim Black's that kind of man."

Joanna's temper flared. "You mean you're asking Jim to go up against seven brutal killers by himself?"

"With his reputation and expertise with a gun, we're bettin' there won't be any shootin'," said Sanders. "Wolfram's gang'll turn tail and disappear for good."

"Yeah," added Wadley. "We're betting when they realize Estes has a lawman named Jim Black and he eyeballs 'em once, they'll crawl back into their holes."

Joanna turned to Jim. The light of the lantern revealed enough for her to see the look on his face. "Don't let them talk you into it, Jim," she said pleadingly.

"Miss Joanna," said Stanley Dent, "without Jim, Sheb Meade will die and so will the town."

Jim's eyes hardened.

"There's plenty of fearless fast guns around," argued Britt Claiborne. "Why don't you hire one of them?"

"We tried Dave McWatters and Al Yates before the last marshal was killed, Britt," replied Henderson. "They don't care about nobody but themselves."

"What about Dan Hyatt?" asked Claiborne. "He's one of the best. He's over in Kansas somewhere."

"Yeah. Six feet in Kansas sod," snapped Henderson. "Ran into Clate Risley in Dodge City. Risley made Hyatt look like molasses in January."

"Maybe you can get Risley," commented Russ Pittman, who had slipped in unnoticed.

"Not a chance," put in Harry Coyle. "I'd rather have Wolfram around than Risley. That Risley is meaner'n a teased bull. He don't have a gang. Don't need one, as fast and deadly as he is."

"Yeah," agreed Tom Sanders, "if we had Risley, we'd have more trouble than we got right now."

All was quiet for several moments.

Jim broke the silence. "I'd like to help you, men, but I gave Joanna my word. I'm not wearing a gun anymore. I intend to help bring order to this country as a lawyer, not a gunfighter. Besides, Joanna and I are going to be married in a few months. I want to get my office opened in Estes Park and build a future for Joanna and raise a family."

Joanna moved close to Jim, slipping her arm in his. The touch of her hand silently voiced the approval of the words he had just spoken.

"There ain't gonna be no future in Estes Park if the Wolfram bunch isn't stopped," said Morris Wadley.

"And what about Sheb Meade's boy?" asked Stanley Dent. "Wayne's only nineteen. I buried his ma two years ago. If Sheb faces those outlaws, Wayne will be all alone."

Joanna felt Jim's body stiffen. Stanley Dent's words hit him hard. Though Jim did not know the Meades, he was touched by the threat that faced the nineteen-year-old. He could never forget his own cold, hard experience.

Finally Harry Coyle spoke again. "Well, Jim, think it over. We only came to ask you, not to force you." Reining his horse in a tight circle, he said, "Let's go, boys."

As the other horses turned, Britt Claiborne said, "Maybe Wolfram won't be back, Harry. Maybe—"

"No maybe about it," cut in Coyle. "They'll be back. I'm bettin' within two days." The sound of the hooves soon died away.

Jim's insides were churning. He spent a few moments alone with Joanna. He reminded her that he would be seeing Mrs. Bennett in the morning about the office, then would have to visit his own farm the following day.

Holding her close, he said, "I love you, Princess."

"And I love you, Attorney J. W. Blackburn." She smiled despite her fears. "Or maybe you ought to paint your shingle *J. William Blackburn.* Don't you think *J. William* sounds dignified and important?"

They laughed together, then kissed tenderly several times. "It's late, Princess," Jim said, stroking her hair and looking into her eyes. "Time for your beauty sleep."

"Oh, you think I need that, do you?" she asked.

"Since you're the most beautiful woman in the world, I don't want you losing an ounce of your beauty."

"Flatterer," she said. Then she kissed him once more and took the lantern in the house.

Jim made his way to the bunkhouse in the dark. Stanley Dent's last words gnawed at his brain.

Chapter Fourteen

Riding a bay mare provided by the B-Slash-C, Jim headed toward Estes Park as the sun began to rise in the morning sky. As he crossed the bridge at the southern border of the Claiborne property, he thought of the day long ago when Joanna was allowed to ride that far with him.

Rounding the corner onto Main Street, Jim saw a sight that made his blood run cold. A small crowd was gathered around the Wells Fargo office. Dangling upside down, halfway up the flagpole, was the body of a man. With sickening certainty Jim knew it was Marshal Sheb Meade.

The few men who stared at the body stood in stunned silence. Dismounting, Jim saw that Meade's hands were tied behind his back. His throat was cut.

Blood streaked the flagpole. Meade's half-clothed body swayed in the morning breeze, hanging by the ankles. Harry Coyle, the head of the town council, stood at the foot of the pole, looking up the street toward Stanley Dent, who was coming with the hearse. Swinging his gaze to Jim, he said one word: "Wolfram."

Stanley Dent pulled the hearse to a halt and eyed the swaying corpse. "Looks like they carved on his chest before they cut his throat," observed the undertaker.

"I don't know how they got him up there, Stan," said Coyle. "Can you shinny up there and cut him down? The blood on the pole is dry."

Already prepared to do so, Dent had two of the onlookers give him a boost. When he had shinnied past the body, he pulled a knife from under his coat and cut the rope. Meade's body hit the ground with a thump.

While Dent descended the pole, Harry Coyle pulled the body from the blood-soaked ground to a patch of grass, rolling the dead man onto his back. Immediately visible to the gathering crowd were the initials *EW* carved in large letters on the naked chest. One man gagged and hurried away. Almost immediately another followed suit.

Jim's eyes ran from the initials to the gaping wound at the throat. Nausea swept over him. Looking at Coyle, he said, "Does his son know about this?"

"Yes. The kid went crazy. Tom Sanders and Morris Wadley are with him over at Doc Pyle's office right now. Doc was giving him something to settle him down."

"How did it happen?"

Pointing up the street, Coyle said, "Meade house is three blocks up on a side street. Wolfram and his gang somehow got into the house and took the marshal out without waking Wayne. The way the blood's dried, I'd say they must've done it not long after midnight. The kid got up at sunrise, found Sheb missing. Started down to the office looking for him. Spied him hanging on the pole. He commenced to screaming."

"Have any idea what the *EW* stands for?"

"Yep. Exactly. Emil Wolfram. He's Del's younger brother. Sick as they come. Faster'n blue lightning with a six-gun. Meaner'n the devil himself with a knife. Runs around challenging fast guns half the time. The other half he hangs out with his brother's gang."

While two men loaded Sheb Meade's body into the hearse, Stanley Dent approached Coyle and handed him a crinkled piece of paper. "Wolfram jammed this into Sheb's pocket, Harry," he said shakily. "Looks like we're in for it."

Jim set his eyes on the note as Coyle read it aloud:

> If you got another tinhorn around, tell him we'll be back at sundown. We're going to drink the saloons dry, then burn the town.
>
> D. Wolfram

Jim's jaw tensed. "They mean it, don't they?"

"Sheb's body is proof of that," said Coyle with despair.

Fury ignited Jim's blood. It showed in his eyes, burning and deadly. Through clenched teeth he said, "They're not going to torch this town."

Harry Coyle looked at him wonderingly. "You mean you're going to help us?"

"They've got to be stopped sooner or later," Jim said. "It might as well be sooner."

Quickly Coyle rushed to the crowd and informed them that Jim Black was going to stand up to the Wolfram gang. They started gathering around Jim, talking excitedly. Stanley Dent voiced his approval and clucked to the horses, pulling the hearse away from the scene.

Looking at Coyle, Jim said, "Any double-barreled twelve-gauge shotguns in this town?"

"I believe there's one at the marshal's office. Should be some at Hedley's Gun Shop."

"Get them for me. Two of them." He paused a moment, then continued, "One other thing. My gunfighting days are over. If I'm going to put on a gun, it's got to be behind a badge. I want you to swear me in as town marshal." As Coyle nodded his approval Jim quickly added, "But understand one thing. As soon as this is over, I'm a private citizen again."

"Sure, Jim," agreed Coyle. "You go on over to the office. Check on the shotgun there. I'll gather the town council and bring a couple more shotguns from Hedley's on my way back." A puzzled look settled on his face. "Jim, how come you want *two*?"

"I'll explain later. Hop to it," said Jim as he started up the street toward the marshal's office.

Ten minutes later Coyle entered the office bearing two brand-new shotguns. He was trailed by Cliff Henderson, Stanley Dent, Morris Wadley, and Tom Sanders.

Pointing to a lone twelve-gauge on the rack, Jim said, "Glad you brought those. That one's rusted out."

After the town council voiced their appreciation for Jim's change of heart, he was sworn in by Harry Coyle. Then Jim examined the two guns and said, "I need to talk to the blacksmith."

"I'll go get him," volunteered the wiry little undertaker, and he disappeared out the door.

Looking at the others, Jim said, "You think Wolfram will come in from the west?"

"Without a doubt," offered Cliff Henderson.

"Then right at the edge of town I want several wagons positioned on the sides of the street so as to squeeze the gang together. I don't want it obvious. Just make them look like they were parked in a hurry. Get it?"

"We got it," replied Morris Wadley.

"I want the people off the streets by two o'clock."

"Yes, sir, Jim," said Coyle.

"Now, as soon as I talk to the blacksmith, I've got to ride out to the B-Slash-C and get my sidearm. I could use another one, but I'd rather have the one I'm used to."

"Hey," said Cliff Henderson, "what about Jim's badge?"

"The only one we had was on Sheb's shirt," answered Coyle. "It'll be wherever the gang ripped it off him."

"I'll find it," said Wadley, moving out the door.

"How's young Meade?" Jim asked Tom Sanders.

"Doc got him settled down. He's asleep now. Doc says he'll probably sleep till midafternoon."

"Poor kid," mused Jim aloud, remembering the day his own family was murdered.

Heavy footsteps sounded on the board sidewalk, then a large bald man entered the office, followed by Stanley Dent. "Jim Black," said Dent, "this is Marv Miller, our blacksmith."

The two men shook hands. "You've changed some," said Miller, "since I seen you cut down Duncan Wheeler."

"A little," agreed Jim.

"What can I do for you?"

Placing his hands on the two double-barreled shotguns on the desk, Jim said, "Can you cut about half off the ends of these barrels?"

Miller's eyes widened. "Sure can, but—"

"I'll be back by one o'clock. Can you do it by then?"

"Yeah, but—"

"But what?"

"With them barrels sawed off like that . . . at very close range they'll cut an army in two."

"Yes," said Jim coldly. "That's what I'm counting on."

Joanna Claiborne trotted the big Appaloosa up and down the fence along the road, her eyes darting periodically toward the south. Something within her was signaling that all was not well. Jim should have been back by now.

The look in his eyes last night was troubling her. The man was a born fighter. Certainly he would do well contending for a client in a courtroom. But somehow he seemed to have some deep, unnamed force within. Of all the men on that train, for instance, why was it Jim Black who stood against the outlaws?

There. She had done it. Even in her own mind Joanna had thought of him as Jim Black. She shook her head. *No,* she told herself. *I will never let Jim Black come into our lives again.*

Suddenly there he was, galloping the bay mare down the road. There was something in the way he rode. . . .

Spurring the Appaloosa, she met him at the gate. "Jim, something's wrong," she said apprehensively.

Nodding soberly, he said, "Wolfram and his gang murdered the marshal last night and strung his body on the flagpole. They're coming back at sundown to burn the town."

The Cherokee face turned gray. Her lips pulled thin. "You've come to get your gun. Jim Black is alive again."

"Joanna, I can't let them burn down our town. You and I have plans—"

"I suppose you'll be all alone," she cut in.

The big man hedged on the truth slightly. "I . . . uh . . . I'll have two friends with me. One on the right and one on the left."

"Who?"

"I don't have time to explain. I've got to get back."

"Why can't they hire another marshal?"

"They did. Me."

The woman's mouth sagged open. Jim reached out and touched her arm. "As soon as it's over I'll resign. We already have that agreement."

Joanna's eyes grew cold. "If you're dead, you won't need to resign."

"Look, honey, somebody's got to do it."

"Why does it have to be you?" Tears were visible in her eyes.

"There's no way I can explain it," said Jim, his jaw squared. "I just have to do what I can to save the town."

"But you promised," she said, her lower lip trembling. "You said you'd never wear a gun again."

Jim shook his head. "I—"

"If you will break promises before we're married, then you'll—"

"No, I won't, Princess," he said, lifting his hand from her arm. "I must go. I love you."

Jim spurred the bay and galloped toward the bunkhouse. Joanna rode slowly to the house and dismounted. As she stepped up on the porch the tall man rode past, the big Colt on his hip. He waved. "See you later. I love you!"

The afternoon passed quickly in Estes Park. Wagons and buckboards were placed at the west end of Main Street, so that seven horses would have to crowd close at that point. Jim loaded the two sawed-off shotguns and walked to an old dilapidated barn at the south edge of town. Thumbing back all four hammers, he held one shotgun in each hand, bracing the butts against his shoulders. Squaring with the side of the barn, he checked his distance and fired one barrel of each gun. The charges tore into the wood, leaving two large holes, edges smoking.

Shifting a few feet to the left and stepping two paces closer, he fired the other two barrels. Jim studied the difference in the holes, thought about it for a moment, then returned into town.

As the sun touched the mountains to the west, the streets of Estes Park were clear. Men crouched behind windows in buildings on both sides of the street. Jim Blackburn, armed with the two sawed-off shotguns and his Colt .45, waited in a doorway at what he had calculated was just the proper distance from the wagons.

Soon the sun dropped behind the mountains. At the east end of the street Russ Pittman appeared, riding alone. Jim threw a quick glance to the west. Seeing nothing, he shouted, "Russ! Get off the street!"

Quickly Pittman slid out of the saddle, tied his horse to the hitching rail, and moved onto the boardwalk. He ran the remaining way until he stood in front of Jim. He wore his revolver. "Miss Joanna asked me to come, Jim. She didn't want you to do this alone."

"Russ, I appreciate it, but you could get yourself killed."

"What about you?" retaliated Pittman.

"It's my job," said Jim, pointing with his chin to the tin star on his shirt. "Now, Russ, when I go in the street, I'm going fast. I've got to time it just right. I've got to catch seven riders while they're between those wagons and buckboards. I want you to stay here. You understand?"

"Yeah, but—"

"No buts," said Jim flatly. Suddenly his eye caught movement on the hills due west. He studied the rugged terrain closely. Abruptly six riders materialized from the deep shadows caused by the setting sun. Jim squinted, counting carefully. Yes, he was right. There were only six. Where was the seventh?

They were riding abreast. Jim hoped they stayed that way. As they drew near, tension built in him . . . a familiar tension, like before a gunfight. Only this was different. Instead of one man, there were six. This time he would step into it with two guns already drawn. Shotguns. Sawed off to be more deadly.

The riders were coming at a slow walk. They were now fifty yards from the target area. Jim thumbed back all four hammers, one at a time. Each made a dry, hollow clicking sound. The comforting weight of the Colt .45 hung at his hip.

Jim waited, peering around the edge of the doorway. He could hear Russ Pittman's heavy breathing. The outlaws approached the place where the wagons were parked. Staying abreast, they crowded closer. Jim's plan, if he had to use the shotguns, was to make sure of getting the four on his left, then using the Colt to bring down the other two.

Bracing the butts of the big guns against his muscular shoulders, he raised the muzzles and made a dash to the center of the street. The six horsemen quickly drew rein, in respect to the four menacing barrels that suddenly stared at them like hungry eyes. The outlaws were positioned exactly as Jim had planned. They sat in one line, side by side, silhouetted against an ominous bloodred sky.

For a brief moment Jim felt a strange sensation as the six horsemen suddenly became blurry. He blinked, and the blur cleared.

"Hold it right there!" he bellowed. "Which one of you is Del Wolfram?"

The man on the third horse from Jim's right eyed him with disdain and gave a predatory grin. "Well, boys," he said, "we got us a punk marshal who thinks he's a man because he could sprout a mustache!"

Wolfram was a large, ugly man. Below his wide-brimmed hat glared a pair of mean, slitted eyes. He had an unsightly crooked nose and thick, purple lips.

As Wolfram's cohorts laughed, Jim said, "You're under arrest, Wolfram. All six of you. Where's the seventh?"

The outlaw leader laughed hoarsely. "Little brother Emil is absent, teacher," he retorted insolently. "He's ridin' over to Montrose to challenge a so-called fast gun." The other riders snickered. "He'll be back with the body in a few days." The snickering turned into laughter.

"I'll get him later," said Jim steadily. "Now, you six boys reach down real easy, lift your guns from the holsters, and let them drop to the ground."

A wicked frown darkened Wolfram's face. "Now, sonny," he growled, "I don't want to have to kill you."

"You're a liar," Jim said. "You'd get just as much joy out of killing me as you did killing Sheb Meade."

Wolfram's hands rested solidly on the pommel of his saddle. "Well, before I kill you, kid," said the large man, "I'd like to know your name. Like to make it as personal as I can when I terminate a tinhorn."

"My name's Blackb—" Jim checked his tongue. "Black. Jim Black."

Wolfram's slitted eyes widened. "Not *the* Jim Black? You're the dude killed Duncan Wheeler? Shot up half the Hench Barkley gang a few days ago in Kansas?"

"The same," said Jim, holding the shotguns steady.

Wolfram looked both ways at his men and started to speak, when from out of nowhere a high-pitched male voice shouted, "Give me one of those shotguns, Black!"

Jim could hear the speaker running up behind him, but dared not take his eyes off the outlaws.

"They killed my pa!" yelled the tall, slender youth as he came alongside Jim. "Give me one of those shotguns. I'm gonna kill 'em!"

"Get back, Wayne," breathed Jim, seeing the glint of opportunity leap into Del Wolfram's eyes.

"They cut my pa's throat," argued Wayne Meade. "Then carved up his chest! I got a right to kill 'em!"

It was evident the outlaws' fingers were twitching, getting ready to make a move. Suddenly the furious youth snatched Jim's Colt from his holster and, pulling back the hammer, brought it to bear.

The six horsemen went for their guns. The .45 in Meade's

hand fired a split second before Jim's two shotguns roared. Right behind the first shots came the other two barrels.

The .45 slug caught Wolfram's horse square between the eyes. The animal stayed erect long enough for Jim's second charge to rip into the outlaw leader's chest. Horse and rider went down together, Wolfram toppling backward from the powerful blow.

Jim's guns killed the other three to the left instantly. Partially stunned, the man to Wolfram's left fell from his horse. Jim whirled to find Wayne Meade while the last outlaw aloft fought his frightened horse, trying to get a bead on the man wearing the star.

Suddenly, from the boardwalk, a gun belched fire and the last outlaw flipped off his horse, dead. The man stung with the buckshot was on the ground swinging his gun on Jim Black. Russ Pittman's revolver roared again. The slug tore a hole in the outlaw's head, flinging him savagely to the ground.

Jim looked at Wayne Meade, who had stumbled and fallen in the excitement. Then he swung his gaze to big Russ Pittman, who smiled at Jim, the gun in his hand still smoking.

"Thanks, pard," said Jim, smiling broadly.

Pittman wiped a sleeve across his mouth. "I owe you one," he said. "Remember?"

The people of Estes Park crawled out of the buildings like cockroaches from the woodwork. A pall of gun smoke hung in the air. Russ Pittman holstered his gun while Jim leaned over and pulled his revolver from the hand of Wayne Meade. The youth sat in the street, expecting a scolding from the man wearing the star.

"I understand how you feel," said Jim softly, "but you went at it the wrong way. You almost got both of us killed."

"I'm sorry, Mr. Black," responded Wayne apologetically. "It's just that—"

"I understand, kid. My whole family was murdered a few years ago."

"They were?"

Jim nodded.

"What did you do?"

"Went after the killers."

"Kill 'em?"

"Yeah."

"There's still one of the Wolframs left," said Wayne Meade, rising to his feet. "The one who carved his initials in Pa's chest after he was dead."

Jim was sure the carving was done *before* Sheb Meade was killed, but he decided to leave well enough alone. It was best that Wayne not know his father had suffered. "We'll let the law handle Emil Wolfram," said Jim flatly.

"What law? Are *you* goin' after him?"

Before Jim could answer, his attention was drawn toward the east end of the street. The spotted white coat of the big Appaloosa looked orange in the glow of the sunset. Joanna road toward him at a trot.

Meade joined Jim in watching the rider draw near.

"Looks like she had to come check on you for herself," observed Pittman.

Joanna drew Chief to a halt, her eyes fixed on the tall, broad-shouldered man. Sliding from the saddle, she rushed into his arms. Clinging to him, she said, "Are you all right?"

"Yes, Princess. I'm fine. Russ helped me. They're all dead."

The woman lifted her head from Jim's wide chest, eyeing the dead horse and scattered bodies of the Wolfram gang. She gasped, burying her face in his shirt.

"It's all right, darling," said Jim soothingly. "The Wolfram bunch won't burn this town or any other one again."

"There's still one Wolfram left," said Wayne Meade. "What about him?"

"His brother said he'd gone to Montrose," answered Jim. "I'll wire the sheriff over there to pick him up."

"And what if he doesn't do it?" said the youth.

Harry Coyle and Morris Wadley detached themselves from the crowd of onlookers and approached. "That was a mighty fine job of shooting, Jim," interrupted Coyle. "How's about signing on as permanent marshal?"

Joanna shot Coyle a hot glare.

"I talked it over with the council just now. We're prepared to offer you double the salary we've been paying."

Joanna started to speak, but before she got the words out, Jim said, "I can't do it, Mr. Coyle."

"Why not?" asked Coyle stubbornly.

"I told you at the ranch. I gave Joanna my word. Would you have a man go back on his word?"

Coyle pursed his lips and thought about it for a moment.

Slowly he lifted his eyes to the beautiful half-breed woman. "Miss Joanna," he said softly, "this town has got to have a lawman. It needs protection. Would you let Jim off the hook?"

Joanna held Coyle hard with her emerald eyes, then shifted them to the man she was to marry. Jim tried to look as neutral as possible. "Is this what you want?" she asked.

"Nothing has changed," he answered steadily. "I plan to be Attorney James Blackburn in this town. I'd be willing to keep the badge on until a new marshal can be hired. The town should not be left unprotected."

Joanna looked back at Coyle. "Would you accept him on a temporary basis?" she asked. "I mean begin looking earnestly for a new marshal tomorrow?"

"Yes, ma'am," conceded Coyle. "We'll start looking tomorrow."

Setting her eyes back on Jim, she said, "All right, darling. I'll let you off the hook. For the sake of our town I'll put up with that gun on your hip until they can find a new marshal."

Grinning broadly, Coyle thanked Joanna. Other citizens who stood nearby expressed their appreciation to Jim for keeping the badge. Russ Pittman eyed the young woman and grinned, but she did not return it.

"You didn't answer my question, Mr. Black," butted in Wayne Meade.

"I'll wire the sheriff in Montrose," Jim repeated.

"If he doesn't get Emil Wolfram," said young Meade heatedly, "I'm goin' after him myself!"

"And get yourself killed," put in Harry Coyle. "Emil is one of the fastest guns around."

Wayne Meade turned away, muttering something no one could hear. Stiff-legged, he headed up the street toward home.

Stanley Dent had arrived with a wagon and was giving directions as several townsmen loaded the bodies.

Turning to Pittman, Jim said, "Russ, I'm going over to the telegraph office and send a message to the sheriff at Montrose. You stay with Joanna. I'll be right back. Then we can head for the ranch."

"You'll have to wait till morning, Jim," said Morris Wadley. "Telegraph office is closed for the day."

Jim threw a glance at the dying light in the west. "Guess it is getting late," he said idly. "I'll ride back in the morning. Have to see Mrs. Bennett anyhow."

As Joanna swung into the saddle and Russ Pittman started down the street toward his horse, the crowd moved toward Jim, voicing their approval of the way he had handled the Wolfram gang.

Chapter Fifteen

A week passed, during which time Jim was unable to talk to the widow of Fred Bennett about renting the office for his law practice. She had gone to Denver and did not return until eight days after the shoot-out. Jim intended to talk to her the morning she arrived. He had already visited his farm near Fort Collins and made arrangements for someone to take care of it until it could be sold.

As interim marshal, Jim was staying at the Water Wheel Hotel as a guest of the town. After breakfast he emerged onto the boardwalk and was greeted by Harry Coyle, who informed him that a new marshal had been hired. Word was expected soon as to just when the new man would be arriving in Estes Park. Jim was elated. He knew Joanna would be happy to hear the news.

Turning from Coyle, Jim looked up to see Britt Claiborne riding up the street. He noticed how the silver-haired man sat in the saddle just like his daughter—straight and proud.

Claiborne raised his hand. "Howdy, Jim." He smiled.

"Good morning, sir," Jim said, returning the greeting. "Have some good news. The town council has hired a new marshal. He'll be coming shortly."

The rancher's smile broadened. "That *is* good news, son. I know of one young lady who'll be mighty glad to hear it."

"Yes, sir." Jim nodded. "I'm sure she will."

At that moment Jim saw Mrs. Bennett coming down the street in her surrey. His heart quickened. "You in town on business?" he asked Claiborne.

"Yes," replied the silver-haired man. "At the bank. I'll see you afterward."

"Fine," Jim said. As Claiborne rode on, the young marshal hurried toward the office of the late Fred Bennett.

An hour later Claiborne's horse was still tied at the rail

outside the bank. Jim hastened toward the building in high spirits. Mrs. Bennett had consented to rent her husband's office at a modest fee to Estes Park's new attorney. As Jim neared the bank he remembered Joanna's words: *"Maybe you ought to paint your shingle J. William Blackburn. Don't you think J. William sounds dignified and important?"*

Jim chuckled to himself. Maybe he would do just that. It might help the town to forget Jim Black, the gunfighter. At any rate, he was excited about closing the deal with Mrs. Bennett. Now he had double good news for Joanna.

Entering the bank, Jim spied Britt Claiborne sitting in front of Steve Shea's desk. The bank president stood and offered his hand as Jim drew near. Shea was a tall, wiry man, with thinning hair and a heavy mustache. Seemingly young for a bank president, he carried a winsome smile. "Howdy, Jim," he said warmly. "Britt was just telling me that you and Joanna are going to tie the knot in November."

"Yes, sir," said Jim, releasing Shea's hand. "I'll be in soon to open an account. Just closed the deal with Mrs. Bennett on her husband's office."

"Good," replied Shea. "We can always use more money in this bank." He rubbed his hands together in a joking way.

While Jim, Claiborne, and Shea discussed the Wolfram shoot-out, the coming new marshal, and Jim's future as an attorney, two somber-faced riders eased their way up the street. One was a short, stocky man in his early fifties. The other was tall and very thin, had a slender nose that resembled an eagle's beak, and a protruding Adam's apple under a sharply pointed chin and bony jaw. He was in his late twenties, with a mean look in his gray eyes. A jagged scar split his left eyebrow. From his narrow hips hung a pair of pearl-handled Colt .45s.

People along the street eyed the two men cautiously while the pair reined in and dismounted at the Salty Dog Saloon. As they passed through the swinging doors, Estes Park's barber thought that one of them looked familiar, but he wasn't certain. He didn't want to spread false rumors that Clate Risley was in town. It would only upset people.

A half hour had passed when Britt Claiborne lifted himself from his chair and said, "Well, Steve, I could keep talking all day, but I'd better head back for the ranch."

Jim rose from his chair and stood to full height. Shea, at six feet himself, looked up at the young man, then at Britt Claiborne. "Joanna landed a big one, didn't she?"

The bank president escorted the two men to the door and pulled it open. "See you later, gentlemen," he said.

"You can bank on it," quipped Claiborne.

As Jim and the older man stepped onto the boardwalk, a booming voice cut the air. "Jim Black!"

Jim stopped in his tracks and turned slowly. Claiborne stood motionless, eyes riveted on the two strangers moving to the middle of the street.

"One of you men call my name?" asked Jim softly.

"Allow me to introduce myself," said the stocky man. "My name is Hench Barkley."

The name registered instantly, but Jim disguised it. "That supposed to mean something?" he asked innocently.

"You were on a train a couple weeks ago. Killed some friends. Kept me from layin' my hands on a lot of gold."

"Wouldn't be a problem if you'd work at making an honest living," said Jim calmly.

"I figure I owe you," breathed Barkley hotly.

"So who's your playmate?" Jim snapped, nodding to the tall, bony man with the expressionless face.

Hench Barkley's eyes widened in cruel enjoyment. He pronounced the name with a smirk. "Clate Risley."

Jim's gunfighting days had taught him how to hold his features cold and impassive. He said evenly, "Don't complain to me. Man has a choice who he runs with."

Risley's gray eyes narrowed menacingly. He looked from side to side, as if gauging the number of gathering onlookers. He wanted as big a crowd as possible. "So Jim Black is wearin' a badge now? Ain't that somethin' to write home about? If you think that badge'll save your skin, you got another think comin'. I'm callin' you, Black."

Jim gave the skinny man a wintry look. "Why are you so anxious to die, Risley? You have no argument with me."

A sneer pulled at the gunman's thin lips. "Think you can outdraw me, eh?"

"No doubt about it, mister. Now, the best thing for you to do is take your friend here and ride on. That way you'll be around to see the sun rise tomorrow."

"Your bluff won't work, Black!" hissed the wiry gunhawk, glancing around at the crowd. "If you don't face me right now, you're yellow!"

"Jim can shoot you three times while you're hunting your gun butts, Risley!" came a male voice from the crowd.

Risley sneered and spat. "Make him prove it," he retorted, eyes glued on Estes Park's marshal.

Jim knew there was no escaping it. Clate Risley was too eager to climb the gunfighter's ladder. Killing Jim Black would give him great stature.

Jim stepped into the street and squared himself with his challenger. Hench Barkley moved toward the boardwalk. The crowd gave the two men in the middle of the street a wide berth.

"You've got your fight, mister," Jim said through his teeth. "Make your play." He had one brief thought about Spence Landford's faceless man, then quickly dismissed it.

Risley wasted no time. His hands darted downward in a swift, smooth movement. At the same moment Jim saw Barkley drawing his gun, a move he had half expected. Risley would be by far the fastest, and Jim's hand was a blur as he drew and fired, the bullet shattering Risley's heart.

Jim swung and fired at Barkley, killing him on his feet, but the fraction of time it took to shoot both men gave Barkley a chance to get off one shot. As Barkley's weapon discharged, the muzzle swung toward the crowd. The slug hit Britt Claiborne in the temple, and he fell to the boardwalk, dead. Women screamed.

The pearl grips were in Clate Risley's hands, the guns still in their holsters. He lay still, his breast unmoving, sightless eyes staring at the blue Colorado sky. Barkley was lying in a crumpled heap.

Jim rushed to where Britt Claiborne had fallen. His heart felt like lead as he looked into the lifeless, ashen face. He stood up slowly and said, "Help me carry him to the doctor's office. Somebody ride out to the ranch and bring Joanna. Don't tell her he's dead. Just tell her he's been shot. Let me handle the rest."

Immediately men stepped in to help, and one jumped onto his horse and rode out of town.

Forty minutes later Joanna Claiborne and Russ Pittman

rode the wagon to a stop in front of the physician's office. As Pittman helped Joanna from the wagon, Jim emerged through the door, his face ashen.

Joanna took one look at Jim and felt a pang of fear. "Jim," she said shakily, "is Daddy . . . all right?"

Jim moved forward grimly and grasped her shoulders. The young woman's heart froze, knowing what was coming.

"He's dead," said Jim soberly, pulling her close to him. "So is the man who killed him."

Joanna's eyes were filled with tears. Pushing herself away, she said angrily, "You think it's all right, just because you killed the man who did it? You think that will bring my father back?"

"Joanna—"

"You and your gun!"

"Joanna . . . I had no choice."

The woman's face twisted. "If you had never worn a gun in the first place, there wouldn't have been some gunslick trying to get you into a gunfight."

Jim was silent, searching for the proper words.

"Well, that *was* it, wasn't it?" she asked, her voice edged with bitterness.

"Yes, but—"

Joanna stepped around him, sobbing, and dashed through the office door.

"Jim, I'm sorry," said Russ Pittman. "I—"

"Why don't you go in there with her, Russ? I'm afraid I can't do her much good right now."

Pittman nodded and went inside.

Several townsmen were gathered around Jim when Joanna and Russ came out ten minutes later. Joanna's eyes were swollen and red-rimmed. She faced Jim briefly and said, "I don't ever want to see you again. Don't ever show up at the ranch. Russ will bring your things into town." With that she stepped to the wagon and climbed aboard.

"Jim," said Russ apologetically, "she don't mean it. She's not herself. She—"

"Let's go, Russ," demanded the young woman.

With his heart aching, Jim watched the wagon move up the street and disappear around the first corner. As Jim turned away sadly, he nearly collided with Wayne Meade.

"Mr. Black," said the youth in his high-pitched voice, "the sheriff at Montrose sent a wire back. Emil Wolfram killed the man he was after and lit out for Grand Junction."

"There's a new marshal coming," said Jim coldly. "Tell him to contact the law in Grand Junction."

Wayne Meade swore. "You know the law ain't gonna do nothin'. I'm goin' after Wolfram myself."

"And wind up gut-shot with his initials carved on your own chest!" said Jim angrily.

"Not if I was taught how to handle a six-shooter properly," came the rejoinder.

Jim tried to control himself. "Forget it, kid. Believe me, even if you learned well and took out Emil, it wouldn't be worth it."

Meade's voice broke from high to low to high again as he swore, saying, "Emil Wolfram's gonna pay, Jim."

Jim's next words spilled out: "Look, kid, once you strap on a gun, you can never take it off." Like a flash, scenes from his own past leaped into his mind. Sheriff Floyd Cashman . . . Spence Landford . . . both had warned him exactly in the same way.

"I don't care," said the lanky youth. "I'll wear a gun till I'm a hundred years old."

"Gunfighters rarely live a quarter that long, Wayne," said Jim, knowing his words would fall on deaf ears. "Most of them are barely past twenty when they meet their faceless man."

"Faceless man?" echoed Wayne.

"Yeah. The one that's faster than you. You don't know who he is, but as sure as May follows April, he's there. Waiting. Waiting for the day when he holsters his smoking gun and walks away, while you lie dead in the dirt."

"I ain't got time to worry about no faceless man," said Wayne. "I just care about one thing. I want to square off with Emil Wolfram. I want him to know who I am just before I kill him."

To Jim it was like listening to himself three years before. "I'm not teaching you, kid," he said. "I don't want you on my conscience."

"Okay," said Wayne sharply. "I'll get somebody else to teach me. One way or another, I'm goin' after Wolfram."

Jim could not believe it. This was like a reenactment of his own bitter past. He did not know what to say or do.

"So I'll be on your conscience either way, won't I?" taunted the youth. Then he turned and ran away.

The following morning Russ Pittman came by the marshal's office and informed Jim that Britt Claiborne's funeral would be the next day.

Jim attended, sitting in the back pew of the church and standing on the fringe of the crowd at the cemetery. If Joanna knew he was there, she did not show it.

A week later Harry Coyle visited Jim at the marshal's office, telling him that the man he had hired as Estes Park's new marshal had learned who his predecessor was and did not like the idea of following Jim Black. Certain he could not fill Black's boots, he'd decided not to come. Coyle had asked Jim if he would consider keeping the badge on his chest permanently.

Jim thought it over. Right now the town needed a lawman more than it needed a lawyer, and he had no desire to go back to his farm in Fort Collins. Since he had lost Joanna, it really did not make any difference what he did. He told Coyle he would keep the job.

Late summer passed into fall. The air in Estes Park took on a brisk feeling. By mid-October snow had already fallen several times and the days were cold and snappy.

Russ Pittman had invited Joanna Claiborne to ride into town with him several times, but on each occasion she had refused. Jezebel had scolded her, telling her she needed to mingle with people, but the moody young woman had offered flimsy excuses for staying at home. It was plain that she did not want to go near Estes Park.

In town, Marshal Jim Blackburn was sitting at his desk, his mind on Joanna, when Stanley Dent stopped in, holding a newspaper.

"Have you seen the paper, Jim?" asked Dent, closing the door against the biting air.

"No," replied the marshal. "Something in particular?"

"Yeah," said Stanley. "About Wayne Meade."

Jim's eyebrows arched. "Wayne Meade?"

"Uh huh. Here, read it."

Jim took the newspaper from Dent's hand and spread it before him. The lettering was blurred. He had been having trouble seeing some things lately but had not let on to anyone. He held his head so Stanley could not see him squinting, trying to make out the words.

"It's not on the front page, Jim," said Dent. "It's on page three."

"Oh," said the marshal. "I, uh . . . I have some things to tend to right now, Stanley. Could you leave it with me? I'll get a chance to read it later."

"Oh, sure." Dent smiled. "Just keep it. See you later." He passed through the doorway and was gone.

Jim waited a few minutes, then put on his mackinaw and walked to Doc Pyle's office. He was glad to find the physician alone. Pyle looked up from a large medical book he was reading when Jim entered.

"Howdy, Jim," the doctor said, smiling. "This social or serious?"

"Serious for a man in my profession."

"Oh?"

"Yeah, I think I need glasses. Can't even read this newspaper."

"Well, I guess I'd better examine your eyes," said Pyle, standing up.

"First I want you to read me something from page three— would you, Doc?"

Pyle took the paper and read to Jim that Wayne Meade had found Emil Wolfram in jail in Utah and had helped him escape. To Wolfram's surprise, Meade had then told him who he was and had killed him in a gunfight. Meade had subsequently gotten into trouble with the law and taken up the gunfighter's life. He was now himself an outlaw and had just killed a gunfighter in Grand Junction, Colorado, by the name of Harley Carter.

Jim was amazed. Carter was one of the best. Apparently Wayne had found someone to teach him who knew his stuff. Jim was sorry for Wayne, knowing he would die one day at the hands of his faceless man.

The physician examined Jim's eyes, then gave him a sight test. He asked if Jim had gotten something in his eyes, and

Jim told him of the kerosene incident on the train and explained that he had not since been to a doctor about it because he thought everything was all right. There had been moments, he said, when his vision had gone fuzzy, but the sensation always went away, so he had figured it was nothing serious.

Grimly, Pyle said, "Jim, it doesn't look good. But I'm not a specialist. You've got to see one though. As soon as possible. There's one in Denver."

"Doc, I can't go to Denver," said Jim. "I've got to be here to watch over this town."

"I know him personally, Jim," said the doctor. "I'll get him to come here. It will cost, but it has to be done."

"I don't mind the expense, Doc," replied the marshal. "You just get him here." Moving toward the door, he added, "You'll keep this to yourself, won't you? It's best that word not get out that I'm having trouble with my eyesight."

"I understand," said Pyle. "I'll tell no one."

Jim thanked the physician and left the office, visibly shaken by the interview.

Six days later Jim returned to Dr. Pyle's office and listened to the verdict of the Denver specialist, Dr. Albert Morrow.

"It's a delayed reaction, Marshal," said Morrow glumly. "I'm surprised you've gone this long without losing your sight. But I must be honest with you—the sight is going. You'll be blind within two months."

The news hit Jim like a sledgehammer. He was quiet for a long time before he spoke to Pyle. "Listen, Doc. I can still see well enough to handle my job for a while longer. You don't need to tell the town council, do you?"

"Telling them is your department, Jim," replied the doctor. "I expect you'll handle that when it's time."

"Thanks, Doc. Let's just keep this like it's been—just between you and me, okay?"

"Sure, Jim," said Pyle. "Whatever you think is best."

Time passed quickly the next two weeks. The deterioration of Jim's eyesight progressed exactly as Dr. Morrow had predicted. Jim could tell it as the days passed. Dr. Pyle was dropping in daily to read his mail to him.

It was nearly noon on the second day of November, and Jim stared blankly out his office window. Dr. Pyle would be by at any moment.

Suddenly the door burst open, letting in the brisk air. "Marshal, we got trouble!" It was the excited voice of Morris Wadley.

"What's the matter?" asked Jim, standing.

"Clate Risley's younger brother just rode into town. He's making no bones about it. Says he's here to even the score with you."

"Where is he?" Jim knew he might just as well handle it immediately.

"At the Pink Lady Saloon. Name's Clint. He's almost a dead ringer for his brother."

"Thanks, Morris," said Jim evenly. "I'll handle it."

"You betcha," said Wadley, then left.

Jim slipped the Colt from its holster, released the cylinder, and ran his fingertips over the six cartridge heads. Snapping the cylinder in place, he stepped outside, easing the gun into the holster.

He was glad it was midday and the sun was shining brightly. With quick, determined steps, the tall man made his way to the Pink Lady Saloon. Standing in the street, he faced the closed door and shouted, *"Clint Risley!"*

Within a few seconds the door swung open and a slender form moved through it. Jim could not bring the facial features into focus but could see the man was built like Clate Risley. The dark shadow of the door made a poor background. He had to lure the man out into the sunlight.

"I'm the sheriff here," said Jim, his voice remarkably calm. "I hear you're looking for Jim Black."

"Yep," said Risley.

"Well, you found him."

"Didn't know you was still wearin' a badge."

"That make any difference?"

"Nope."

As Jim talked he backpedaled slowly. As if drawn by a magnet, Clint Risley stepped off the board sidewalk into the dust of the street and the brilliant November light. Huddling in the brisk air, a crowd gathered.

"Now that you've found me," said Jim coldly, "what's next?"

"You die for killin' my brother," snapped Risley.

"He came looking for me," said Jim. "Just like you."

"Only this time it's *your* funeral," said the gunman through his teeth.

"He didn't have a funeral," said Jim. "We don't hold funerals for—"

Jim's failing eyes caught the movement of Risley's hand. His own gun was out and spewing fire before the thin man could put his into use. Jim's slug tore into the bony chest and out the back. Lying on the ground, Risley coughed twice. Blood trickled from the corners of his mouth. He groaned, coughed again, and died.

Chapter Sixteen

On November 18 a lone horseman rode through the gate of the B-Slash-C Ranch. Dismounting at the house, the young man tramped through the snow, ascended the porch steps, and knocked on the door. To the black woman who opened the door, he said, "I have a letter here for Miss Joanna Claiborne. The marshal in Estes sent me with it."

"Thank you, son," said Jezebel. "Y'all look a little cold. Would you like to come in?"

"Thank you, ma'am," said the messenger, "but I need to get back."

As the young man rode away, Joanna emerged from the kitchen. "What is it, Jezebel?"

"A letter from Mr. Marshal Burntblack, honey," she replied, extending the envelope.

Joanna took it without comment and walked up the stairs. Stepping into her room, she closed the door and tore open the envelope. Having received dozens of letters from Jim while he was in school, she immediately noticed the marked difference in the handwriting.

November 18

My Darling Princess,

We were to be married one week from today. I love you.

Always,
Jim

Joanna did not come downstairs for lunch. Jezebel waited until nearly suppertime. Still the young woman had not left her room. Sighing, Jezebel mounted the stairs, tiptoed to Joanna's door, and listened. There was no sound within. The black woman tapped lightly on the door. "Miz Joanna," she called softly. No answer. "Miz Joanna."

The bed squeaked and footsteps approached the door. As it opened, Jezebel fixed her gaze on Joanna's swollen, red-rimmed eyes. "Aw, honey," she said, "why cry yo' heart out? Why don't you just give in and go to yo' man?"

Joanna dropped her tear-stained face on the big woman's shoulder. Jezebel held her close, patting her back.

"Oh, Jezebel," said Joanna, "I want to see him so bad. I love him so much." She sniffed. "But it would only make matters worse. I just couldn't be the wife of a man who lives by the gun. I couldn't stand it when he died by the gun. There's no way I could live with that dreadful moment hanging over my head. It's better that I don't see him."

Jezebel bit her tongue.

Later at the supper table Joanna picked at her food. Jezebel had invited Russ Pittman to eat with them, hoping he could somehow cheer up the despondent young woman.

"You're going to waste away to a shadow, Miss Joanna, if you don't eat," said Pittman.

"I guess I wouldn't really care," responded Joanna.

"Why don't you let me ride into town and bring Jim back with me?"

Fear registered in Joanna's face. "I don't want to talk about it, Russ," she snapped.

Silence prevailed for several moments, then Pittman introduced another subject. "I was talking to Stanley Dent in town yesterday."

"Mmm-hmm," Joanna commented with no enthusiasm.

"Seems Wayne Meade has become a ruthless, blood-hungry gunfighter."

"Oh?"

"Been challenging the top guns from Cheyenne to Albuquerque. Killing them right and left."

"Too bad," mused Joanna. "He was a nice boy." She thought quietly for a moment. "I really couldn't blame him for feeling as he did about Emil Wolfram, after what that man did to Sheb. Too bad he couldn't have thrown the gun away after he killed Wolfram."

"Actually," said Pittman, "Wayne and Jim were forced into the same situation. Only Jim turned out good. He put a badge behind his gun. But Wayne, he hasn't turned out . . .

too good." Pittman let the last few words trail off. The mention of Jim stiffened Joanna's face.

Without a word the young owner of the B-Slash-C laid her napkin on the table and ran from the kitchen. Pittman and Jezebel looked at each other, shaking their heads.

Jim Blackburn had set November 25 as his last day as marshal of Estes Park. The town council had been made aware of his failing eyesight a month earlier and had been sworn to secrecy. He wanted to give them time to find a new man. The same day Jim sent the note to Joanna, Harry Coyle informed him that a new man had been hired. He would be in Estes Park to take over on November 26.

Jim had managed to conceal his growing blindness from the townsfolk. But now he was beginning to bump into furniture and fumble for door handles.

The big man had pondered much about his future of late. One thing was sure—as soon as he resigned, word of his blindness must be spread fast or he'd be gunned down helplessly. Once his blindness became known, he would be a has-been. No longer would he be a potential stepping-stone for young gunslicks. For them he would be the same as dead.

But what to do? Where to go? Whatever the future held for him, it would include an aching, dark loneliness. Without the beautiful half-Cherokee woman who had once so brightened his life, there would be a haunting void. At least up till now he had had his profession. He was the champion and protector of the people. As of November 25 even that would be gone. Of course, he still had his legal education. But who would want a blind attorney?

One thing Jim would always carry with him—the sweet memory of Joanna; that, and the dream they had once had. But fate had dealt him a savage blow. Even the emptiness where the dream had once been was a vain remembrance, a fleeting wisp of something that never was to be.

Jim had made his mind up to one thing. He definitely would leave Estes Park. There was too much there to remind him of Joanna. He felt that a new location somewhere would ease the pain in his heart.

It was November 25 when Dr. Hugh Pyle sat in the marshal's office reading the mail to Jim Blackburn for the last time. When the task was finished, Jim said, "I've made up my mind, Doc."

"About what?"

"I'm riding out to the B-Slash-C this afternoon."

Pyle's eyes widened. "You what? Why?"

"I can still make out the outline of facial features if I stand close to a person in direct sunlight. Won't be able to much longer."

"What are you getting at, Jim?" Pyle asked.

"I've only loved one woman in my life, Doc. She's the most beautiful creature God ever made. I want to see her face one more time before my sight is gone."

Pyle shook his head and looked at the floor. "It's too bad she doesn't feel the same about you."

Jim nodded but said nothing.

"If it will help, go out there and torture yourself."

Jim had no plan about approaching Joanna. He would just take it as it came. Reining his horse through the gate, he squinted at the big white house and outbuildings. They were a vague shape in the midafternoon sun. The structures sharpened slightly as he drew near.

From the front porch of the house he caught sight of a large, dark-faced object moving down the steps. "Mr. Marshal Burntblack! Bless yo' soul, you came back!"

Jim dismounted and warmly embraced her. "Jezebel! It's good to see you," he said. His horse nickered.

Jezebel turned her face toward the house and shouted, "Miz Joanna! Miz Joanna!"

Jim's heart jumped to his throat as the screen door burst open. A dark-haired blur dressed in yellow came through saying, "Goodness, Jezebel, what on earth are you—" Joanna's eyes fastened on the tall, handsome man.

Jim swallowed hard, concentrating his failing eyes on the vague form of the woman he loved.

Jezebel hoisted her skirts and climbed the porch steps. "I think Jezebel left some dirty dishes in the kitchen." She slipped through the screen door, pulled it shut, rolled her back to the wall, and listened.

"Hello, Princess," Jim said cautiously.

"Hello, Jim," Joanna replied. "You're looking fine."

"You too," he said. "More beautiful than ever."

"Er . . . everything all right in town?" she asked, for lack of something to say.

"Uh . . . yes. Everything's fine."

Joanna was still on the porch. Jim wanted to get closer to her, to feast his eyes on her for the last time.

"Princess, I . . . well, I haven't seen you for a long while. I just rode out to see you. I know you told me never to come here again, but I just had to come this once. I just—"

"It's all right, Jim. I shouldn't have said those awful things to you. I want you to know that after I had time to think it over, I couldn't blame you for Daddy's death. It wasn't your fault."

"Thank you, Joanna. I'm glad you feel that way." He was trying to think of a way to get her down on his level so he could see her better. Neither spoke for a long moment.

Joanna solved the problem for him. "The badge looks good on you," she said, trying to fill in a wordless gap.

"Oh, it's, uh . . . it's a new kind. Did you ever see one with scrolls along the edge?"

"No."

"Come down here and I'll show it to you."

Nervously Joanna descended the steps and moved closer. Jim turned slightly, causing the sun to strike her entire face. His heart drummed against his ribs. His arms ached to hold her.

"Mmm-hmm. Real nice," she said, looking from the badge into his angular features.

"You always did look good in yellow," said the big man softly. He thought he detected a smile. "And pink . . . and white . . . and black . . . and red . . ."

A slight giggle escaped her lips. She looked into his eyes. He was looking at her, but it almost seemed he was looking *through* her.

Neither spoke for a moment. Joanna felt her heart burning within. She wanted Jim to take her in his arms. She wanted him to kiss her . . . and breathe the words *I love you* in her ear.

Knowing this was the last time he would ever see the beautiful face he loved so much, Jim wanted to squint and sharpen the focus. But it would be a dead giveaway. He didn't want Joanna to learn of his malady until word drifted from Estes Park. By then he would be gone.

Joanna came within a heartbeat of reaching toward him, when sunlight glinted on the handle of his Colt .45. Abruptly she was reminded of his way of life.

"Things all right here on the ranch?" Jim asked, enjoying the warmth of her presence.

Joanna nodded. "Everything's fine. Russ handles the men and the work. I'm afraid I don't do as good a job as Daddy did in managing the finances though. Guess I'll have to hire a business manager one of these days."

Silence prevailed.

"Chief all right?"

"Mmm-hmm. Showing his age a little, but still the best horse in Colorado."

Silence hung in the air again. Jim took one long look at the Cherokee features, then said, "Well, Princess, I guess I better get back to town. Somebody might be looking for me. Thanks for letting me see you."

"It was good to see you again, Jim," she said shakily.

As Jim hesitated for a moment, Jezebel was peeking through the screen, saying under her breath, "Kiss her, man! Grab that pesky female and plant one on!"

Jim Black forced himself to turn away. Jezebel swung her fist as if to punch the big man.

As he settled in the saddle, Jim said, "I wish it could have worked out. Makes me hate this gun. I love you, Princess . . . Joanna. I always will."

The beautiful woman could not answer. A hot lump in her throat was choking her breath. Jim could not see the scalding tears on her cheeks.

Joanna wiped her eyes as she watched the big man ride off. Just as he disappeared from sight Jezebel came through the door. Stepping up beside Joanna, she put a strong arm around her.

"Oh, Jezebel," sniffed Joanna. "I'm so mixed up."

"You wouldn't be, honey," the black woman said firmly, "if you would just do what's right."

"What do you mean?" asked the confused young woman, sniffing again and wiping tears.

"This ol' stuff about you couldn't stand bein' married to a lawman."

"Well—"

"I've been bitin' my tongue fo' a long time, Miz Joanna. I

can't bite it no more. You listen, now, and you listen good. Just who you thinkin' about anyway?"

"What do you mean?"

"When you says you can't be the wife of a man who packs a gun."

"Well, *me*, I guess."

"No guessin' about it, chile. What about Mr. Jim?"

"What?"

"That man loves you so much it's killin' him."

"I know."

"Is it fair to let him live alone, eatin' his sweet heart out 'cause you're afraid he's gonna get killed?"

"Well—"

"Look at it this way—you love him just as much as he loves you. Right?"

"Yes, Jezebel. Just as much."

"Then wouldn't it be better to have every minute together that you can latch on to?"

"Yes, I—"

"Think, girl. Yo' lettin' time get away. This is the day you and that handsome hunk of man was to get married. Why don't you jump on Chief and ride after big Jim and tie the knot right now? You can still get married today. The day ain't over till midnight."

Joanna took a deep breath and exhaled, coming to a decision. Turning to the large black woman, she wrapped her arms around her and said, "You're right, Jezebel. Oh, what a fool I've been! I've been so selfish. I'm going to fix myself up nice and ride Chief into town. If Jim will still have me, we'll get married tonight!"

"Whoopee!" exclaimed Jezebel. "There ain't no question he'll have you!"

Joanna kissed Jezebel's plump cheek. "If you'll help me, I can be ready to ride in half an hour."

"Then let's get to it!" breathed Jezebel. "Time's a-wastin'!"

The marshal of Estes Park gazed at the blurred splendor of God's handiwork as he rode back to town. It hurt to know that soon he would not be able to see any of this beautiful country. He would memorize it, just as he had memorized the face of Joanna Claiborne. Those fascinating features would be engraved in his mind until the day he died.

The sun was already behind the western peaks when Jim rode into town. The streets were virtually deserted. Dismounting in front of the office, he squinted at three dark figures who stood in the shadows against the door. Two of them parted, one to the right, the other to the left.

One obscure form remained centered before the marshal. From it came a deep, throaty voice. "Evenin', Jim."

Jim wanted to squint again, but he dared not. "Do I know you?"

The man gave a humorless chuckle. "That's funny, Jim." He paused a moment, his face marked by dark shadows. "I gotta know."

"What's that?" Jim asked. A raw wind came off the snowcapped peaks and swirled through the town, chilling him to the bone.

"If you're still the fastest man alive," came the cold answer.

Halfway up the block Doc Pyle stepped out of his office, instantly taking in the shadowed scene in front of the marshal's office. He stood motionless, breathless. He knew Jim would never see the man go for his gun in the gathering dusk.

Jim knew it too.

His challenger moved slowly from the boardwalk to the center of the street. Jim could hear the boots grating on the crusty earth. The man's change of position helped a little, but there still was not enough light. He could barely make out the shapes of the buildings, which stood like great formless towers on both sides of the street.

Something cold slithered down Jim's spine. He peered with difficulty at the man with the deep voice. He seemed to blend with the shadows. His features were vague. It was as if the man had no face.

No face!

It came home like a bolt of lightning. *Here was his faceless man.* The unseen nemesis who had lurked in the shadows, biding time, stalking him since the day he first strapped on a gun.

Jim knew it. The time had come.

"It's eatin' me inside, Jim," said the heavy voice. "You understand."

Joanna's face flashed through Jim's mind. Suddenly his ears picked up a slight grating sound from the faceless man's boots. Jim's hand flashed downward. Two shots rang out, one behind the other, throwing a curtain of fire across the dark street.

The earth seemed to erupt under his feet. A hot, mysterious force lifted him in the air, spinning him around. The hard surface of the street, like a monstrous fist, slammed his back. The purple sky overhead was spinning as a dark curtain came over him like a shroud.

Doc Pyle knelt beside the inert form of Jim Black. The faceless man slid his gun into the holster as his two companions joined him.

People were instantly in the street. The first man to reach the kneeling physician was Harry Coyle. The three gunmen started toward them as Coyle said, "Doc, is he—"

"He's dead," said Pyle.

The three men checked their stride, turned, and walked away. "Funny thing," said the victorious challenger.

"What's that?" asked one of the others.

"He beat me to the draw. His gun fired first . . . but he missed."

"So what?"

"He's never missed in his life. I just don't get it."

"You worry too much, Wayne. So he beat you to the draw. He's dead and you're alive."

"Yeah, Meade," added the other companion. "You're the fastest gun now."

"It's not the same," came the deep voice. "He outdrew me. I'll never live it down. It'll eat my guts out."

"You just wait'll we tell how you killed the great Jim Black!" said the first one.

"I don't care," snapped Wayne Meade. "He outdrew me. That's all I know. He outdrew me!"

Chapter Seventeen

Joanna Claiborne's heart pounded as she rode into Estes Park. She was glad she had been able to slip away from the ranch without Russ Pittman knowing. He would have insisted on escorting her into town, and she needed the time alone to rehearse what she was going to say to Jim.

Her heart pounded harder as the stallion rounded the corner and headed up Main Street. Jim would probably be eating supper at the hotel dining room. She drew up in front of the Water Wheel and slid from the saddle. As she tied the reins to the hitching rail, two middle-aged women whom she recognized were coming down the boardwalk. They were sisters, partners in a dress shop.

"Why, Sadie," said Sylvia Fraker, "I do believe it's Joanna Claiborne."

"Good evening, Miss Sadie . . . Miss Sylvia," said Joanna.

"We haven't seen you in a long time, my dear," said Sylvia. "Not since your father's funeral, I think."

"Yes, ma'am," said Joanna.

"What brings you to town at this time of the day?"

"I've come to see Marshal Blackburn," said Joanna.

The two middle-aged faces blanched. "Then you haven't heard?" Sadie asked.

"Heard what?"

"Oh, dear," gasped Sadie. "Sylvia, help me. Joanna and Jim Black were engaged once."

Sylvia Fraker touched a nervous hand to her cheeks. "Well, dear," she said shakily, "there was a gunfight in front of the marshal's office about an hour ago. . . ."

"Where's Jim?" demanded Joanna, a coldness overtaking her body.

"He's—"

"*Where is he?*" The young woman's voice was piercing.

"A gunman shot him, honey," said Sylvia, attempting to steady her voice. "He's dead."

Joanna put her hand on the hitching rail. The lamplit street seemed to whirl. The two women gripped her arms. "Come, dear," said Sadie tenderly. "We'll take you over to the shop, where you can sit down."

"Does Stanley Dent have the body?" asked the stunned young woman.

"No, honey," answered Sylvia. "It's at the doctor's."

Bounding down the street, Joanna dashed toward the doctor's office. The sisters were calling to her, but she did not hear them.

Dr. Hugh Pyle was sitting at his desk in the front office when the door flew open and Joanna's face appeared, pale as death. Rising to his feet, he started to speak.

"How did it happen, Doctor?" Joanna asked, her mouth dry. "Who killed him?"

"Sit down, Miss Claiborne," said Pyle, adjusting a chair beside the desk.

The young woman dropped into the chair and wiped her face with a sleeve.

"Three gunmen were waiting for Jim when he got back from your place. One of them challenged Jim and shot him."

Joanna pressed her temples with her fingertips. She felt numb all over. She could not even cry. Memories of Jim flooded her brain. Today's scene at the ranch stood out vividly. His last words echoed in her mind. *"I love you, Princess . . . Joanna. I always will."*

Suddenly words were coming from her mouth, words over which she had no control. "Oh, Jim! Jim! Jim! Why did I do it? Why?" Her throat pinched tight. She closed her eyes. "Oh, Dr. Pyle, I've been so awful. And now . . . now it's too late! If only I could have told him!"

Joanna suddenly felt two strong hands squeezing her shoulders. She opened her eyes. The doctor looked at her straight, then smiled.

She was totally baffled.

"You *can* tell him, Joanna," Pyle said, broadening his smile. "Jim is not dead."

Joanna's mouth froze open. Her emerald eyes widened. "But . . . but Sadie and Sylvia said—"

"Right now the whole town thinks he's dead, honey. Except for the two men who carried him in here."

"But why?" she gasped, throwing a glance at the closed door of the infirmary.

"Those gunmen were bound to check on Jim after he was shot. I didn't know what they might do to him if they knew he was still alive. So I got to Jim first and loudly told Harry Coyle he was dead. The gunmen heard me, climbed on their horses, and rode out. I don't know how far they may be by now, but I'm keeping it quiet awhile longer."

Joanna sprang to her feet and started for the infirmary door. Pyle intercepted her. "Wait a minute now. I need to talk to you."

"He's back there, isn't he?" she asked impatiently.

"Yes. But I need to tell you something first."

Reluctantly, Joanna returned to the chair. "What's wrong, doctor? I can take anything. Just so he's alive."

"He's very much alive, Joanna," Pyle said firmly. "In fact the bullet wound was not all that serious. Caught him in the right shoulder."

"I don't understand, Dr. Pyle," she said, studying the physician's face.

"Joanna, a moment ago you were saying that you'd been wrong. You thought Jim was dead, and you were lamenting that you couldn't tell him."

"Yes."

"How much do you love that man, honey?"

"With everything that's in me," insisted Joanna. "I love him as much as any woman could love a man."

"I think you know that he feels the same way."

"I know how Jim feels."

The physician's face grew serious. "Do you know why he broke your command and rode out to the ranch today?"

"Because he wanted to see me."

"He wanted to see you for the *last* time in his life."

Puzzlement captured the young woman's face. "I . . . I don't understand."

Pyle took hold of both of her hands. "Joanna," he said solemnly, "Jim is going blind."

The words seemed to burn her ears. She sat in silence while the physician told her of the kerosene, the temporary loss of sight, the beginning of the permanent loss, and the

Denver specialist's verdict. "So you see, Joanna, that man in there wanted to see your face before his sight was too far gone. He'll be stone blind within a few weeks."

Joanna's lip quivered. "Oh, dear God."

"The only reason that gunslinger didn't die this afternoon is because Jim couldn't see him. Young fool, whoever he was, thinks he outdrew the great Jim Black."

Joanna stood up. "Let him think it, Dr. Pyle. Let the whole world think it. Because Jim Black *is* dead."

"What?"

"Jim Black was a gunfighter, Doctor. A blind man cannot be a gunfighter. He was Jim Black whenever he wore that gun. He was J. William Blackburn without it."

"Guess you're right about that."

"I rode in here just now to tell Jim I would marry him in spite of the gun. But now the gun is no longer an issue. If he'll still have me, I'm going to marry him, Doctor. In fact, if I can talk him into it, we'll get married tonight. This is the day we'd set to be married. But for my selfish foolishness, it would have happened."

Dr. Pyle was beaming from ear to ear.

"Furthermore," said Joanna, "Jim can now open his law office. I'll be his eyes, if he'll let me. We'll build the greatest law firm west of the wide Missouri."

"Tell you what," said the elated physician, "you go in there and see Jim, and I'll go after the preacher."

"Better let me ask him first," she replied.

"I know what he'll say." The doctor smiled, heading for the door. "I'll go after the preacher. While I'm at it I'll send someone to the ranch to tell Russ Pittman and Jezebel to hurry to town for the ceremony." With that he was gone.

The door clicked shut. Joanna promptly flipped the sign in the window, exposing the side that said The Doctor Is Out. Rushing across the room, she opened the infirmary door. The big dark-haired man was propped up in bed, his shoulder bandaged and his arm in a sling.

Joanna hurried to his side. "Oh, Jim," she blurted, "I'm so sorry for the way I've been. Please forgive me. Please—"

With his free hand Jim reached up and found her mouth, pressing his forefinger over her lips. "You don't have to repeat it, Princess," he said softly. "The good doctor's walls are thin. I heard every word. Let's forget the past. We'll begin our future right now, as that team you were talking about. I have a good name for the firm."

"You do?"

"Uh-huh. Since you're going to be my eyes, I think we should call it Blackburn and Blackburn."

Bending close, Joanna said, "Then Blackburn and Blackburn it is, partner."

Moving his hand to the back of her neck, he pulled her close. Their lips met and blended, her warm tears moistening his face.

Squinting hard into her eyes, he said, "What's taking that preacher so long to get here?"

She planted another soft kiss on his lips and whispered, "I love you, Jim."

"I love you, Princess," he said warmly. "And I always will."

THE BADGE: Book 3

THE BLACK COFFIN

by Bill Reno

Outlaw Dave Starr, alias Dave Bradford, finds himself in a peculiar situation when he kills a trio of bank robbers outside Georgetown, Colorado, and is mistaken for his twin brother, the famous gunfighter Dan Starr. Rather than admit his true identity, he pretends to be Dan and agrees to serve as town marshal until the new marshal arrives.

The ruse gets out of hand when Dave meets Jo-Beth Taylor, who from afar has secretly loved the real Dan Starr. Not revealing his true identity, Dave finds himself falling in love with the beautiful young woman. The situation is futher complicated when the brother of one of the outlaws killed by Dave brings his gang hunting the famous Dan Starr in order to extract vengeance. To carry out the plan, the gang takes hostage the family of a wealthy mineowner and demands that he send Dan Starr with a large ransom in gold. It falls to Dave Bradford to try to rescue the family, not realizing that he will be walking into a deadly trap.

When the real Dan Starr arrives in town and discovers that his brother and an innocent family are prisoners of the ruthless gang, he sets out to right the wrong. But it is a mission in which only one of the brothers will survive—and only one will win the love of the beautiful Jo-Beth Taylor.

Read THE BLACK COFFIN, *on sale March 1988 wherever Bantam paperbacks are sold.*